VEILED SPIRITS

HAUNTED MAGIC
BOOK ONE

E. L. FINLEY

FOXTROT WRITING

Published by Foxtrot Writing LLC
Cover art and design by Silviya Andreeva of Dark Imaginarium Art
Editing by Raven Quill Editing
Proofreading by Autumn Reed

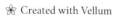 Created with Vellum

To all of you who never felt like you fit in anywhere.
It wasn't you.
You just hadn't found your place or people yet.

INTRODUCTION

This book contains mentions of sexual assault, attempted sexual assault on page, death of a loved one, strong language, mature content, and violence. Please read at your own discretion.

VEILED SPIRITS PLAYLIST

Tis the Damn Season - *Taylor Swift*
We Are Never Ever Getting Back Together - *Taylor Swift*
Dying For - *Rain City Drive*
Making the Bed - *Olivia Rodrigo*
Happier - *Marshmello and Bastille*
Shake It Out - *Florence + The Machine*
Hits Different - *Taylor Swift*
Half of Forever - *Henrik*
You Belong With Me - *Taylor Swift*
Gasoline - *Nic D and Connor Price*
Just Pretend - *Bad Omens*
Aerials - *System of a Down*
Numb Little Bug - *Em Beihold*
Granite - *Sleep Token*
The Albatross - *Taylor Swift*

CHAPTER 1

IZZY

*P*ushing out of the classroom, I walk toward the front of the Gallagher building, where I have most of my Hawthorne Grove University classes.

I glance down at my homework for the evening, startled when a hard shove to my back sends me flying. All the books and papers I'm holding soar through the air.

"Defensare," I whisper under my breath. One of the perks of being a mage is that I'm able to shape the raw magical energy that powers our planet to my will. In this case, I quickly form it into a barely there shield that flickers into place underneath my knees. It saves them from the worst of the fall.

As soon as my knees hit the dingy beige tiles with a loud thud, I let go of my shield. My knees throb where they connect with the ground. Tears prick my eyes at the flash of pain, but I'm able to battle them back for now.

My golden-blonde, wavy hair falls like a curtain in front of my face. I gaze at the purple and blue ends of my shoulder-blade-length hair to distract myself from Danielle Fletcher and her clones.

1

Danielle is Hawthorne Grove's resident mean girl and the bane of my existence. Making my life hell seems to be her favorite pastime. She should really try getting a normal hobby, like knitting or jumping off a cliff.

Hawthorne Grove is a small town in New England. It has lush, tree-lined streets, historic architecture, and a main street that's so cute it makes me sick. Hawthorne Grove is also a short distance from the frigid waters of the Atlantic. The only thing that makes Hawthorne Grove stand out from other small towns around here is that it's populated with mages, instead of normal humans, unfortunately for me.

"Watch where you're going, *vilis.*" Danielle sneers at me, flipping her stick-straight platinum-blonde hair over her shoulder. She narrows her dull brown eyes at me when I glance up through my lashes.

Wow. How original. Calling me the mage slur for magic-less, *vilis.* I haven't had someone remind me that they think I don't have magic in a whole five minutes. If she's going to insist on tormenting me, the least Danielle could do is come up with creative insults.

For some reason, mages feel the need to use Latin for everything. Insults, spells, swearing—you name it—mages have a Latin word for it. At least Latin words for spells make sense because it helps focus magic. Most mages don't have enough control over their magic to cast without a focus word.

"No one wants you here," Madison Redman informs me in a shrill voice. She's wearing the same country club house-wife outfit as Danielle and Tina Ward. Only, her button-down and matching skirt are pink. Danielle's are yellow, and Tina's are powder blue. "Why don't you just leave?"

Oh, trust me, I would if I could.

If I don't finish school, the mage council will hunt me

down and drag me in for testing. That's just about the last thing I want.

The mage council is the governing body for all mages. They make the laws, enforce rules, prosecute offenders, and execute those convicted of the most serious crimes. Having one group of old guys acting as judge, jury, and executioner ends up being pretty corrupt. Shocker.

Hawthorne Grove is the council seat for the mage council of North America. I'm counting down until I can leave here and never see the council or the mages of this town again. I only have one more year of this hell left. One hundred and forty-six more days. I can totally do this.

Maybe if I keep telling myself that, I'll start to believe it.

"You're such an embarrassment to your family. They'd be better off without you," Tina adds. With brown hair, lightly tanned skin, and deep brown eyes, Tina could be pretty. That is, if you ignore all the ugliness on the inside.

Tina's dig is the only one that lands. My family isn't embarrassed of me in the slightest. They couldn't care less that the town thinks I don't have magic. But she's right about my family being better off without me. I put them all in danger just by existing.

The hot tears I've been trying to contain finally leak out of my eyes and cascade down my pale cheeks at her barb. As the silent tears splash onto my ripped jeans, I curse the fact that I cry at everything. Happy, sad, angry, frustrated, you name it, and I cry because I feel it.

I hate it.

It's hard to be a badass when I cry at literally everything. I don't bother wiping up the tears, because I don't want to clue Danielle and her minions in that I'm leaking. Hopefully they'll get tired of this soon and leave. Lord knows I'm fucking tired of dealing with it every day.

My magic stirs in my chest at my strong emotions. It

crackles in agitation behind my breastbone. Unlike what everyone in Hawthorne Grove thinks, I do have magic. Enough magic to level this and surrounding towns without breaking a sweat.

But I can't tell anyone that. It's bad enough my family knows.

Danielle huffs at my lack of response. *"Accendere,"* she says, pointing at my books and papers. They light on fire with a *whoosh*. With a cackling laugh, Danielle and her groupies stride away, ridiculously high heels clacking on the tile.

Sighing, I mutter, *"Restinguere."*

The fire instantly goes out. My books and papers are perfectly fine. I learned a long time ago to spell all of my belongings to protect them. A simple defensive spell on everything keeps the worst of the attacks from destroying my stuff.

The assholes here love to fuck with me. I get away with magically protecting my things because people think my brothers do it for me. They still enjoy lighting my stuff on fire, dumping water on it, or covering it in caustic goo.

It's super fun when people mess with my stuff while others watch. I totally love having to deal with their magical attacks without any magic. All while the peanut gallery laughs at my struggles.

I fucking hate this town.

"You need help?" a deep voice asks from behind me. My shoulders sag in relief that it's not one of my other main tormentors, Mason, Richard, or last year's new addition, Tyler. It's just Levi, my combat teacher. He's one of the only people in this hellhole who is actually kind to me.

"Yeah, that'd be good. Thanks." My voice is rough from crying, but Levi doesn't comment on it. Instead, he just walks around in front of me and kneels down, uncaring about getting his dark-wash jeans dirty. We work in silence to pick up all my papers and books.

Once we have everything gathered, Levi unzips my backpack and puts his stack inside. I follow suit. As I'm zipping up the backpack, he pushes to his feet. He doesn't offer me help up, but that's not unusual for him. Levi always makes sure not to touch me anywhere, skin on skin. It's a little weird, but I assume it's so he doesn't get into trouble for perving on students.

My worn white Chucks squeak on the tiles as I stand. When I'm steady, I crane my neck up and up to meet Levi's gaze. He is probably the tallest person I know, clocking in at around six-and-a-half feet tall. When my eyes finally land on his face, I meet his otherworldly eyes. They're obsidian, with a thin red ring around the pupil.

"Was it Danielle, Tina, and Madison who did this?" he rumbles. I look away and press my lips into a thin line, refusing to tell him. Levi sighs. "I'll report them if you'd just confirm who it is and what they do."

I scoff. "You and I both know this school won't do jack shit about it, Levi. Reporting them will just make my life harder." Since I supposedly don't have magic, Hawthorne Grove University doesn't particularly care what happens to me. Bullying, insults, and attacks are all fine and dandy with the administration, as long as it's only lower mages or me subject to it.

Mage society is separated into higher and lower mages. Higher mages are the ones with money, power, status, and clout in the community. They have access to the best jobs, preferential legal treatment, and make the decisions for mages as a whole. They're also incredibly snobby and stuck-up, thinking their family name makes them better than everyone else.

Lower mages, on the other hand, are the everyday mages.

They don't come from prestigious mage lines or hold high mage offices. Instead, they're just regular people who happen to have the ability to harness raw magical energy.

Because the council is located in Hawthorne Grove, there are way more higher mages here than other mage cities. Here, the lower mages are treated particularly badly. Since everyone thinks I'm magicless, I'm automatically lumped in with the lower mages.

Levi shakes his head at me, resigned to the way things are but not liking it any more than I do. "The option is always open if you change your mind."

"I appreciate it. I better get going," I tell him reluctantly. While I hate spending time at HGU, I do weirdly enjoy hanging out with him.

"I'll see you tomorrow." He gives me a crooked grin before walking off.

"See you then," I whisper to his retreating back.

Slinging my bag over my shoulder, I make my way to the front of the school. I push open the heavy front doors and step out into the blinding sunlight. It's so bright, I have to squint and blink my eyes for a few seconds.

When I can finally fully open my eyes, I start the trek home. Keeping up appearances that I don't have magic means I can't just portal to my house. Instead, I have to do it the old-fashioned way—walking. That's one thing I don't mind, though. Hawthorne Grove is full of forests, shrubs, flowers, animals, and more to keep me entertained on the fifteen-minute trip.

Halfway home, I feel my phone buzz in my pocket. My lips tip up into a small smile, already knowing who it is. Pulling out my phone, I glance at the screen.

BISHOP

Wanna go to the Poisoned Vine 2nite?

Bishop is my best friend in this shithole town, and he enjoys beating things up, just like I do. The Poisoned Vine is our favorite MMA gym. It's a few towns over, so I get a break from Hawthorne Grove for a little while.

> Hell yeah, I do. What kinda question is that?

BISHOP
I'll pick you up in 30 mins.

> K

I walk the rest of the way home with a goofy smile on my face. While my day has sucked, at least I'll get to hit things tonight.

CHAPTER 2

IZZY

"*Y*ou look like shit, kid," Agatha, or Aggie, as I call her, informs me as I push open the door to my room. I live with my parents and two older brothers, so my room is really the only place I have to myself.

Aggie's spectral form hovers over my bed. She has her legs crossed and her petticoats primly arranged around her lap. While she was only a few years older than me when she died, Aggie insists on calling me *kid*. It drives me crazy, which is probably why she does it.

"Thanks. You always say the nicest things to me, Aggie," I deadpan. The ghost just cackles at my sarcasm.

Seeing spirits sounds pretty cool. Until you realize that ghosts are just as much of assholes as the living. Aggie should have crossed over ages ago. But she's still here, annoying the shit out of me.

She follows me wherever I go, which can make it hard to keep the whole seeing ghosts thing a secret. At least Aggie has been leaving me alone at school recently. That makes it somewhat easier.

Shoving my door closed, I drop my backpack onto the

ground near my desk. Walking over to my closet, I warn, "Close your eyes or turn around if you don't want an eyeful of my boobs."

Not bothering to check if she listened, I strip out of my violet tee and light-wash jeans. I dig through the dresser in my closet and find a black sports bra. Pulling it out, I put it and my favorite lilac workout leggings on.

I snag a black hoodie I stole from Bishop and pull it over my head. Burying my nose in the soft, worn fabric, I take a deep inhale of Bishop's rainy forest scent. It always calms me when I've had a rough day.

Once I'm finished changing, I grab my guitar and flop onto my fluffy purple comforter. I lie on my back with my legs and socked feet on the lavender wall at the end of my bed. Turning my head, I look out the window over my bed while I softly strum my acoustic guitar.

"What are your plans for the night?" Aggie floats over to my desk as she talks.

"Go to the gym with Bishop, murder a punching bag, and cross over some ghosts," I say while I stare at the elm trees in my backyard.

"You know, you can take the night off, kid." When I glance over at Aggie, her forehead is pinched in concern. While she gives me shit on the regular, Aggie also cares about me, in her own way.

"And who's going to cross them if I don't?" I ask, already knowing the answer. There's no one we know of who can do what I do. So, the responsibility falls to me. That's how I spend most of my nights.

Aggie gives me a sad nod, letting me know she'll do her part so I can cross those who need it tonight.

I get lost playing my guitar and singing for a while. I'm playing "'Tis the Damn Season" when Aiden, one of my older brothers, comes crashing through my door.

"Lover boy's here, Iz." Aiden leans against the door and stares at me for a beat. With the same golden-blond hair and gray eyes, we're often mistaken for twins. But he's a good half a foot taller than me and three years older.

Rhys is my other brother. He's seven years older than me and takes after my dad. Aiden and I both look like our mom, Maggie. With brown hair, hazel eyes, and his six-foot-two height, Rhys is the spitting image of our dad, Sean.

"Why do you always sing such depressing songs?" Aiden whines.

"I don't!"

"You really do."

"Fine," I huff. To prove him wrong, I start belting out "We Are Never Ever Getting Back Together" as loud as I can. That'll teach him to criticize my song choice.

"Ah! My ears! They're bleeding!" Aiden exclaims dramatically. He hates pop music and any popular songs. I roll my eyes at him and keep singing. "Stop! Uncle! I give up! You were right, Izzy!"

I stop singing as soon as he admits I'm right. Grinning at him from my spot on the bed, I savor my victory over my annoying older brother.

"You're such a pest, Izzy," Aiden tells me with a wide smile, nowhere near as annoyed as he tries to seem. "Do you want me to send lover boy up, or are you meeting him downstairs?"

"You can send him up." I sit up and put my guitar down. Getting off the bed, I bend over and gather my hair into a high ponytail. After securing the hair tie, I straighten up and shove my feet into my sneakers, blowing the strands that are too short to be in the ponytail out of my face.

"Okay. Just keep the door open. You know Mom's rules. You can only fuck him with the door open." Aiden flashes me a cheeky grin before bounding out of my room.

I snort at his interpretation of Mom's open-door rule. Although, I'm pretty sure she'd be thrilled to come home and find me doing Bishop. She's been pushing us together for years, but that's never going to happen.

"You ready to go?" Bishop rumbles in his smooth, deep voice as he steps into my room. With his sharp jaw, muscular frame, and megawatt smile, Bishop is one of the most eligible bachelors in Hawthorne Grove. But he has exactly zero interest in his legions of admirers, preferring to hang out with me, the town reject.

Bishop shoves a hand through his unruly brown hair that's constantly falling in his baby-blue eyes as he looks around my room. He spots my guitar sitting by my bed. Trying, and failing, to be subtle, he runs his gaze over my face. He's probably checking for signs I've been crying. Singing is a way to let out my emotions, so I often cry when I play guitar.

"Yep," I chirp, trying to seem upbeat so Bishop doesn't worry. Snagging my wireless earbuds, I tuck them in my hoodie pocket, along with my ID holder. Glancing around my room, I make sure I'm not forgetting anything.

When I'm confident I have everything, I murmur, "*Aperire*." Out of habit, I speak the phrase aloud to open the portal. My weird magic means I don't need an incantation to do the spell, unlike other mages. Instead, I just need to visualize what I want to happen. My magic takes care of the rest.

The portal to a back alley a few minutes from the gym swooshes open. Bishop walks through first. Once he's on the other side, he holds out his hand for me as I step through. Ignoring his hand, I hop through on my own. Touching Bishop is dangerous. I like it way too much.

While I resisted it for a while, I can't deny that Bishop is my best friend now. I don't know how he broke through my defenses, but here he is, being all smug and shit about it. It'd be safer for him not to hang out with me, but he doesn't seem to care. Nothing I do makes him stay away, and, trust me, I've tried.

Letting go of the portal, I watch it snap closed. Shoving my hands into my stolen hoodie pocket, I take off for the gym. Bishop falls into step beside me.

"You wanna spar or use a punching bag?" Bishop slings his arm around me as I walk. At six-foot-three, he towers over my five-foot-six frame. I poke him in the ribs to get him to remove his arm. With how much muscle he has, I doubt he even felt my jab. We start walking with me tucked into his side.

"Punching bag. I'm too angry to spar. I don't want to break your pretty face. You need it to pick up chicks." I grin up at him.

He just rolls his eyes at me. "You know I'm not picking up women."

"You should," I tell him quietly, earlier mirth gone. "Or dudes. I really don't care, as long as you're with someone."

Bishop hums in disagreement but doesn't say anything further. We walk the rest of the way in silence, both of us lost in our thoughts.

The red-brick front of the Poisoned Vine comes into view. I pick up my pace when I see the MMA gym's black awning decorated with crimson thorns and lettering dripping with blood.

Bishop chuckles at my excitement. He pulls open the glass-and-metal door before waving me through. I practically skip inside.

It's a huge space, complete with three sparring rings, a wall of punching bags, and a padded area for practice. The gym has black tile floors, black mats covering the walls, and red mats on the floor of the sparring rings and practice area.

With the wall of windows and fluorescent lights in the industrial ceiling, the gym is well lit.

I start toward the hanging bags when a cheery voice calls out. "Hey, Izzy and Bishop!"

"Hey, Reggie," I say with a smile as I turn toward the eager wolf manning the front desk. His curly brown hair complements his mocha skin and deep brown eyes. Reggie's earnest smile makes it impossible to be in a bad mood.

Mages aren't the only ones with magic. The same magic that allows mages to cast spells also powers animal shifters, like wolves and bears, fae, vampires, sirens, and more.

Usually, different magic users keep to themselves. But the Poisoned Vine is open for anyone, other than normal humans, to use. As long as the rules are respected. The average human has no idea we exist, so we try to keep separate from them.

The Poisoned Vine is owned by some wolves. That's part of the reason I chose it. I'm sick of all the elitism of mages. When I'm on my own time, I don't want to interact with a single mage, outside of Bishop and my family. No Hawthorne Grove mage would be caught dead in a wolf-owned gym, so I'm in the clear here.

"What are you doing tonight?" Reggie enthusiastically asks.

"Just some punching bag work," I answer for both Bishop and me. Bishop usually only spars when I do. He likes to stick close to me, so he'll likely take the punching bag right next to mine.

"Cool! The owners are going to be here tonight. Stop by before you leave, and I'll introduce you!" Reggie is so excited at the prospect of introducing us that I don't have the heart to refuse him. Giving him a small nod, I head over to the punching bags.

"Don't forget gloves, Izzy," Bishop calls. I nod, while having no intention of following his advice.

Shoving my earbuds into my ears, I put on my favorite gym playlist. "Dying For" blasts in my ears as I push up the hoodie's sleeves, so they won't get in my way.

I aim a bare-knuckled punch at the black bag hanging in front of me. My fist lands with a satisfying thud. My knuckles sting, but I don't pay them any attention. Instead, I lose myself in the music and violence, punching out all my pent-up frustration from the week.

When my knuckles are too bruised and sore to keep going, I reluctantly step back from the swinging bag.

While beating up an inanimate object helped some, it didn't do nearly enough to calm the storm raging in me. It's a constant battle to keep all my emotions inside at school. Reacting to the insults and taunts will only encourage the power-tripping mages.

Any reaction chances letting my magic out to play. I have to use every shred of self-control I possess to keep my magic chained up when it wants to lash out at the other mages. While it would be satisfying to pay them back for the daily pain they cause, it's not worth it.

Nothing is worth Bishop's and my family's safety.

The daily struggle against my magic is exhausting. Add in the lack of sleep from spending most nights crossing ghosts, and I'm hanging on by a thread. I can't keep going like this much longer.

Something has to give.

I'm just not sure what.

Scrubbing my battered hands over my face, I attempt to force back the frustration and exhaustion trying to drown me. I refuse to cry here. Guys are so quick to judge a girl for crying. In a gym full of dudes who are already judgmental about me being the only girl, I don't want to give them another reason to look down on me. Women like hitting things, too, so I don't know why they're so uppity over it.

"You okay?" Bishop asks as he stops in front of me, brown brows slanted in concern.

"Just peachy," I mutter behind my hands. Letting my arms fall from my face, I don't resist the hug Bishop pulls me into. He always seems to know what I need. It just makes staying away harder.

After a moment, I step out of his hold. Bishop reluctantly lets me go, his blue eyes still crinkled with worry. I try to rearrange my face into something that says I'm fine. By Bishop's grimace, it doesn't work.

Huffing, I give up on trying to appear anything other than done with life. Turning, I stride toward the door before remembering that Reggie wanted us to meet the owners. I veer toward the front desk instead. Reluctantly, I walk up to the smiling wolf.

The last thing I want to do tonight is meet people. But for the wolf who has shown me more kindness than the entire town of Hawthorne Grove, I'll do it. "Where are the owners you want us to meet, Reggie?" I ask tiredly.

"I'll go get them. One sec!" Reggie sprints off, leaving Bishop and I staring after him. I glance at Bishop, and he's wearing the same bemused expression I am.

Reggie's a character, that's for sure.

It's only a minute or two before Reggie comes out of the back office, followed by three massive wolves.

Jesus Christ, those dudes are built.

The largest one is probably six-foot-five and made of pure muscle. His sun-bleached blond hair is trimmed short, and he has a day's worth of blond stubble. Together, with a jaw sharp enough to cut granite, flinty aquamarine eyes, and tattoos peeking out of his black tee, his whole appearance screams *don't fuck with me*.

Duly fucking noted, wolf.

To his left is a man who looks like a slightly shorter and much friendlier version of the bigger one. The same blond hair, blue-green eyes, and angular bone structure make me think they're siblings. His golden hair is longer and messier than his brother's, though.

Whereas the tall one is intimidating, this wolf wears an easygoing smile. It matches his laid-back band T-shirt and jeans. His eyes are still sharp, constantly assessing his surroundings. On second thought, I'm not sure how much friendlier he actually is.

The third wolf stands somewhere in between the other two in height. His jet-black hair curls around his ears, and his moss-green eyes are narrowed on me. He's just as good-looking as the other two, with a model-like square jaw, high cheekbones, and slightly crooked nose. Instead of a tee and jeans, he wears a charcoal button-down and black slacks.

I swallow uneasily as they get closer. My instincts are screaming at me to run away from the three predators prowling closer.

Rather than running, I stand my ground. I tip my chin up, refusing to show how unnerved I am. Wolves respect courage. I'll be damned if I give them a reason to look down on me. Enough people already do.

When the three wolves and Reggie reach us, Bishop tips his chin slightly in deference. I look at him with wide eyes. Since when does Bishop show respect to anyone or anything other than me? He has almost as big of a problem with authority as I do.

"Luca." He nods to the largest one. "Archer and Cain, good to see you."

He knows these wolves?

Of course, he does. There's no way he'd let me come to a

gym owned by randoms. Bishop is meticulous when it comes to my safety.

"Bishop," Luca growls in a deep voice. He turns his startling aquamarine eyes on me. Arching one blond brow, he asks without words what my name is.

I bristle at his wordless demand. Shoving my annoyance down, I answer, "I'm Izzy." I'd really like to keep coming to this gym. Pissing off the owners will definitely get me kicked out. I can play nice for one conversation.

Luca sticks out one large palm, clearly intending to shake my hand. I don't really want to touch the big wolf, but I'm trying to seem polite here. With an internal sigh, I place my pale hand in his tanned one.

Familiar tingles shoot up my arm from where we touch.

No. No fucking way. This can't be happening.

My wide eyes bounce up to meet his, and he doesn't look surprised. I forgot that wolves can tell through smell. He's likely known since he stepped foot into the gym.

Shit. Shit. Shit. What the fuck am I supposed to do?

Run away and hope to never see him again is really my only option. But freaking out right now will only clue him into my plans. Smoothing my expression, I try to look like I'm unaffected by him. I'm pretty sure I fail, but it's the best I can do right now.

Turning toward his brother, I make hesitant eye contact with Archer. He also sticks out his hand, and I pray to anyone who will listen that I don't feel anything when we touch.

It doesn't work.

I feel the same tingles as I did with his brother. Briefly closing my eyes, I will the frustrated tears away. I don't want to give away my emotions right now.

When I'm sure I won't burst into tears, I extract my hand

from the smiling wolf. I stick my hand out for Cain to shake, already knowing what's going to happen.

My hand tingles.

Un-fucking-believable.

Why does the universe hate me so much?

"It was nice to meet you," I lie between gritted teeth before grabbing Bishop's hand and tugging him toward the door.

"Wait!" Luca calls.

I ignore him and focus on getting to the door. When I hear footsteps behind me, I turn to Bishop and yell, "Time to go!"

Breaking out into a sprint, I drag Bishop behind me as we burst through the doors to the gym I'm never coming back to.

His wide eyes meet mine after he looks over his shoulder at the three pissed-off wolves trying to follow us. "Izzy—" he starts.

"There's no time! I'll explain later. We need to fucking run. Now!" I scream.

CHAPTER 3

IZZY

"Izzy! What the fuck is going on?" Bishop asks breathlessly as we sprint toward the alley we always use to portal to and from here. That's one thing I appreciate about Bishop. He is always there for whatever I want to do, including running away from three wolves.

Man, I'm really going to miss this gym. It has some of the nicest facilities of any MMA gym we've gone to.

Really? The gym is what I'm going to focus on right now? Instead of the three massive problems chasing us down?

I guess so.

Sighing, I debate how to answer Bishop. The truth is probably the best. "All three of them are my mates."

Mates are fate's gift to supernaturals. Fate chooses the person or people who are a perfect match for your soul. Men typically have one mate, and women have multiple. There aren't as many women as there are men, so women generally end up with several mates.

Bishop turns wide eyes on me before slowing as we hit the alley. I throw up a portal and continue heading toward it until Bishop tugs me to a stop. "Izzy. You can't run from your mates like this."

"Like fuck I can't." Running away from my problems is my favorite form of exercise.

Letting out a deep sigh, Bishop informs me, "Luca's the alpha of Pack Nightshade. Archer and Cain are his betas. They'll just find you if you run."

Goddamn it. No! I refuse to believe that the universe hates me this much.

How the fuck did I end up with one of the scariest alphas in the country and his two terrifying betas as my mates?

I'm a twenty-one-year-old mage, fumbling my way through life. There's no way I'm fit to be a fucking alpha mate.

And the Nightshade Pack has a reputation for being especially brutal. Wolf shifters tend to be violent by nature. But the Nightshades are bloodthirsty, even by wolf standards. They are not people to fuck with.

"You don't know that," I try to protest as I watch the three enraged wolves round the corner to the alley.

They don't look pleased to see us. I can't imagine why. It's not like their mate just ran off on them.

"I do know that. You do, too, Izzy. Do you want to talk to them now or have them find you when you're at school?" Bishop turns to look at me while still keeping an eye on the wolves slowly making their way to us. Though they're pretending like they're not listening, I know they can hear every word we say.

"Fucking fine," I grit out while avoiding Bishop's gaze. I don't need him seeing just how messed up I am over all of this. This is the absolute last thing I need on top of the dumpster fire my life is already.

Letting go of the thread of magic keeping the portal open, I hear it snap closed.

"You ran," Luca rumbles out as he reaches us. He crosses his muscular arms over his chest, making his biceps bulge. My eyes briefly dip to the impressive display before I yank them back up to meet his burning aquamarine eyes.

"Wow, really? I hadn't noticed, Sherlock," I snark. It's probably not a great idea to antagonize Luca. But if I'm not hiding behind anger and sarcasm, I'm going to cry.

Luca's eyes narrow at me in annoyance. Good. He should be as irritated at this situation as I am. "Why?"

Not really sure how to answer him, I grind my teeth so hard my jaw aches. Looking over, I meet Bishop's somber gaze to see if he has any idea how I should start. "Just tell him the truth, Izzy," Bishop encourages me, like it's just that easy.

Unfortunately, the truth is one thing I can't share with these wolves. At least, not the whole thing. Groaning, I shove the few loose strands of hair out of my face. Since I don't have anything else to offer them, I give them the only truth I can. "I ran because I can't mate with you."

Deep growls fill the air at my announcement. The hairs on the back of my neck stand up at the eerie sound. My magic perks up at the prospect of a fight. Squashing it down, I glare at Luca as I wait for him to say something.

"Why? Because we're wolves?" Cain is the one to speak, his deep, melodic voice curling around me.

"What? No! That's not it at all." I'm mildly offended they think I'm so racist. Or is it speciesist? I don't know. My brain is too tired to figure it out right now.

Although, I can't exactly blame them, because mages are, on the whole, elitist pigs.

Luca hums, clearly not believing me.

I roll my eyes at him. "St. James over here," I start, gesturing over to Bishop. He raises his hand, and I give him a look.

What the hell is he doing?

Catching my confusion, he slowly lowers his hand. His expression turning sheepish, he gestures for me to continue.

Huffing at his weirdness, I start again. "As I was saying, St. James is also my mate. He's from one of the most powerful mage lines in Hawthorne Grove. Mating with him would vastly improve my status in town. My parents would pass out from joy if I did. I'd barf at how cute we'd be. Yet, I'm still not mating with him."

Archer tilts his blond head at me as I speak, studying me. "Why would he help your status in town? Are you not from a good mage family?"

I snort at that. Gallagher is *the* mage family in Hawthorne Grove. We helped found the town hundreds of years ago. That's part of why people enjoy picking on me so much. Most mages would never dream of going against a Gallagher. We tend to be really powerful. But because they think I don't have magic, they can torment me and feel better about their subpar pedigree.

"No. My family is prominent. I don't have magic, so I'm at the bottom of the social ladder." Maybe if the wolves learn I'm defective, they'll reconsider mating with me. My pathetic heart squeezes at that.

I know it will kill part of my soul, having three of my mates reject me, but it's necessary. It's not like I have a very long life expectancy, anyway. Maybe it'll just expedite the process. Then my family will at least be safe.

"That's a lie, little mate. That portal reeks of your magic. Try again. This time, don't lie. It won't end well for you." Luca's voice is soft yet somehow super threatening. I wonder if he'd teach me how to be that intimidating without yelling. It would help with all the mages who mess with me.

Swallowing uneasily, I glare at Luca as I steel myself. I refuse to cower to the intimidating alpha who could prob- ably kill me with very little effort. There's what looks like a flash of respect in his eyes as I don't back down. But it's gone too quickly for me to be sure.

"It's not a lie, as far as the not-so-good people of Hawthorne Grove know," I respond.

"Why do they think you don't have magic, then?" Luca demands. He's clearly used to getting his way and having people fall over themselves to obey him. He's in for a rude awakening when it comes to me. I have a problem with authority. And I'm awful at following orders I don't agree with. It gets me into trouble at school more often than not.

My mind blanks at his question. I can't think of any plausible reason why, other than the truth I can't tell him. So, I blurt out the first thing that comes to mind. "I have a degradation kink."

Oh my fucking God.

I can't believe I just said that.

There's nothing wrong with it, but that's very much not my thing. It's also a weird thing to tell people you just met.

As soon as the words are out of my mouth, I close my eyes in embarrassment. I want to smack myself, because surely, there was something better I could have said. Literally anything would have been an improvement.

A bark of laughter from my right startles me. I open my eyes to see Bishop laughing so hard he's doubled over. Aggie hovers behind him, also cackling in delight at my horrible answer.

Oh, good. More people to witness my humiliation.

Just what I wanted.

I don't even know when she got here. I've been so focused on the wolves that I haven't been paying attention to my surroundings. At least my brothers aren't here. I'd never live this down. Bishop better not tell them about it.

As Bishop's laughter dies down, I raise my brows at him. "You done, St. James?"

He wipes a few stray tears that leaked out from laughing off his face. "Yep. Sorry."

I snort. "No, you're not."

"You're right, I'm not," Bishop tells me with a grin. "You always have such a way with words."

I flip him off for enjoying my raging embarrassment. Scrubbing my hands over my face, I blow out a breath before looking at the wolves. Archer and Cain are grinning at my predicament. Luca smiles slightly, and I wonder if he ever grins fully or laughs.

"So, where was I?" I ask rhetorically, trying to remember what the point of the whole kink debacle was.

"You were telling us about your degradation kink," Luca informs me dryly. My cheeks grow pink in embarrassment.

"Oh, yeah, that." If the universe wants to take me out tonight, I really won't object.

"That's the story you're sticking with?" Luca arches a golden brow at me skeptically.

While it's embarrassing as all get out, it's not even close to the worst thing I could have said. "Till the day I die," I confirm with a nod. "Anyway, the fucking point of all of this is that I can't mate with you. And it's not because you're wolves."

"Why?" Luca growls as he advances on me a few steps. I have the urge to back up, but I stand my ground in the face of the massive wolf coming closer.

"I can't tell you that." My voice is thick with frustration. It's not like I want this. I want more than almost anything to be just a normal person for once. I want to be able to celebrate finding my fated mates, not mourn the life I'll never have.

But I'm not, and I can't.

There's so much more at stake than my petty wants and wishes and hopes.

"Can't or won't?" Luca presses.

"Can't." Somehow, I keep my voice from breaking. I refuse to be weak in front of them. I may not be able to mate them, but I still want the wolves to respect me.

"Until you can give me an honest fucking answer, I won't accept that. So, you're stuck with us, little mate," Luca growls.

"No," I grit out as I close the distance between us. "You're going to fucking leave me alone and go on your merry wolfie way."

"Or what?" Luca questions, his voice laced with amusement. It's clear that he's underestimating me like everyone else.

Anger bubbles in my chest, sparking at my mate thinking I'm weak. I breathe through the emotion, not wanting to do something I regret in the heat of the moment. My magic also stirs in my chest. A little trickles out at my agitation. It's enough to make the strands that escaped my ponytail float in a non-existent breeze.

Luca's eyes widen as he feels the electric charge of my magic skate over his skin. His aquamarine eyes narrow in consideration. He finally realizes he and his wolves aren't the only predators in this alley tonight.

"Izzy, rein it in," Bishop demands. I glare at him for acting like I'm the problem. But he's already turned to Luca. "Back the fuck up. You're not helping this situation any."

I don't see if Luca backs up at all, because I'm too busy trying to pull back my magic.

But I can't.

Ah, fuck. This is why I don't let it come out to play. My magic won't be satisfied until it destroys something to prove to our mates how strong we are. Casting spells doesn't require much of my power. So, I can do them while still keeping my magic contained. Once I give it a little freedom, it tries to take over.

"I can't," I whimper as I struggle with the magic flowing through my veins.

Unlike with other mages, my magic hasn't ever felt like a part of me. Instead, it feels like a separate entity that's hitching a ride in my body. Once it gets out, it often won't listen to what I want, and it turns me into a much more violent version of myself. I'm already violent enough, without the extra encouragement from my magic.

"Isabel. Look at me." Bishop's sharp voice calling my full name makes me snap my gaze to his. I get lost in his baby blues as they flick between my gray ones. "You're safe, sweetheart. They're not going to hurt you. I'm safe. Your family is safe. Your magic isn't needed right now."

His words help calm the roiling storm inside me slightly. But it's not enough. My magic screams inside of me to prove how strong we are so our mates will still want us. Normally, I'd roll my eyes at it. But it's taking everything I have to keep my magic from razing the buildings around us in a show of power.

"Prove. Strong," is all I can get out past the stranglehold the magic has on my airway.

Bishop's forehead crinkles in confusion as he tries to puzzle out what I need. His eyes eventually light with understanding about what my magic needs. "Fuck, sweetheart. Well, leveling this town isn't an option, so what will work instead?"

I shrug because moving my limbs is exponentially easier than trying to talk right now.

"Hmm. Would sparring work?" Bishop asks after a moment of thought.

I consider it. Laying the three wolves on their asses would be super satisfying. It would be pretty hard for them to deny how strong I am if I beat them in a fight. My magic agrees, and I breathe out a sigh of relief. "Yes."

"You need to pull your magic back. Otherwise, you'll hurt them. Can you do that for me, sweetheart?" Though Bishop tries to keep his body language relaxed, to lull my magic into compliance, I can still see how tense he is.

My magic slowly slithers back through my veins to where it normally sits behind my breastbone. I sag in relief when it finally goes back to where it's supposed to be.

Bishop crushes me to his chest once he feels my magic disappear. His hand shakes where it cups the back of my head. Anytime my magic gets out, there's always a chance it won't let go again. We don't know what happens to me if my magic keeps control of my meat suit. "You okay?" he mumbles into my blonde hair.

I give him a jerky nod, not trusting my voice to stay steady. My heart is galloping in my chest, and I'm breathing heavily, like I ran a marathon. I'm not sure I'm okay. But I'm back. That's really all that matters.

"What the fuck was that?" Luca asks way too calmly for someone who almost witnessed the destruction of a small city. While his voice is even, his eyes warily watch me from a few steps away.

Good.

Maybe the dumbass won't provoke my magic in the future.

"That was a preview of why I let people think I don't have any magic."

CHAPTER 4

IZZY

"*W*hatever it was, it was fucking epic!" Archer interjects from behind Luca.

A half smile crosses my lips at his praise. "Thanks."

"So, can you take us all out with your magic?" he asks while bouncing on his toes. His aquamarine eyes dance in delight.

Bishop snorts. "She can obliterate your entire pack, Arch, and still have magic left over."

I glare at Bishop. He just smirks at me in response. I really don't need the wolves knowing any more about my magic than they already do. Yet Bishop is throwing out clues like they're confetti.

He's infuriating. As is Luca.

It seems to be a theme with my mates.

"Oh, man! That's so cool!" Archer grins at me. We must have different definitions of cool. Someone being able to destroy my entire family doesn't really seem cool to me.

Archer wanders closer as he talks, stopping beside Luca, who didn't back up as much as I thought. They're way too close to me now.

"Why would your magic worry about the safety of your family?" Luca asks shrewdly.

I groan. "Dude. Really? I just told you I can't tell you. I have eight million other problems I have to take care of tonight, so can we just spar and get this over with?"

Luca prowls back into my space as he pushes me for information. "What are these other problems?"

"Stuff. And things," I answer evasively. It's not like I can tell the wolves what I spend my nights doing.

Bishop doesn't know, either. He only knows about my magic because my parents told him after finding out he's my mate. He definitely wouldn't be happy to know what I've been doing in the forest.

"Wow, kid. You're really good at not arousing suspicion," Aggie sarcastically comments from behind Bishop. I turn my head to give her a death glare. When she catches my narrowed eyes, her spectral ones widen in understanding. "Oh. Right. They don't know you can see me. You can't talk to me now. I'll just...be quiet."

Rolling my eyes at her, I turn back toward Luca. Oh, goodie. Cain is now in my personal space as well.

Does Cain have any other expression other than glaring? Because I haven't seen his captivating face without his eyes narrowed on me.

Luca doesn't say anything for a beat. He just clenches his jaw, causing a vein to throb on the side of his stupidly handsome face.

Why couldn't the universe give me ugly mates?

At least it would be easier to stay away if they didn't look like models.

"I'll spar with you," Luca finally concedes. "On one condition. You have to go on a date with each of us at a time of our choosing."

My mouth pops open at his ridiculous demand. "What?

29

No! I am not going on a date with any of you. Besides, what are you, like eighty?" I ask. I know full well he isn't anywhere close to that. Even with wolves aging much slower than humans, there's no way he's that old.

"Cute," Luca tells me, clearly unimpressed. "No. I'm thirty."

My brows raise in surprise. He's really young to be an alpha, maybe the youngest one in recent history. Usually, wolves are around fifty to sixty when they take over their packs. With their slow aging, wolves still look around thirty at that age.

I blank my face to cover up how impressed I am. I have a feeling Luca doesn't need a bigger ego. "Wow. You really are an old man. Who knew the Nightshade Alpha was a cradle robber?" I tell him in as serious of a voice as I can manage, just to irritate him. He's really not that much older than me. It's fun needling the overbearing wolf, though.

Luca glares at me and opens his mouth to say something. Bishop beats him to it. "Izzy," Bishop groans. "Could you try not to antagonize Luca for a whole five seconds, please?"

"You wanted me to talk to them. I'm talking!" I protest. I am technically following his instructions.

"Is she always this mouthy?" Luca asks Bishop with a raised brow.

My mouth pops open at the audacity of this wolf to talk about me like I'm not here. I'm also not mouthy. I just have a sarcastic streak. I growl and send a punch of magic to the infuriating wolf's midsection. He doubles over with a satisfying groan.

Straightening up, Luca advances on me a step, the promise of violence in his eyes. "You want to play, little mate?"

My eyes widen. I flounder for something to say in response to his threat and invitation. Half of me wants to say *hell, yes*. The other half actually has an ounce of self-preservation and screams *no*.

When I don't say anything, Luca chuckles, the sound menacing. "You either agree to go on a date with us, or you can deal with the consequences of your magic alone."

My mouth drops open again that he'd do that. I know he just met me, but I thought maybe he'd care about me, since I'm his mate and all.

Apparently not.

I don't even know why I'm surprised. Most people don't like me, much less care about me.

My heart squeezes at his callous disregard for how dangerous it is for me to let my magic out. I logically know he doesn't have any idea what could happen to me. But it still feels like someone shoved jagged glass around my heart, which tears into the organ with every beat.

I whirl around before he can see just how much his lack of concern guts me. "Goddamn it," I softly growl to the brick in front of me, wanting to kick the wall in frustration. The last thing I need right now is to get emotional in front of my bullheaded mates.

"I don't think he means it, kid. Even if he does, he doesn't know what it could do to you," Aggie says, attempting to reassure me. Her words echo my own thoughts.

Jesus. I must really be a mess if Aggie's being nice to me.

This entire night has been a shit show. I'm so ready for it to be over. My shoulders slump in defeat as I realize I have no other option but to agree to his terms. I turn around, ready to agree. Instead, I come face to face with Bishop's chest. He's standing between me and the wolves, giving me a moment to process everything in peace.

A lump forms in my throat at his thoughtfulness. I let my head thump against his hard chest as I try to absorb his strength. His warm arms wrap around my back, squeezing me comfortingly.

"You okay?" Bishop asks me again.

"I'm just so tired," I whisper brokenly. I'm so tired of taking the whole town's shit. I'm so tired of having the safety of everyone I care about resting on my shoulders. I'm so tired of having to spend all night, every night, crossing ghosts. And all that comes with it.

I'm just fucking tired of it all.

"I'm so sorry, sweetheart. What can I do to help?"

I just shake my head. There's nothing he or anyone can do about it. I'm the only one who can fix anything. That fact just makes me feel more overwhelmed. But I don't have time to fall apart right now. I need to get my shit together and get this over with. There are ghosts I need to cross tonight.

After a moment in Bishop's arms, I'm able to stuff my feelings down. I step back from his hug, swiping my hands over my cheeks. Hopefully, I don't look like I've been close to crying. There's really nothing I can do about it, though. I'm too scared to pull on my magic, even for a simple spell, right now. At least when I'm not blinded by rage at Luca for being an asshole.

"Thanks," I tell Bishop before stepping around him. All three wolves are staring at me with concern. Even Luca.

"I'll go on a date with each of you." There's no snark or fire anywhere in my words. All of it is gone and replaced with bone-deep exhaustion.

Luca's eyes crinkle in worry, instead of flashing with victory, like I thought they would. "What just happened, little mate?" he asks.

"Nothing," I answer, too done with tonight to come up with a creative lie.

Luca frowns at me. "You're a shit liar."

"Yeah. I know."

He huffs out a laugh at my admission.

Bishop looks down at me for a moment before turning back to the wolves. "You basically told her you didn't give a shit if she died. No one wants to hear their mate say that, Luca."

I glare at Bishop for spilling my secrets. He just can't help himself with the wolves tonight, it seems.

"What?" Luca exclaims. "I never said that!"

"You did when you told her you'd leave her to deal with her magic on her own. If Izzy loses control of her magic, she can die. Every single time her magic runs the show, there's a risk she won't ever come back." Bishop's voice gets choked up as he talks about something happening to me. My heart squeezes, seeing my normally stoic mate and best friend close to tears.

I give into the impulse to hug him, wrapping one of my arms around his back. Bishop breaks out into a huge grin at me being the one to initiate it. He bands his muscular arm around me and pulls me tighter into his side.

After dropping a kiss on the top of my hair, Bishop rests his cheek on my head for a moment. I allow myself a second to enjoy his comforting touch and scent.

"I thought losing control of magic was just an inconvenience for mages?" Luca is likely thinking of how young mages frequently lose control right after coming into their power at sixteen. Those control losses are little more than an annoyance. Certainly not a threat to entire towns.

"For most mages, yeah," I confirm bitterly. Not only is my magic weird, but it also came in way too early. I got my magic at seven, which is unheard of. I've had to hide it for almost fourteen years, two-thirds of my life.

Luca tilts his head in consideration. "But not for you?"

"No." I don't want to say anything else and invite questions I can't answer.

"Fuck. I'm sorry, little mate," Luca tells me seriously. My eyebrows jump almost to my hairline at him apologizing. From what I understand, alphas never apologize. I don't have much experience with wolves, though. "I'd never do anything to put you in danger. I'll spar with you, without any conditions. Whatever you need, I'll do it." Luca rakes his hand through his short blond hair as he talks.

I'm taken aback by his concern. It soothes some of the jagged edges of my heart. The pathetic organ feels less like it's a torn, bloody mess. With my sappy heart softened a little toward him, I try to compromise. "How about, if I win, no dates. If you win, then I'll go on a date with each of you."

Luca shook his head, seeming surprised more than anything. "You don't need to do that, little mate."

"I know. Do we have a deal or not?" I ask impatiently. He should agree before I change my mind. This is the only way they'll ever get a date with me. And let's face it—I'm going to lose. Without my magic, I have no hope of winning against the behemoth.

Is going on a date with each of them a spectacularly bad idea?

Yes, yes, it is.

Does my idiotic heart scream at me to spend as much time with them as I can?

Yes, yes, it does.

Hopefully, one date each will be enough to tide me over once I have to stop seeing them. Or it could just make the whole thing more complicated.

Who knows?

I'm winging it here. There's no cheat sheet for getting through this. I just have to make it up as I go.

Luca flicks his aquamarine eyes between mine a few times before nodding. He sticks his hand out to shake. When I grasp it with mine, Luca says, "We have a deal."

CHAPTER 5

IZZY

*T*ucking the loose strands of hair behind my ears to get them out of my face, I start walking out of the alley.

"Where are you going?" Luca questions as he reaches me in a few strides.

Man, having long legs seems super handy. He takes one step to every one of my two. Walking next to him like this, I'm reminded of just how colossal he is.

How does someone even get that tall and built?

Did he sacrifice virgins or something?

Footsteps behind us break me out of my internal musings. Glancing behind me, I see Bishop, Archer, and Cain following a few steps behind us. "To the gym to spar," I tell him. "But I don't want to spar until the gym closes for the night."

"Why?"

"You're, like, seven-feet tall and four hundred pounds of solid muscle. I'm getting my ass beat tonight. I'd rather the whole gym not witness it." I could win against him with magic, but that's pretty much the only way. With how aggressive my magic is tonight, there's no way I'm pulling on it. I'll have to do this without the speed or strength to match him. It'll be impressive if I last even a few minutes against him.

Luca barks out a startled laugh. When I turn to look at him, I see a small grin playing across his lips. He's handsome as hell when he smiles. The rough edges soften just enough to make his face inviting. With his teal eyes crinkled with laughter, he actually looks his age.

What has he been through that his eyes are so hardened normally?

Not that I'm going to ask him. That's dangerously close to giving a shit, and I'm on a strictly no-shits-given diet.

"I'm not seven-feet tall, and I don't weigh four hundred pounds. If you know you're going to lose, why offer me the deal?" Luca peers down at me curiously.

I shrug. "I don't know. It was an impulse decision. I can always take it back if you want."

"No," he immediately growls.

I snort. "Okay, then, wolf boy. No more questions, and I'll hold up my end of the bargain."

We reach the front door to the gym. Luca quickens his steps to get to the door ahead of me. He pulls it open before gesturing for me to go first. Shaking my head at the confusing wolf, I step through while mumbling, "Thanks."

Bishop follows behind me. Turning to him, I ask him something that's been bugging me all night. "How do you know the wolves?"

Bishop's eyes widen at my question. He scrubs his hand over his face, seeming reluctant to answer me. Blowing out a breath, he says, "I've been doing some work for the Nightshade Pack."

My lips part in shock.

"Are you fucking kidding me, St. James?" I ask louder

than I mean to. But I'm hurt that he's been keeping things from me. It quickly turns into anger, an emotion I'm infinitely more comfortable with. "What the fuck happened to no secrets?"

Bishop's annoyance flares in response to mine. "Like you're one to talk. I know you don't tell me everything you do."

He's not wrong. But that's really not the point here.

Rounding on him with my hands on my hips, I hiss, "Those are secrets I have to keep to protect you!"

He leans down so we're practically nose-to-nose. "Why do you think I'm working with them, Isabel? To fucking protect you!"

"What?" I breathe.

"When they come for you," Bishop tells me, not needing to explain who *they* are. They haunt every one of my nightmares, after all. "You'll need allies. Why the fuck do you think I'm working with one of the most dangerous packs out there? To find someone strong enough to protect you because I'm not! And I fucking hate it!"

Bishop is breathing heavily. His chest rises and falls rapidly as he stares me down.

All the wind is knocked out of my sails at his admission. "It's not your job to protect me, Bishop," I tell him quietly.

"Like fuck it isn't, Izzy. You're mine. And I'll protect you till my dying breath," Bishop promises, his voice brooking no argument.

"Don't say that," I plead, my voice breaking. "You know I'm a lost cause. You're going to have to let me go one of these days."

Dying will suck. It'll probably be violent and painful and brutal. It'll likely do irrevocable damage to my soul, keeping me from finding peace in the afterlife. But it'll be worth it because Bishop, Aiden, Rhys, Mom, and Dad will all be okay.

Knowing that everything I do keeps them safe is the only thing that keeps me going. Especially lately, when I've wanted to curl up and just let everything drown me.

"I'm never fucking letting you go, Isabel," Bishop rasps.

I shake my head in denial. "You have to." My voice wobbles, and my lips tremble, thinking about Bishop being dragged down with me. I press my lips together to hide their shaking.

Bishop doesn't say anything else. He just pulls me into a hug. After a moment, I push away from him.

He's getting too attached to me.

Why?

I honestly don't know. I'm a sarcastic bitch most of the time. He has his pick of anyone, and for some unknown reason, he wants me. I need to do better at keeping my distance from him. It's the only way to keep the infuriatingly stubborn man safe.

Glancing to the side, I see the three wolves staring at us. Each of them wears a thoughtful expression. They obviously heard way too much.

Awesome.

Archer is the first to shake it off. "While Luca and Cain clear the gym, you wanna check out our office with me, sunshine?" I raise a brow at his nickname. I've been called many things, but a ray of sunshine isn't one of them. One side of his mouth tilts up at my confusion. "Your hair looks like strands of sunlight. And your disposition is just so sunny, I thought it fit perfectly."

I snort. The man gave me an ironic nickname. He clearly knows the way to my little black heart. Archer's more dangerous than he looks, that's for sure. I'll have to keep an eye on him.

He reaches out his hand for me to take. I hesitantly place mine in his. Exuberant tingles shoot up my arm, dancing and sparking because of his touch. When a mage meets their mate, they feel tingles when they touch for the first twenty-four hours. After that, touching them is like touching anyone else.

Gritting my teeth, I try to shove the feeling away. It doesn't work.

Archer's already turned around, tugging me behind him. He doesn't see the struggle on my face. He pulls me down a plain corridor with black walls and carpet. It has a single steel door at the end. Punching in a code I can't see, Archer quickly unlocks the door and pulls me into the room.

Bishop follows, closing the door after him. He leans against the cool metal of door with his eyes closed, looking exhausted.

Me fucking too, dude.

The office has gray walls, a black carpeted floor, and one small window. Along with a shiny walnut desk and black chair, the only two other items of furniture are two deep ruby chairs.

"Wanna play *Would You Rather?*" Archer asks from his perch on the desk. He's swinging his legs back and forth as he looks at me expectantly. His arms are braced on the desk behind him. When he leans back, I get a flash of washboard abs.

I dart my eyes away before he can catch me staring. Shoving his defined abdomen out of my mind, I focus back on his question. "No," I tell him. I don't want to give him more information about me, even if it's just silly likes and dislikes.

"Mountain or beach?" Archer asks, like I didn't just refuse.

"Forest," I answer to be difficult, unwilling to pick either option. The forest, especially at night, is my favorite place, though.

"Coke or Pepsi?"

"Boylan Bottling Co." Again, an honest answer because their sodas are way better than Coke or Pepsi. But I'm mostly just saying it to annoy him.

"Sweet or salty?"

"Umami." That's the only one that's a lie. I love sweets, especially pastries. They're the one guilty pleasure I allow myself to indulge in.

Archer isn't pissed off with me ignoring the rules of his little game. Instead, he's grinning like a hyena, clearly pleased with me. I narrow my eyes at him, trying to figure out what has him so amused. It only causes his smile to grow larger, lighting up his entire face.

Archer looks like a quintessential surfer dude, with his sun-streaked blond hair and twinkling aquamarine eyes. Even smiling, there's still something dangerous about the wolf. Like my magic can sense he's a threat, even when he's trying his hardest not to seem like one.

Before Archer can ask me any other questions, the door pushes open behind Bishop. He quickly moves away from it to avoid being squished. Luca steps into the room, his eyes roaming over all of us before settling on me. He stares at me for a long moment without saying anything.

I start to fidget under his intense gaze. Noticing my nervous movements, Luca shakes himself out of whatever thoughts he was lost in. "The gym's cleared out. I need to change, then I'm ready to spar."

"Cool. You changing in here?"

He gives me a nod in confirmation. Not saying anything else, I pull open the heavy steel door and step out into the hallway. Bishop and Archer are hot on my heels.

CHAPTER 6

IZZY

*W*hen we reach the main gym space, I snort at what I see.

Cain's doing some sort of punching drill, throwing punches and kicks at empty air. Aggie's pretending to be his opponent. She's landing ghostly punches on him and crowing her victory.

Aggie looks up as we enter. I raise my eyebrows to ask her what she's doing. Aggie shrugs. "I'm bored. It's not like I have a lot to entertain me, kid."

Fair enough. Aggie's been dead a long time. I imagine it gets boring and lonely watching everyone else live their lives while you're frozen in one moment of time. Subtly dipping my chin, I let her know I heard her.

"Which ring does he want to use?" I ask Archer.

The Poisoned Vine is one of the biggest MMA gyms I've seen. It makes sense that it's owned by the Nightshade Pack, since they're wealthier than God. The Gallaghers are well off, but I'm not sure even we match them.

Then again, I'm not entirely sure their money comes from legal sources. There are rumors the Nightshades deal in arms and contract killing. Remembering their reputation just makes me angry all over again that Bishop's been working for them without telling me.

What if he got hurt?

I'm not worth it. I wish he would just realize that.

"Probably the middle one." Archer points to the ring smack-dab in the center of the gym. I'm doubly glad they cleared out everyone. With where Luca wants to spar, the whole gym would get a front-row seat to my beat down.

"Sounds good," I respond before striding toward it. I strip off my hoodie as I walk. Having a loose top will just give Luca something to grab on to. He doesn't need any more advantages over me than he already has.

Someone makes a strangled noise to my right. Turning, I see Cain roving his eyes over my torso. "You're not wearing a shirt," he grits out.

"Um. Yeah. I have a sports bra on," I reply, confused about why he's staring at me like I'm naked. My high-rise leggings come up to right over my belly button. With my sports bra, there's, at most, six inches of my torso showing.

The boy needs to get out more if this is what gets him going.

After one last look at my bare midriff, Cain scrubs his hand over his face and turns away. I stare at him for a beat, wondering what his deal is.

"Your neck and shoulders are exposed, Izzy. You're taunting his wolf," Bishop informs me helpfully.

My eyes widen in realization.

Whoops.

I totally forgot wolves like to chow down on their mates to show possession. Usually, wolves mark their mate in the crook of the shoulder. My strappy black sports bra definitely shows off my neck and shoulders.

But I don't have anything else with me to wear. He's just

going to have to deal with it. Shrugging, I continue to the boxing ring. It has a square perimeter blocked off by ropes. I wonder why Luca doesn't want to spar in the octagon, which is usually used for MMA fighting.

I duck under the ropes to get into the ring. When I straighten, I turn toward the hallway we just came out of.

Luca prowls out of the corridor as I turn. I almost swallow my tongue when I see he's wearing a pair of blue-and-white fighting shorts and nothing else. The entirety of his tanned torso is on display. My gaze bounces between his huge pecs, starkly defined abs, and the V that peeks out of his shorts.

Holy hell. He's even bigger and more muscular than I thought.

I'm also distracted by his tattoos. On his left pec, he has a snarling wolf wrapped in vines. The vines have thorns and star-shaped flowers. Luca has more of the spiked vines trailing down his left arm.

I'm so distracted by my perusal of him, I don't notice he's reached the ring until he's stepped inside it. "Like what you see?" Luca asks in an amused voice. My eyes bounce up to his, and my cheeks burn slightly at getting caught checking him out.

Scoffing, I retort, "I've seen better." That's a big, fat lie. He's, by far, the most muscular man I've ever seen. I'm not going to give him the satisfaction of knowing that, though.

He chuckles at my obvious lie. "First one to tap out loses. That good with you?"

"Yep," I chirp, more than ready to get my humiliation over with.

"You want any protective gear?" Luca asks, glancing down at my bare hands and shins in worry. He's not wearing anything, so I don't see any reason I have to.

I open my mouth to refuse when Bishop pipes up. "Wear

the damn gloves, Izzy. Your hands are already bruised enough."

He chucks a pair of MMA gloves at me before I can refuse. Luckily, my reflexes are fast enough to catch the gloves before they smack me in the face. I glare at Bishop, who just grins at me in return. Shaking my head, I put them on without complaining. Bishop's not going to leave it alone until my hands are protected.

Giving Luca a nod to let him know I'm ready, I walk to the center of the ring. I hold out my fists for him to bump. He walks up and gently taps my comparatively tiny hands with his own.

We circle each other, each observing the other and looking for an opening. Watching Luca doesn't make me feel better about sparring with him. There aren't any obvious weaknesses I can exploit. He's faster, stronger, and better trained than I am.

Sighing, I decide to go on the offense. In a burst of speed, I rush toward him. When I reach him, I hook my leading leg under his weight-bearing leg. Pulling on his leg doesn't topple him to the ground, but it does unbalance him. As he stumbles, I dart in and land a jab to his gut. Before he can react, I dance out of his reach again.

Luca raises his eyebrows at me, surprised I managed to land a hit. I snort. "Did you think I didn't have any experience sparring? I'm not a complete idiot to challenge you to something I've never done before."

He just shrugs with a small smile, not saying anything. We circle each other once more. I rush him again, faking him out with a low kick. He dodges it but can't dodge the second low kick I aim at him.

I quickly get out of his reach once I've kicked him. With how giant he is, I can't get too close. If he has a chance to get me to the ground, it's over for me.

Luca rewards me with a full smile this time.

What a weirdo. Why does me kicking him make him grin?

He rushes me, not giving me any time to think about it. Luca lands a soft hit before retreating.

We continue like this for a while, trading kicks and hits. He pulls his punches and kicks. I don't, and it still doesn't seem to make a difference to the wolf. It feels like I'm hitting solid marble anytime I connect with his body. I'm pretty sure it hurts me more than it hurts him.

Eventually, I'm worn out from the back and forth. "Stop fucking playing with me, wolf boy. Just finish this." I'm too tired to keep up with him.

He stares at me intently for a moment or two.

Then he charges. There's no warning he's about to move. One second, he's on the opposite side of the ring from me. The next, he's crashing into me, taking me to the floor. I don't even have a chance to react. Much less dodge.

Luca sticks a hand behind my head to keep me from banging it on the floor when he takes me down. He straddles me, his heavy hips pinning me to the ground.

But it's not Luca I see over me.

Instead, I'm bombarded by flashes of unwanted bodies pinning me to hard surfaces. I can almost smell their rancid breath and feel their cruel hands grabbing places they shouldn't.

Fuck! Nope. Not today. This is not fucking happening right now.

I'm a goddamn idiot.

Bishop has pinned me so many times while sparring, and it never made the memories surface. So, I thought I was safe to spar with Luca. But a man I just met pinning me down is apparently a different scenario to my fucked-up brain.

I need him to get off me before I break down. Bucking

my hips doesn't do anything, and I'm too lost to the memories to remember my grappling training. So, I gasp out, "Get off me!"

Luca smirks at me before seeing my wild eyes. He immediately scrambles off me, kneeling and holding his hands up in surrender.

I want the floor to open up and swallow me now that Luca's seeing this piece of me that I keep hidden from everyone, including Bishop and my family. Closing my eyes, I try to hold off the tears that want to spill down my face. When I realize I can't, I hop up.

"I need a minute," I shout before rushing off toward the locker room.

CHAPTER 7

IZZY

I slam the door behind me and lean my forehead against the smooth surface. Tears run down my cheeks and silent sobs rack my frame. I haven't mastered not crying, but I have perfected crying silently.

Nothing even happened to me. Lots of people have gone through so much worse.

What gives me the right to be so messed up about a little over the clothes touching?

Nothing.

I'm just a crybaby.

"You need me to get Bishop, kid?" Aggie asks as she floats through the wall next to the door. I can give her enough juice for her to interact slightly with Bishop. He knows the signs of Aggie trying to get his attention.

I shake my head. "No. He doesn't know."

Aggie sucks in a surprised ghostly breath. "You didn't tell him?"

"No," I rasp past the emotion choking me. "What the fuck am I supposed to tell him? He'll absolutely lose his shit if he finds out." Bishop is crazy protective over me. If he finds out

47

some of the boys at school have tried to force me into things, he won't be able to stop himself from killing them. That's a one-way ticket to mage jail. I won't allow that to happen to him.

It's been six months or so since anyone's tried it. I should be over it by now. But I'm clearly not. Even worse, I just made an absolute ass of myself in front of all four of them.

"I don't know, kid. But it's not healthy to keep things like that inside," Aggie says sagely.

Scoffing, I ask, "What about my lifestyle is heathy, Aggie? We both know I'm not going to make it to thirty, maybe not even twenty-five. If *they* don't kill me, my nightly activities will. So, what does it really matter?"

"Don't talk like that, kid," Aggie gently admonishes. She's in almost as much denial as Bishop is. They both think there's a future for me. They're both wrong.

Not saying anything further, I ride out the emotions until I finally stop trembling. The tears dry up, and the sadness ebbs away. In its place is white-hot anger. It burns my insides and makes me feel something other than shame and self-loathing.

Some of the anger is at those guys who touched me without consent. Most of it, though, is at myself.

I should be stronger.

I shouldn't have let myself get into those situations.

Needing an outlet for my anger, I pull my fist back and aim it at the white wood door. "Kid!" Aggie yells before I can make contact with it.

"What?" I snarl, too lost to my rage and pain to be polite.

"They have punching bags here. Don't break your hand punching a door!" Aggie's words manage to break through the anger suffocating me.

Giving her a sharp nod, I pull open the bathroom door. I don't look at any of my mates as I head over to the punching bags. When I reach the bag, I rip off my gloves. I attack the bag bare knuckled, needing the pain to ground me and keep me from drowning.

After a few punches, Bishop walks up behind me. I brace myself for him to try to stop me or make me wear the gloves. "Here," is all he says as he thrusts my headphones and phone at me. A lump forms in my throat at his thoughtfulness. Bishop always knows exactly what I need.

Would he still want me, knowing how weak I am?

I can't think about that. I've cried enough for an entire lifetime tonight. Thinking about that just makes the tears threaten to spill again. So, I shove it out of my mind as I snatch the earbuds and phone from Bishop.

None too gently putting my earbuds in, I put on "Making the Bed." I don't see if Bishop walks away, because I'm too focused on punching. With my music going, I lose myself to the rhythmic thumping of my fists against the bag.

After a particularly hard punch, I feel my left pinky and ring finger knuckles crunch as they hit the bag. Bright, intense pain flares in my hand. It feels like a lightning bolt hit those two knuckles and set them on fire. "Fuck!" I shout, partly from the pain and partly from frustration at myself.

It was stupid not to use the gloves. Now I can't keep punching, because I'm pretty sure they're broken.

Yanking my earbuds out, I carelessly toss them on the ground near their case. I scrub my other hand over my face as all four men come rushing over.

"What happened?" Archer asks, as he's the first one to reach me.

Blowing out a breath, I debate not answering any of them. But I need Bishop to heal it for me. I'm not in control of myself enough to use my magic right now. "I broke my knuckles," I grit out.

Archer's eyes widen at my admission, but his brother is the one who asks, "Can I see them?"

Nodding, I hold out my left hand for Luca to inspect. His warm hand gently grabs my wrist. The other supports my palm as he gets a look at it. His gentleness surprises me, especially coming from the guy who was a major asshole in the alley.

The other three lean over to see it too. It's already starting to swell. My knuckles are bruised from earlier, so my hand looks a mess. "Yeah. Those are broken," Luca confirms with a nod, his aquamarine eye jumping up to mine. "You're handling the pain well. You break your hands often?"

Somehow, I refrain from snorting. If only he knew. Broken knuckles are a walk in the park compared to what happens nightly in the forest. "Something like that," I reply evasively.

Luca assesses me for a moment. But he doesn't push for me to answer, surprising me again. Maybe he's not as much of a jackhole as he seemed.

"Need me to heal that for you?" Bishop asks tiredly. Looking at his drawn eyes and lips flattened into a harsh line, I feel awful for putting him through this. I know he hates seeing me hurt.

If the roles were reversed, I'd be fucking pissed at him. But Bishop is used to dealing with my recklessness. He's not even angry anymore, just resigned.

"Yeah," I answer, my voice small and pathetic.

Bishop notices the change in my voice. "I'm not mad at you, Iz." He tries to reassure me as his hand hovers over my damaged one. Luca's still carefully holding it, keeping it steady for Bishop. Warming blue light surrounds my hand, knitting together the broken joints. I sigh in relief as the pain slowly fades away.

"I know. It'd be better if you were," I tell him.

Bishop huffs out a laugh. "You'd rather I yell at you?"

"It's better than your quiet disappointment," I whisper, feeling the damn tears threaten again.

"I'm not disappointed, Izzy. I'm just worried. So fucking worried, it makes me sick. You're going to get yourself killed one of these days, and I don't know what to do to stop it." Bishop's voice breaks at the end, and he closes his eyes to gather himself.

He's not wrong, but I don't know what to say to make him feel better. While I desperately want to reassure him, I also refuse to lie to him.

Aggie saves me from having to figure it out. "I'm sorry to interrupt, but we have to go, kid. The ghosts are getting antsy. They'll wander off before long."

Sighing, I ask Bishop, "Can you open a portal for me to my backyard?" He doesn't know exactly where I go in the forest behind my house. I'd like to keep it that way, so I'll just hike the rest of the way to my clearing.

"Yeah." Bishop turns away from my now mostly healed hand. I still can't punch with it, because the insides aren't fully healed. Mage magic fixes most of the damage and accelerates healing, but wounds still take time to heal, even with magic. But it doesn't hurt anymore, which is a win in my book.

Now that my hand is as healed as it's going to get, I gather up my earbuds and phone. Walking over to the sweatshirt I stole from Bishop, I pull it on and shove my stuff in the pocket.

"Where are you going?" Luca asks, sounding almost as tired as Bishop.

Christ. I sure do have a way with boys if I can wear on Luca that much after only a few hours.

"Into the woods." I can't help but softly sing the iconic

line from my favorite musical. I love anything that subverts your expectations. *Into the Woods* is excellent at that.

Luca's brows furrow in confusion, my reply not really answering his question.

Before he can ask anything else, I turn on my heel and head for the portal Bishop just opened. I call over my shoulder, "Well, I wish I could say it was nice to meet you. But, quite frankly, it was soul destroying."

I'm about to step through the portal when Cain softly asks, "Was it really that bad to find out we're your mates?" The imposing wolf's voice wobbles a little.

Way to make me feel like shit, dude.

Sighing, I turn back to the three wolves. Dropping the attitude I usually use as a shield, I let them see some of the exhaustion and sadness I try to hide.

"No, Cain. It's not about you. If I were a normal girl, I'd be fucking thrilled to be mates with you. But I'm not normal. And finding three more men who were meant for me that I can't be with is a special kind of torture," I tell him simply.

Because it is. It takes every ounce of self-control I have to keep Bishop at arm's length. Now, I have to find the strength to keep three determined wolves at a distance too.

"Do yourself a favor, Cain, and forget about me. Forget about the fucked-up mage that fate hated you enough to pair you with. Go find yourself a nice, normal wolf to have nice, normal babies with and live a nice, normal, *safe* life together. It'll be better for you that way," I finish as I turn back toward the portal.

Before I step through, Cain calls, "And where will you be while I'm living this normal life you dreamed up for me?"

I let out a humorless chuckle. "Dead," I whisper, so quietly, I'm not sure they can understand me. Without waiting to see if they heard, I step through the portal.

CHAPTER 8

LUCA

"Well, that was a shit show," Bishop mutters as he watches our little mate walk through the portal. He scrubs both of his hands over his face before closing the rip in space.

Even though she's out of our sight, Izzy is burned into my memory. When I close my eyes, all I see is her delicate heart-shaped face, small button nose, and kissable pink lips. Her gray eyes are striking, in part because of the pain swimming in them. Even when she's smiling, Izzy's eyes are still drowning in heartache.

Her anguish kills me. She's so young. There's no reason she should be hurting so much. But I'm probably the last person she wants to open up to about it now.

How small Izzy is also triggers my protective instincts. Nightshade wolves tend to be tall and pack on more muscle. She's almost a whole foot shorter than me and four inches shorter than most women in my pack.

Yet, even with her small stature, Izzy refused to back down. I could tell we scared her multiple times. She never cowered or ran, though. Izzy just tipped up her chin and wordlessly dared us to do our worst. That takes a hell of a lot of courage.

Archer laughs. "That's one way to put it. Would it kill you not to be a prick, for once, Luca?"

I wince because he's right. For the millionth time, I find myself wishing my parents were still here. My dads were always the charmers. They'd know exactly what I should say to get Izzy to forgive me and what I shouldn't say going forward.

My mom would have loved Izzy's fire. She'd have cackled at Izzy's sarcastic remarks and given her tips on how to get under our skin even more. Mom would have been overjoyed at finally having a daughter to do girly stuff with. She'd love someone to share all the Nightshade family recipes with.

All four of them are missing out on so much. I sometimes wonder if all the good parts of me died that night. It never bothered me until I met Izzy.

The only thing I can say in my defense is, "She ran."

"Yeah, dickhead, we know," Cain grumbles. "How you acted just makes her want to keep running."

I groan because he has a point. I certainly didn't do myself any favors by being a dick to Izzy.

I'm surprised Cain gives a shit about me scaring her off. With everything he's been through, I would've thought he'd be happy that we made a horrible first impression on her.

Most people would be shocked I let Cain and Archer talk to me like this. As the Nightshade Alpha, I have a merciless reputation. Outsiders think I rule our pack with an iron fist and don't tolerate dissent.

While I'm not a pushover, I don't rule the pack through fear. They're my family. A good alpha listens to his pack and meets their needs. A weak alpha uses his pack to meet his own needs. I just have to hope my dads would be proud of how I'm leading our pack, because everything I do is for their sake.

After what happened to my parents, I realized the Night-shade Pack needed to be stronger to prevent anything like that from happening again. That's why I've created the reputation I have. Although I'm not violent with my pack, I am with anyone who poses a threat to us. I've earned every inch of my murderous, cruel reputation. The things I've done to keep my family safe have tainted my soul. It's worth it to protect everyone.

Shoving a hand through my hair, I try to think about how to fix the mess I made with Izzy. But first, I need to know something. "Did you know she was our mate, Bishop?" I growl at the mage.

He barks out a humorless laugh. "No, Luca, I didn't. If I had, I sure as hell wouldn't have introduced her to you like this. I actually want her to like you assholes."

"I always wondered what made you ballsy enough to approach us in the first place, Bishop. Now I know," Archer comments with a chuckle.

Two years ago, Bishop approached our pack about working for us. I was skeptical of him at first, but he's been invaluable in protecting our pack. Without his spells, our pack would have been an easy target for our many enemies. His magic is also a massive help in running our businesses. The mage doesn't shy away from dirty work.

At first, Bishop was a threat. Now, he's as much a brother to me as Archer, just like Cain. Bishop's proven his loyalty over and over again, and he's repeatedly shown that he's a good man. We're lucky to have him on our side.

"I'd do anything for Izzy. The woman has no idea she holds my heart in the palm of her hand. She still encourages me to fuck other people," he says while shaking his head.

My brows jump up in surprise. "Why?" That's not normal

mate behavior. Most mates are extremely jealous. I haven't even known Izzy for a day, but I'll kill anyone, other than her mates, who touches her.

Bishop sighs. "She thinks it'll keep me safe."

"Why would it keep you safe?" Cain interjects. He pushes his floppy onyx hair out of his eyes. It's always getting in his way, but he refuses to cut it. Even though I know why, I still wish he was able to. The past still has such a hold on him. Maybe our little mate can help him break free of it.

"I can't tell you," Bishop growls, fury seeping into his voice. He takes an agitated swing at one of the punching bags in front of us, his fist connecting with a solid thump. Muttering under his breath, he asks, "Why can't Izzy ever catch a break?"

"Why can't you tell us?" I press, trying to understand what's going on. I can't keep my little mate safe if I don't know what's threatening her.

"Izzy would never forgive me. Telling you would put the three of you in danger. I'm willing to do almost anything for Izzy's happiness, but betraying her trust isn't one of them." Bishop hangs his head when he finishes.

"Fair enough, man," Archer replies, trying to defuse the situation. He's a natural peacekeeper, always trying to make everyone happy. "Can you at least tell us about what she meant with her last comment?"

My heart rate kicks up at the reminder of our mate talking about her death like it wouldn't kill us too. She clearly doesn't understand what mating means if she thinks we can just find someone else to replace her. From the moment we met her, she's all there will ever be for us.

Bishop clenches his jaw and closes his eyes. He scrubs a hand over his face before opening his eyes again. "People like Izzy don't have a long life expectancy. Part of what she can do is also dangerous. She swears she's stopped doing it after she almost died, but I don't know if I believe her. That's the thing about her. Izzy will always put everyone else before herself. Even if it kills her."

I trade concerned looks with Archer and Cain at what Bishop is sharing. What the fuck does he mean, our mate doesn't have a long life expectancy? It also worries me that Izzy's so quick to put everyone else before her own well-being. That's a recipe for burnout.

I won't press Bishop for more information on what she is, because I respect him protecting her trust. But I do have one other question about her. "What caused her reaction to me pinning her?" The sheer terror on her face as I pinned her down will haunt me for the rest of my life. I never want my mate to be scared, but it's so much worse when I'm the one who did it.

Other than the end, I enjoyed sparring with her. I'm impressed with her skills. Izzy was so sure she'd lose, but she put up a good fight. Her technique was spot on, both with sparring and her punching bag work earlier.

As soon as I came into the gym tonight, I knew my mate was here. Instead of rushing over, I observed her as she pounded on the punching bag. Her form was nearly perfect. I'm surprised she was able to hit the bag for almost two hours straight. Most mages don't have that stamina.

After our sparring, her punching was sloppy. That's probably why she broke her damn hand. I'm not sure what worried me the most—the fact that she fractured two knuckles or that she had a minimal reaction to the pain. There's no reason she should be so accustomed to pain that broken knuckles barely phase her.

"I don't know. I've pinned her many times before. She's never had a reaction like that. But I'm damn well asking her the next time we're alone." Bishop's blue eyes are swimming with both rage and pain. I understand the feeling when it comes to Izzy. The little mage has turned me inside out in a matter of hours.

"Let us know what she tells you or at least what we can do to avoid triggering her. What's the best time for us to take her out on the dates?" Cain's the planner out of us. Without his meticulous organization, there's no way our pack would be thriving like it is.

"If you don't want Izzy to hate you, ask her yourself. She can't stand people deciding things for her," Bishop informs us. He squints his eyes in thought. "Izzy should be free Monday afternoon. If you head down to Hawthorne Grove, we can all hang out together. Hopefully Izzy will be a little more receptive to you three after cooling off this weekend."

Both Archer and I look at Cain. He knows our schedule better than either of us. After thinking for a moment, he nods to himself. "That'll work. Text me the address and time, and we'll be there."

Bishop gives us a curt nod in response, clearly lost in his own thoughts. I bet he's worrying about Izzy. That'll be the norm for all of us from now on. I can already tell she'll make me go gray way before a hundred.

He opens up a portal ringed in blue magic almost the same color as Izzy's. Bishop starts toward it before turning back to me at the last second with a half grin. "Bring the Charger, Luca. Izzy will get a kick out of it, and you could use all the brownie points you can get with her right now."

I huff out a laugh, wondering if my little mate likes cars as much as I do. "I can do that. We'll see you Monday, Bishop."

CHAPTER 9

IZZY

"You're really pretty," Billy, the ghost I just finished healing, tells me. With floppy curly brown hair, a baby face, and a lanky build, he looks far too young to be dead.

"Um. Thanks." I look at Aggie to see if she has any idea what to say when a dead kid hits on you. She shrugs her shoulders at me. Not sure how to respond, I just ask, "Are you ready to move on?"

I never force the ghosts Aggie brings to me to move on. Once I heal them, though, most want to cross over.

Billy nods while staring at my boobs. I roll my eyes at him. Even dead, boys are all the same, I guess. Turning to the horizon, I point out the road that leads over the lime green hills. "Follow the yellow brick road. It'll take you where you need to go."

He looks off into the distance, probably taking in the lavender sky and fluffy baby blue clouds for the first time. With a bright orange sun, chartreuse and hot-pink plants, and blue rocks, the spirit realm is an interesting experience. It's kind of like if a preschooler colored our world with only markers from the neon pack. Everything's super saturated, and the colors don't always make sense.

"Like *The Wizard of Oz?*" Billy questions, his brows pulling down in confusion. His brown eyes are clear now, unlike when Aggie first brought him to me. He's not deathly pale anymore, either.

I chuckle. "Yep, just like that." Whoever created *The Wizard of Oz* either had to have been to the spirit realm or heard about it from someone who had. It's too much of a coincidence to be anything else.

"Is it scary? The afterlife?" Billy nervously looks at the yellow path disappearing over the hill. Most ghosts are a little scared of crossing over. It's understandable to be worried. No one really knows what's on the other side, not even me.

"I don't think it's any scarier than what you've already been through. If it helps, the people I've seen cross over always do it with a smile." I usually let people cross over in peace. But some ghosts want someone there with them. Whatever I can do to ease the transition, I try to do.

"Okay," Billy hedges, kicking the blue dirt with the tip of one of his beat-up Vans. Rolling his lips between his teeth, he rocks on his heels for a moment before coming to a decision. "I'll go. I'm ready to see my family again." My heart squeezes at everything the kid's been through. I usually don't ask ghosts what happened to them. Billy wanted to share, so I was happy to listen.

With a wave, Billy trots off down the yellow brick road. Aggie and I keep watching, even after he's out of sight, until we see the flash of purple lightning. That's how we know he's successfully crossed over.

Turning to Aggie, I take in her wild red curls, vibrant blue eyes, and deep green velvet dress. Unlike when I'm in the land of the living, I can see Aggie in full color here. "You ever think about crossing over?"

Aggie's been dead for nearly one hundred and fifty years. That's a long time to be stuck in limbo. "Sometimes. Maybe once I know you're settled, I'll cross," Aggie tells me as she stares at the brick pathway. I nod, even knowing that won't ever happen.

We stand in silence for several beats, just listening to the wind blow, the birds squawk, and the insects chirp. For being a gateway between the living and the dead, the spirit realm is surprisingly full of life.

"Was Billy the last one?" I ask Aggie.

She nods, fiery curls bouncing at the motion. "Yep. Your power keeps growing, kid. That was the eighth ghost tonight." I used to struggle with healing and crossing one ghost every week. Now, I can do up to ten a night without being completely drained.

It doesn't seem to make a difference, though. No matter how many I cross, there are still so many who need my help. When people are killed in especially brutal ways, like being tortured or ritualistically murdered after watching their whole family be killed, it damages their soul. When souls are too messed up, they can't cross over. They're perpetually stuck in limbo, never finding peace.

With my magic, I can heal these soul wounds. I'm the only one who can, as far as we know. One twenty-one-year-old is responsible for healing all of the fucked-up ghosts on the planet. Whoever decided that was a good idea should be sacked. There's no way I can keep up with the demand, but I keep trying.

"Yeah. I just wish I could do more."

"You do great, kid. Now, stop stalling. You need to go to class today," Aggie reminds me.

I scoff. "Easy for you to say, when you're not the one that

has to do it." But I know she's right. I don't really have time to waste.

With a deep breath, I throw myself backward. This flings me out of the spirit realm and back into my body. For a single moment, everything's peaceful. Blissful, even.

Then my abdomen rips open, and I scream. My back arches off the forest floor as I experience the injury that killed Billy. Blood gushes from the wound, soaking into my running shorts. I'm pretty sure my intestines are spilling out of my belly, but I don't really want to know. All I can focus on is the pounding, throbbing pain in my stomach.

The price I pay for healing ghosts is experiencing every agonizing physical injury that killed them. Through my magic, I experience the same injury without any lasting damage. I can be gutted and healed within an hour, as long as I have enough magic left. If I run out of magic, then I die from the mortal wound. That possibility is why I keep what I do every night secret from Bishop and my family.

In Billy's case, he was gutted and bled out. When Aggie brought him to me tonight, his eyes were hollow and his face blank. His spirit was completely shut down from the trauma of his death. Poor Billy wasn't just murdered. He also watched a psycho kill his parents and baby sisters before the same guy tortured and killed him.

While his family was killed just as horrifically as he was, none of them had trouble crossing over. It doesn't always make sense which ghosts have too much soul damage to move on.

I scream until my voice is too hoarse to scream anymore. Then I scream silently and writhe on the forest floor. The stabbing pain pours over me in waves. It spreads to the top of my head, all the way down to the tips of my toes. Every single inch of me feels like it's getting battered by a spiked bat. Repeatedly.

Unfortunately, I can't retreat into my mind to get away from the pain. If I do, it stops the process, waiting for me to fully experience it before continuing. Why I have to feel the full extent of the pain, I don't know. But I do it every single night to help people who no one else can.

My penchant for screaming is why I always put up a silencing dome before healing ghosts. It would be awkward if anyone heard me screaming and stumbled upon me in the middle of the forest, bleeding profusely.

After who knows how long, the pain stops. My insides knit themselves back together with an audible snap. I'm left a bloody, but healed, mess. I pant quietly as I lie there. "What time is it?" I croak to Aggie, who's hovering at my feet. Her eyes are pinched with worry after watching me heal a fatal injury for the eighth time tonight.

She floats over to my left wrist before peering down at the watch I wear for this exact purpose. "It's five in the morning."

"Fuck my life," I groan. I've spent yet another full night healing ghosts, so I don't have time to get much sleep before class today. "Wake me up in an hour, please."

I drift off, exhausted from healing so many injuries in such a short time.

IT FEELS like I just close my eyes when Aggie shouts, "Kid! Get up!"

"Five more minutes," I mumble, too tired and sore to get out of bed right now. What the hell did I do last night that made me hurt so much?

"No can do, kid. Get up, now! You can't afford to miss school!" Aggie yells at full volume. It startles me enough that I blink open my eyes. I see trees and a blue sky above me, instead of my purple room. That's when I remember that I never made it to my bed last night.

I groan. Today's going to suck. Thursday night was the last night I managed more than an hour or two of sleep. I'm running on empty on this not-so-delightful Monday morning.

Rolling over onto all fours, I'm able to struggle to my feet. Once I'm standing, I sway side to side, staggering like a drunk.

The first order of business is cleaning up the blood. My mom would flip if she found bloody laundry in my hamper. "*Purgare*," I whisper while thinking about cleaning off the blood and forest gunk caked on my abdomen. A gentle breeze blows over my stomach. When I look down, everything's cleaned up, including my shorts and sports bra.

Since that's taken care of, I need to go home. Luckily, I don't have to walk back. I'm able to focus long enough to open a portal to my room. I gratefully stumble through the opening, falling back to my knees once I reach the plush carpet.

"What can I do, kid?" Aggie questions as she hovers next to me, wringing her hands anxiously. Aggie's the only one who sees what I do every night and the toll it takes on me. It's hard for her to witness me in so much pain, night in, night out.

"There's nothing you can do, Aggie. I just have to power through today. Then I can fucking sleep."

Rubbing my gritty eyes, I push to my feet again. I shuffle to my closet and pull out the first top and pants I find. Shrugging on one of Bishop's faded black band tees, I step into my high-rise dark jeans next. Once I shove my feet into my Chucks, I'm ready to go.

"You need the rest. I'm not bringing any ghosts for you tonight. You can't keep going so many days without sleep."

Aggie stares me down, daring me to argue with her. I'm not planning on it. She's right. I can't keep pushing so hard. It's not sustainable, and I'm going to burn out one of these days.

Nodding to show I heard her, I sling my plain backpack over my shoulder and head for the door. "Your shirt's on inside out, kid," she tells me. Looking down, I see she's right.

"Fuck my life." I sigh as I quickly change it around and tuck it back in. I have a feeling that's how the whole day is going to go today.

CHAPTER 10

IZZY

I blink open my eyes to see my family, Bishop, and the wolves in a line, with their hands cuffed in front of them. Glancing down, I take in the plain white dress I'm always wearing in these damn dreams. Even though I know it's a dream, I'm powerless to do anything to change it.

Still, I try to yank my hands free of the magic-dampening cuffs. All I succeed in doing is wrenching my shoulders, the cold metal not budging an inch. Even though I'm currently magicless, the two burly guards grip my shoulders like I'm a flight risk. There's no way I'd run and leave everyone I care about behind.

"Isabel Magnolia Gallagher, the council hereby finds you guilty of every crime you were charged with. You are sentenced to execution," the smarmy voice booms from somewhere behind me. I can't turn around to see which councilman it is. "Your family and friends are sentenced to execution by magic as well. It is your fault they have to die. Such a shame the selfishness of one mage will lead to the extinction of two prestigious mage lines."

"No!" I scream as I buck and twist to speak face-to-face to the man doing the sentencing. The two guards prevent me from turning around. "Leave them out of it! They didn't do anything wrong." My begging and pleading never changes anything, but I have to try.

"Carry out the sentence for everyone but her. Let her watch the consequences of defying us," the disembodied voice orders.

One guard steps up to Bishop, the first person in the line. His blue eyes turn accusingly toward me. He doesn't have to say anything for me to understand he blames me. "Meeting you was the worst thing to ever happen to me," Bishop tells me. I flinch at his words, not because they're too harsh but because they're true. He deserved so much more than me.

Then the guard casts a spell. A sickly green light encircles Bishop's head. He can't breathe through the bubble, and he claws at his throat, trying to get air in. It doesn't work. After a few minutes, Bishop stops struggling. His limp body drops to the ground with a thud.

"No!" I wail, with tears running down my cheeks. My shoulders shake with sobs as I scream in devastation, "Bishop!" I fight the cruel hands holding me, wanting to go over to my best friend and the only person who really knows me. No matter how much I struggle, I can't get free.

Instead, I have to watch the guard kill everyone I love, one by one.

"I wish you were never born," my mom hisses at me before she's killed.

"You are our greatest regret," my dad tells me solemnly before being suffocated.

"Our family was better without you," Rhys informs me before he, too, asphyxiates.

"We never loved you," Aiden shouts before he's choked to death.

I scream and cry and beg and plead for all of their lives. It never does anything. By the time they finish with my family, I'm sobbing so hard, I can barely breathe. It feels like someone took a sledgehammer to my chest, and all my bones are shattered and poking my heart. I wish they'd just kill me already. Dying is better *than living with a gaping, ragged wound where my heart is supposed to be.*

The wolves are a new addition to this horror show. While I just met them a few days ago, they already feature in my recurring nightmare.

Great.

"I wish I never met you," Luca grits out.

"We deserved a better mate than you," Archer says without his signature smile.

"You weren't worth it," Cain spits, driving the final spike into my already shredded heart. The guard kills all three of them at once. By the time their bodies hit the ground, I'm numb. I don't feel anything anymore. My mind is too overwhelmed to process the all-consuming grief.

"I'm sorry," I gasp out to the row of dead bodies. Not that it'll do anything. Nothing I do will ever undo all the carnage I cause just by existing.

"Save your apologies. Your kind doesn't deserve to live. Nothing you say will make us spare you," the voice behind me booms. "Throw the girl on the pyre."

I don't try to fight the guards as they drag me to the burning funeral pyre. I don't try to stop them from throwing me on top of it. I don't try to escape the flames licking across my body, charring my clothes and skin. Instead, I welcome the oblivion of death.

"Miss Gallagher!" A nasally voice yanks me out of my nightmare.

My head jerks up off my desk at hearing my name, breaking me free of my dream. I look around, dazed and confused, having no idea where I am. It takes me a moment to realize I'm in my advanced magic theory class. I guess I fell asleep during the lecture. Subtly, I wipe my hands over my eyes to clean up any tears that leaked out from my dream.

"Am I boring you, Miss Gallagher?" Professor Moore sneers. He's a stout man with a round belly. His black hair is thinning, and his brown eyes remind me of a weasel. As a mage from a lower family, he especially enjoys tormenting me during his classes.

"Absolutely," I reply honestly. Advanced magic, my ass. I was doing spells more complex than this at ten years old. Plus, after being awake for nearly three days and just having a soul-crushing nightmare, I have no tolerance for his petty bullshit.

Professor Moore sputters, and his face turns red in anger. I don't think he expected me to answer honestly. Unfortunately for him, apologizing isn't my default setting. "Out of my classroom! I won't tolerate this behavior! Go to the dean!" Professor Moore screams at me.

"Yep," I reply, not even fighting it. Instead, I shove all of my stuff back in my backpack and get up. I don't bother to glance around the classroom to see the smug faces of my classmates. They love whenever I get in trouble. My suffering is these entitled assholes' preferred entertainment.

Don't they realize there's so much more going on in the world than petty mage politics? How can they spend all their time social climbing when so many people are suffering?

Sometimes, I want to scream at all of them. I want to shake them out of their safe little bubble and make them look at real problems. Everything my classmates care about— status, money, and power—doesn't matter in the grand scheme of things. Even the richest and most powerful people still die. Instead of using their resources for good, the people of Hawthorne Grove live their lives selfishly. They use their gifts for personal gain, never to help others.

It drives me crazy. I can't wait to never see this fucking town again. Once I graduate, I'm moving to some normal human city and never thinking about these horrible people again.

Shaking my head, I stalk out of the classroom, tuning out the laughter that follows me.

While I try to walk steadily, I stumble once I'm out of the room. The short nap did nothing to alleviate my exhaustion. I feel like I'm about to pass out, and the hallway spins like a gravity ride at an amusement park.

Hopefully I can keep it together enough to avoid puking on the dean. He wouldn't be happy about that. Dean Murphy already hates me enough as it is. I'm sure he would expel me if he could. The only thing stopping him is the sizable donation my family makes every year. If he kicks me out, HGU will lose their biggest donor.

While Dean Murphy can't expel me, he can make my life hell. He's a pro at making this school even worse than it is. I'm super excited to see what punishment I get today. Not.

"You don't look so good, kid," Aggie chimes in suddenly from beside me.

I stumble and crash into the wall at her appearing out of thin air. "Jesus fuck!" I hiss in surprise. "What the hell, Aggie! Where did you even come from?"

"Well, you see, when two mages love each other very much—" Aggie breaks off as I make a gagging sound at the thought of her parents getting it on. I very much don't need to picture two old people banging. She grins at my theatrics. "You pulled me to you. You're running on empty with how much magic you used this weekend."

"Don't I know it," I mutter as I rub my hands over my tired eyes. It doesn't help.

Sighing, I shuffle down the curving stone stairs of Gallagher Hall. Aggie floats silently next to me. We don't talk, in case someone is near enough to hear me.

The door to the courtyard is right next to the stairs, so I'm out in the bright sunlight in no time. Blinding light stings my gritty eyes and causes my head to throb painfully. Luckily, it's only a quick walk to the Byrne building, which houses all the administrative offices.

I heave open the heavy, dark-wood doors and trudge up to the third floor. The dean has his own floor in the building because, of course, he does. How could a pompous asshole be expected to share a floor with peasants? That would just be agony for him.

As I push open the jet-black doors to his personal office, I'm greeted by the sight of one of my two favorite people on campus.

"Isabel, lovely to see you!" Judith, the dean's assistant greets me. She's a tiny woman, and she has her gray hair pulled back into a perfect bun. Her blue eyes always twinkle with joy behind her glasses. Today, she wears a deep purple dress with a lacy black cardigan.

Judith hops out of her chair and walks to me with surprising speed for an old woman. It takes her no time at all to move from her antique walnut desk and across the thick navy carpet to where I'm standing. She wraps her thin arms around me, enfolding me in a grandmotherly hug. I hug her back, needing some comfort after the dream I just had.

"What are you doing here, dear?" Judith asks me kindly. She knows I never venture to the dean's office willingly.

"I got in trouble for falling asleep in class," I tell her with a wince. Judith is one of two people I respect here, so I want her to think positively of me. I don't want her to think I'm a lazy bum like the rest of the school does.

"Have you not been sleeping well, dear?" she asks, not judging me for falling asleep in class. My shoulders slump in relief, and I shake my head no. "I can tell. Let me talk to the dean for you. You're not in any shape to deal with that nasty man. What's the easiest punishment for you right now?"

I snort at her calling her boss a nasty man. She's not wrong. Dean Murphy is a pathetic excuse of a mage.

Humming, I try to think of what I can do in my half-dead state right now.

"Probably running laps for Levi. Other than you, he's the only one here who doesn't hate my guts." Levi doesn't allow any of the usual bullying in his class. That's why I'm taking another one of his classes this semester. It doesn't hurt to learn more self-defense techniques, either.

"They're just jealous. I'll go talk to the dean. Have a seat, dear. You look like a feather could knock you over." Judith points out the row of black velvet chairs across from her desk. As I head over to the chairs, Judith pulls open the gold door to the dean's office and slips inside.

I sink onto the cushy seat and lean my head back against the royal blue paisley wallpaper. My eyes slip closed as I wait for her.

CHAPTER 11

IZZY

*M*inutes later, I hear the door creak open. Prying my burning eyelids apart, I squint at Judith as she walks toward me. "The dean agreed to twenty laps. I hate to rush you out, dear, but it's best if you leave before he comes back out."

"Thanks, Judith. You're a lifesaver," I tell her with a tired smile.

While running five miles when I can barely stand won't be fun, at least it's doable.

Some of my past punishments include cleaning the entire school and cooking food for all students and staff for a week. Both of those tasks are usually done with magic. My brothers have come in to help me do tasks that are pretty impossible without magic. The dean hates it.

Pushing to my feet, I give Judith one more hug before heading out. Once I'm out of the building, I pull my earbuds out of my backpack and put them in. I put on "Happier" and shake out my limbs. With my music on, I start jogging to the Walsh Athletic Center, hoping it will help me wake up. I feel like I could fall asleep standing up right now.

A little less than ten minutes later, I arrive in front of the glass and steel building. Whereas most of the other buildings at HGU look like they're from the seventeenth century, the Walsh Athletic Center is all modern glass, right angles, and cold gray metal. Whoever designed it did not understand the assignment to match the rest of campus.

I pull open the glass and metal door and am immediately smacked in the face with cool air. Since it's September, the air is muggy and humid outside. The rapid change causes me to shiver and wish I brought a sweater with me.

"I'm so fucking tired," I mumble as I walk around the red track toward Levi's office. A few students are working out on the fake green grass in the middle, but most people prefer to use the weight rooms upstairs. Beneath the main floor are two pools for competitive swimming.

I'd think physical activity would be beneath mages, but the mages here get super into sports competitions. Since mages don't have naturally enhanced strength, speed, or reflexes, HGU can play against normal universities.

"I know you are, kid. Maybe Levi will let you rest a bit before doing the laps," Aggie suggests as we round the corner to the coaches' offices. Levi doesn't coach any sport. Instead, he's in charge of all the physical education and combat classes. He only started last semester, so he's a fairly new instructor. Maybe that's why he doesn't hate me like the rest of the school.

"A short rest isn't going to do anything. It's better to get it over with now." We walk the remaining distance in silence, each of us lost in our own thoughts.

I'm relieved to see Levi's door open, the light on. At least I don't have to wait around for hours. I can get the laps over with and go on to my other classes.

Unlike other coaches or professors, Levi goes by his first

name instead of his last name. It was a little weird at first, but I've gotten used to it.

I knock on the doorframe and pull out my earbuds before stepping into the space. Levi's office is decorated in shades of black and gray. His gray walls are bare, and his ebony wood desk is devoid of anything personal. I've wondered why he doesn't decorate, but it's not really my place to ask.

"Hey," I greet Levi as I step inside his office. He jerks his gaze up from his computer when I step in. My eyes meet his obsidian ones. With his irises being pitch-black, the only way I can tell he even has pupils are the red rings around them. Levi wins the award for coolest eyes, hands down.

"What are you doing here, little raven?" Levi asks with his lips tilted up in a small smile. He pushes his black hair out of his eyes as he talks. With it cut shorter on the sides and longer on top, the onyx strands frequently fall in his striking eyes. His olive skin keeps him from being washed out by his dark hair and eyes.

My tired brain flashes back to the first time he called me that.

I can't believe I have to take gym class as a junior in college. If I were allowed to participate in any of the sports, I wouldn't have to take a gym credit. Without any magic, I'm banned from all school-sponsored activities.

I had the choice between weightlifting and combat class. Obviously, I choose combat. A school-sanctioned opportunity to beat up the other mages at HGU? Sign me the fuck up.

There's a new professor teaching P.E. classes this year. He'll probably be just as much of an insufferable asshole as the rest of the faculty here, but there's always a chance he might be better. Just like there's always a chance that T-Rexes will become unextinct and eat all of my classmates, which is probably a more likely scenario, honestly.

With a deep sigh, I push the heavy wood doors to the gym open.

I choose a spot along the back wall, so I don't have to get too close to any of the other mages.

It's a few minutes before the professor walks in. I'm lost in my thoughts, so I don't notice him enter until he says, "Good morning, class. I'm Levi, your new combat teacher. For our first class period, I'm going to do individual sessions with each of you to assess your skills. Once you've completed your assessment, you can leave. The rest of you can talk quietly amongst yourselves as you wait."

Levi calls the first person up, and everyone else breaks off into their little cliques. I stay where I am against the wall. Class is going pretty well until Tyler Giles sidles up next to me. "I'm surprised they let a magicless nobody like you in a combat class."

I roll my eyes so hard, it's a wonder they don't get stuck. "It's a surprise they let an unoriginal, marginally more intelligent than a toaster, b-level mage like you in combat class."

Tyler's face turns almost purple in anger as he sputters at my insult. Before he can respond, the new combat teacher is suddenly standing in front of us. I let my head thump against the blue mat behind me, already knowing I'm going to get yelled at for this encounter. It doesn't matter that I didn't start it. I'm always the one at fault.

"I don't tolerate bullying in my class," Levi barks.

My eyes snap open and my mouth parts in shock. I'm not the one bullying anyone. As I suck in a breath to argue, I realize the combat teacher is glaring at Tyler, who's almost as shocked as I am. "I wasn't bullying her. She's the one who was insulting me! I was just trying to make conversation."

"I heard what you said to her, so don't try to lie to me, boy. You're dismissed from today's lesson. You can arrange time with me outside of class for your assessment." When Tyler just opens and closes his mouth like a fish, Levi growls at him. "Leave. Now!"

At Levi's bellow, Tyler goes as white as a sheet. He almost trips over himself to leave the gym. After glaring at me one last time, he storms out.

"Are you okay, little raven?" Levi asks gently.

I raise my eyebrows at the endearment. "I'm fine, thanks. That was, by far, not the worst thing someone has done to me at this school. My name's Izzy, by the way."

Levi's fists clench at his side when I mention prior bullying. He seems to shake himself out of his anger. "That type of behavior will not be allowed in my class. I can't change what other instructors do, but you won't have to deal with it here. And I know your name, little raven."

I'm not sure how he knows my name when I haven't told him yet. Maybe he was warned about me by other professors. "Why are you calling me little raven, *then?"*

"It suits you," he tells me with a shrug.

I narrow my eyes on him. I don't look anything like a raven, so I don't know what he means by that. "Fine. If you're going to call me a raven, then I'm calling you a screech owl." That's the most annoying sounding bird name I can come up with on the spot.

Levi grins at me. "Deal."

"I got in trouble in class, screech owl," I tell him as I shake myself out of the memory.

"For what?" he questions in his deep baritone. As he speaks, Levi stands from his chair, unfolding to his full towering height.

He's incredibly muscular. I've had the pleasure of seeing him without a shirt a time or two. The glistening dips and ridges of his rock-hard abs are forever burned into my mind. The only person I've met who's more muscular is Luca, but I'd rather not think about my frustrating wolf mate.

"For falling asleep in class." When Levi cocks an eyebrow in disbelief, I sigh. "And telling Moore that his class is boring."

He barks out a laugh. "Sounds about right for you, little raven. What're you supposed to do here as punishment?"

"Run twenty laps." I rub my hands over my face, trying to

make my eyes feel a little less gritty and tired. If I'm going to run five miles, I need to be at least somewhat awake.

"Seems a bit harsh," Levi comments as he stretches his arms over his head. His black long-sleeve tee rides up above his black jeans, showing a glimpse of his cut Adonis belt. I yank my gaze away before he can catch me staring.

I huff a laugh at his observation, which is the most I have the energy for at the moment. Anything involving me and the school is always extreme.

"Let me grab my phone, and I'll run with you," Levi tells me, already turning back to his desk before he finishes his sentence. I shrug off my bag and lean it against one of the chairs, knowing it'll be safe here while we run.

"Damn. That is one fine specimen of a man," Aggie declares from beside me. "If I were still alive, I'd jump that man faster than you can say, 'Aggie, you're dead. Stop hitting on the living.' You're lucky to be alive when you are. They didn't make men like that back in my day."

I choke on my spit at Aggie's commentary. Turning my head, I glare at her. When she turns to look at me, I widen my eyes in a *what the hell* look. Aggie shrugs and continues to check out Levi's ass. I totally don't look at it with her until he turns around.

When I drag my gaze up to his face, I see him wearing an amused smirk. My cheeks pink at him catching me checking him out.

Turning on my heel, I flee his office to escape the embarrassing encounter. This is all Aggie's fault. Unfortunately, I can't exactly blame it on my ghost friend to Levi. I don't need one of the only nice people at this hellhole thinking I'm crazy.

With his long legs, Levi easily catches up to me. We don't say anything as we reach the track and start running. I put my earbuds back in because physical activity is always better with music. "Shake it Out" starts playing. As I run, black spots dance in my vision. I ignore them the best I can. The longer I run, the more lightheaded I feel. My body feels all floaty and untethered from the ground.

When a wave of cold rushes over my scalp and down my spine, I realize I'm going to pass out. I don't have time to brace or even slow to a stop. One moment, I'm running. The next, my vision goes completely black.

The last thing I hear before I fall headfirst into oblivion is Aggie shouting, "Kid!"

~

"KID! WAKE UP! NOW!" Aggie screams in my ear.

I snap my eyes open and bolt upright at her yelling. Looking around, I expect to see my room or the forest. Instead, I'm greeted with a masculine bedroom that I've never been in before. Dark wood floors and navy walls give the room a cozy feel.

Glancing down, I see I'm lying in the middle of an absolutely massive bed. The thick blue comforter and white sheets are softer than anything I've ever felt. While the bed is luxurious, I have no idea where I am or how I got here.

"Um. What's going on?" I ask Aggie as I struggle out of the plush mattress. It feels like I'm sitting on a cloud. While it's comfy, it's super hard to get out of. After what feels like five minutes of fighting the stupid thing, I finally get out of the bed and stand up. My bare feet land on a thick oriental rug I hadn't noticed before.

"You passed out while running. Levi kidnapped you. Now, you're here, and all four of your mates are at HGU, wondering where the hell you are." Aggie paces back and forth across the room as she fills me in. Her spectral form hovers a few inches above the floor as she walks.

"I don't even know where to start. What the fuck do you mean, Levi kidnapped me? Where even am I?" I scan the room for my shoes as I question Aggie. None of what she said makes sense, other than the passing out part, of course. On top of not getting enough sleep, I also haven't eaten nearly enough this weekend to keep up with my magic usage.

"After you collapsed, he carried you to his office. Levi then conjured something that looked like a gateway to hell and dragged you through it. I followed and we landed here. He tucked you into bed and then left the room. I've been drifting between here and school, waiting for you to wake up." Aggie is breathless by the time she finishes filling me in.

"A gateway to hell? You mean, a portal?" I question. Maybe Levi just has red magic that makes it look like flames. Usually, Aggie's pretty good about recalling things, but she might be confused this time.

"No, I don't mean a portal! It was pitch black and ringed with flames! The other side was just a black abyss, not the normal view of where you're going with portals." Aggie gestures wildly as she talks, clearly unnerved by the whole experience.

"Huh."

"Come on! We need to go before he gets back," Aggie prods me. She tries to push me toward the door to leave. It doesn't work since she's a ghost, obviously. Aggie huffs in frustration, and I can't help the giggle that comes out at her antics.

At Aggie's glare, I raise my hands in surrender. I try to placate her. "Let me just find my shoes. Then I'll portal us out of here."

"They're right here," a deep voice informs me from the doorway. I cringe, realizing my window for leaving has closed. Turning from Aggie, I face Levi, who's leaning against the doorframe, watching us. My white Converse dangle from his fingers. That explains why I couldn't find them.

With a sigh, I tell him, "Look, if you're planning to murder me, can you just not? I have a ton of shit to do, and I really don't have time to get killed. I'll pencil you in a few days after never happening, and we can circle back around then to this whole killing me thing."

Levi's eyes dance with amusement when I finish. "Good thing I'm not here to kill you. Your survival skills need work, little raven. That speech wouldn't convince anyone to spare you."

Aggie snorts next to me. "You think that's bad? You should see what she does in the forest every night. It's only by some miracle she isn't dead yet."

"What is it she does in the forest, spirit?" Levi asks as he switches his gaze to Aggie.

"She heals gh–" Aggie starts to reply before turning wide eyes on me. My lips part in shock at Levi addressing her. There's no way he can see her. I'm the only mage with that ability we know of. Aggie whispers, like it will stop Levi from hearing her, "Can he see me?"

"No," I reply, at least sixty-two percent positive of my answer.

"Yes," Levi confirms at the same time.

Aggie and I look at each other in utter disbelief before we both turn to Levi with wide eyes. "That's not possible. I'd know if another mage could also see her," I protest. There's no way there's been someone like me under my nose for almost a year without me noticing it. I'd like to think I'm not that oblivious.

"You're correct. There isn't another mage in Hawthorne Grove who can see ghosts," Levi informs me, before continuing. "I am not a mage, little raven."

CHAPTER 12

IZZY

*A*fter Levi drops that bomb, the lights in the room begin to flicker. A black mist seeps out around him before it crawls across the floor toward us. Levi's eyes glow red and a skeletal face appears over his face, making his features hazy. Electricity whips in the air around him, and the hair on my arms stands straight up.

"Holy hell," I whisper, wondering what on earth is going on. Maybe Aggie wasn't too far off with Levi opening a gateway to hell. He sure looks like a Grim Reaper right now. All he's missing are a scythe and black robes.

As quickly as the creepy effects start, they end. With a bright flare of light, Levi returns to normal. It's like the mist and skeletal features never existed. But I know what I saw.

"What are you?" I breathe, less confident I can get Aggie and me out of this situation unscathed than I was before. If it comes down to pure power, I'm not sure who would win. Normally, I'm confident I'm the one with the most magic. Not this time.

Although Levi is definitely scary when he lets his power out, I don't feel like he'll really hurt me. For some reason, I've always felt safe around him. Hopefully, I won't need to find out if I can beat him in a fight.

"I'll tell you when you tell me what you do in the forest," Levi bargains with me. I press my lips into a thin line and look away. I'd rather not tell anyone what I can do. "That's what I thought. Come get your shoes, little raven. We need to get you back to school."

I hesitantly approach Levi. When nothing happens as I draw near to him, I get braver. I close the last few steps between us quickly. My hand darts out to grab my shoes from his outstretched hand. As I close my fingers around the shoes, my hand brushes his. Familiar tingles race giddily up my arm.

No. Not again.

I snap my gaze up to his. "You're my mate?" I croak.

"I am," he confirms, his black eyes bouncing between mine.

Releasing the shoes, I let them drop to the floor with a bang. I rub my hands over my face and tunnel my hands into my hair. Spinning away from him, I look at the ceiling and mutter, "Why does this keep happening to me? What the fuck did I do to you, universe?"

Honestly, I'd like to know. The universe seems to love fucking me over. In a past life, was I a dictator who ate babies for breakfast? Or someone who put toilet paper under instead of over? I must have done something awful to deserve all the shit the universe piles on me.

One of the two people I actually like being around at school is my mate. Now, I have to avoid him to keep him safe. Although, with his creepy Grim Reaper party trick, he might be able to keep himself safe.

"Are you displeased because I'm not a mage?" Levi asks evenly. I'd expect him to shout or get angry or something. Instead, he just calmly asks the question.

"What? No!" I whirl to face him as I talk. "Why does everyone think that? All of the mages here suck ass. Why would I want one as my mate?" It's honestly a relief that Bishop is the only mage I've been paired with thus far. Then again, if I were matched with a random mage from Hawthorne Grove, it'd be a piece of cake to stay away.

Although, I didn't know fated mates could be from different species. Different species can't have kids together, so a mage can't have a child with a shifter, vampire, fae, or whatever the hell Levi is. I would've thought fate would only pair people with the same race for that reason, but I guess not.

"Why are you unhappy, then?" Levi questions. His jet-black eyes narrow in thought as he considers me.

I sigh and rub my hands over my face. It's only as I'm rubbing my eyes that I realize I'm not exhausted anymore. Sure, I'm a little tired, but it's nowhere near the bone-deep fatigue from before. Instead of answering his question, I ask one of my own, "How long have I been asleep?"

"You slept for almost six hours, kid. That's why your other mates are waiting outside Gallagher Hall." Aggie eyes Levi warily. I almost want to laugh at the change in her. She sure flipped quickly from thinking Levi's hot to viewing him as a threat.

"What? Fuck! I missed my other two classes." I groan, already knowing my professors are going to speak to the dean about my absence. I'm probably not going to get away with only laps this time.

"I covered for you, little raven," Levi informs me. "The dean was thrilled to hear that I've been making you run laps all day until I determine you regret your actions."

I snort. Of course, he was. Me having to run for six hours straight was probably the best news Dean Murphy heard all day.

Shaking my head, I bend down to grab my Converse I dropped earlier. I plop down on the rug and put them on. When I've laced my sneakers, I stand back up and look at Levi. If I leave, maybe he'll just forget this whole mates thing. "Well, as fun as getting kidnapped by you was, it wasn't. Let's not do this again."

"You can't open a portal here," Levi calls as I turn away from him and start drawing my magic.

I laugh.

Sure, I can't, buddy. Imagining a portal in my mind, I let my magic flow out of me. Instead of forming a rip in space like normal, it feels like it slammed against a brick wall. Like a crash test dummy, my magic jerks back from the hit and rebounds into me. It feels like a bunch of rubber bands snapped in my chest at once.

"Ow," I mutter and rub my breastbone, under which my magic huddles currently. It seems... scared, which has never happened. Turning to Levi, I ask, "Where, exactly, are we? And why won't my magic open a portal?"

Levi winces in sympathy at my pained expression. "Here and there," he replies evasively. "I'll tell you why your magic doesn't work if you tell me why you don't want me as a mate."

He really seems to love bargaining. Blowing out a breath, I decide it doesn't hurt anything to tell Levi about the mate stuff. "You already know I can see ghosts. That type of magic is essentially a death sentence if anyone finds out. Being my mate just puts you in danger. I can drag you down with me if I am found out. That's why I'm upset. It's nothing about you."

Levi's eyes soften at my explanation. "You don't need to worry about me, little raven. I can take care of myself. As for your magic, mage magic doesn't work on this plane."

Plane?

"Where the hell are we, Levi?" I demand. Only I could

manage to get kidnapped by my P.E. teacher. My teacher, who turns out to be a Grim Reaper and takes me to another dimension.

"A question for a question. Tell me what you do in the forest that has the ghost so worried, and I'll tell you where we are." Levi advances on me as he talks, only stopping once we're toe to toe.

He stares down at me, and I gulp. How have I never noticed how intimidating he can be before now? Levi does an excellent job playing the laid-back combat instructor. That freaks me out more than if he were always intimidating. Someone who can hide their true nature is far more dangerous than someone who is upfront about who they are.

Instead of replying, I shake my head. Levi would probably try to stop me from healing the ghosts if he knew. I know it's dangerous, but I'm the only one who can help them. It would make me pretty selfish to put my own safety above the thousands of ghosts I've helped.

Levi just nods, already expecting my response. "Are you ready to go? We should get you back before your other mates worry."

"Yeah, I'm ready to go, as long as Aggie can come too." I don't know whether this realm can trap Aggie at Levi's command. Aggie may be a pain in the ass, but she's my pain in the ass. I'm not going to leave her in some alternate dimension.

His lips twitch up at my assertion, but he doesn't respond. Levi ducks out of the room, leaving me unsure what to do with myself. It's not like I can leave. Glancing at Aggie, I see if she has any idea what to do. "Don't look at me, kid. He's terrifying. I'm just going to hide behind you and hope he forgets about me."

"I'm not that scary, ghost," Levi says as he walks back into the room. Aggie lets out a ghostly screech and huddles behind me. I snort. I'm not sure hiding behind me works the way she thinks it does. But I'll let her do her.

Levi holds his hand out to me. I hesitantly put mine in his as black mist swirls around us. The floor feels like it's dropping out from under me, and I squeeze my eyes shut. Here's hoping I'm not falling to my death. That'd be inconvenient.

"Open your eyes," Levi rasps from in front of me. Peeking one eye open, I see that we're back at school. When I open both eyes, I realize I'm plastered against Levi's front. I can feel every inch of him, including his hard dick.

I stumble back in shock and crash into the wall behind me. Because, of course, I do. I'm apparently incapable of looking like anything other than a mess in front of my mates. Not that it matters what they think of me.

It's probably better if they do think I'm a garbage gremlin. It'll hurt when my mates finally realize I'm not worth it, but I can deal with all the pain in the world to keep them safe.

On that depressing note, I should probably stop hiding in an alcove with my combat instructor and a ghost. Straightening, I brush past Levi and head for the front of the building. He transported us to an alcove near the door, so it's a short walk outside.

Levi is hot on my heels as I push open the door. Once my eyes adjust to the overeager sun, all I see is Bishop. He notices me as soon as I leave the building, and he starts walking toward me. Bishop has his hands shoved in his jeans pockets, and he's wearing a similar band tee to the one I'm in.

I completely forget I'm supposed to play it cool around him, so people won't know we're mates. After my nightmare earlier, I'm just so relieved to see that he's okay. Taking off at a run, I close the distance between us in no time. When I'm close enough, I leap at him, wrapping my arms and legs around him like a spider monkey.

Bishop catches me with a grunt. He supports my ass with one arm and bands the other around my back. "Hello to you, too, sweetheart," Bishop says with his lips pressed against my ear and a smile in his voice. His warm breath fans across my neck, causing me to shiver slightly.

"You're okay," I whisper. Even though I know it was just a dream, it's still hard to see everyone I care about being killed. Seeing Bishop in one piece and unharmed soothes a part of me I don't really want to acknowledge. This is totally how friends feel about each other.

"Of course, I am," Bishop responds. "Hey, what's wrong, Izzy? Did something happen?"

"Nightmare," I answer, refusing to release my death grip on him so we can talk like normal people. In his arms is one of my favorite places to be. For totally platonic, friend reasons. That's all I can ever feel about him. If only my stupid heart would get the memo.

"Oh, sweetheart. I'm sorry. I'm fine, as you can see. So are the wolves, who are starting to get a little jealous at all the attention you're giving me."

I groan at the reminder of my other mates. I'm not sure why they're here, but I can't deny that I'm relieved to see them after the dream earlier. Bishop doesn't put me down until I'm ready to let go of him. After another minute of enjoying his hug, I wiggle to be put down. He slides me down his body.

Spinning around, I take off toward the wolves. Archer is the first one I see. I crash into him at full force, and he doesn't budge even an inch. That's one solidly built wolf.

While I'm hugging him, I breathe in his vanilla citrus smell. After a quick hug, I whisper to him, "Tell anyone I hugged you, and I'll shank you." He barks out a startled laugh at my threat but doesn't say anything.

I move on to Luca next. When I wrap my arms around

him, his arms hesitantly enfold me in a hug. The man is great at giving hugs, unfortunately for me. I bury my nose in his chest and inhale his dark, woodsy scent. When I pull back, I meet his aquamarine eyes with my gray ones. "You heard what I said to your brother. The same applies to you, wolf boy."

Without waiting for a response, I walk over to Cain. He's more reserved than the other two, so I don't hug him at first. His green eyes flick between mine before he opens his arms in an invitation. I slowly approach him, not wanting to freak him out. When I'm in reach, he startles me by grabbing me around the waist and hauling me into his body.

After a moment of breathing in the burnt marshmallow scent of the wolf, I tell him, "I'd rather not kill you, so keep this whole lapse in judgment to yourself." When I pull back, Cain gives me a half smile as his arms drop away. That's the most positive emotion I've seen directed my way from him.

"Why, exactly, are you threatening us if we tell anyone you hugged us?" Archer asks while trying to smother his amusement. The wide grin stretching across his handsome face betrays him, though.

I roll my eyes. "I have an image to uphold. Who's going to believe I have the personality of a cactus if it gets out that I give hugs and shit?" I huff and cross my arms as all three wolves smile at me. It's a reasonable concern. I've spent a lot of time carefully constructing my image of a heartless porcupine. It keeps people away. In this town full of assholes, that's a good thing.

"I don't think anyone would believe them, anyway, little raven," Levi interjects from behind me. I totally forgot he was here; I was so caught up in Bishop and the wolves.

"Who the fuck is he?" Luca rumbles as he advances on Levi.

89

CHAPTER 13

ARCHER

"*I*'m her m—" the guy as tall as Luca starts to answer from behind our mate. Izzy throws her arm back and connects with him. She groans, and he grunts as her elbow hits his solar plexus.

Izzy turns to face him and whispers, "Not here. There are too many ears." He gives her a nod and straightens up.

Elbowing people in the gut is more like my sunshine. With her blonde hair, delicate bone structure, and pale skin, Izzy does look like the embodiment of the sun. She also smells like berries and sunlight. It's only when you look into her eyes that a few clouds appear. Izzy's eyes are like the ocean during a hurricane, emotions constantly swirling and crashing in the gray depths.

Despite her prickly personality, Izzy's emotions flit across her face. She's horrible at hiding what she's thinking. It's adorable, but I'm pretty sure she'd stab me for calling her that. It might be worth it, though.

Speaking of shanking me, I wondered if Izzy had been body snatched when she ran over and crashed into me. Her tiny arms banding around me in a hug caught me off guard.

When she whispered that she'd stab me if I told anyone, I barely held back my laugh. At least I knew it was, in fact, my sunshine.

She probably didn't mean for us to hear her whisper to Bishop about her nightmare. With our enhanced hearing—perks of wolfing out—we could all hear what Izzy said. I have the urge to hug her again, but I doubt she'd be open to it.

That's okay. I'm an expert at slowly wearing down people until they have no choice other than to accept my affection. Just look at Cain. I only get punched twenty-five percent of the time when I try to hug the guy. That's a huge improvement.

Izzy sighs before spinning to face us. As she's mid-spin, she stops and looks at something over Bishop's shoulder. From where I'm standing, it looks like she's staring at three girls who are giving her death glares. I wonder what the fuck their problem is. "Fuck me six ways to Sunday," she says with a groan.

That's certainly an image my dick didn't need. I can't get the thought of fucking Izzy over and over out of my mind. Now, I'm hard. Cool, cool. Not awkward at all. "Gladly," I respond, knowing that's not what she meant.

Izzy looks at me in confusion for a moment. Her cheeks, dusted with freckles, turn pink when she realizes what I was talking about. She rolls her eyes at me. "Hilarious," she comments dryly.

"I wasn't joking, sunshine." I give her a wolfish grin. Izzy's eyes widen before she ducks her head in embarrassment. It's cute. Her looking away also gives me an opportunity to adjust myself without her noticing.

"Who are they?" Luca asks with a head nod toward the three girls. Izzy avoids eye contact with him, suddenly finding something on the ground fascinating.

"Those are the girls who love to make Izzy's life hell." Bishop is the one to fill us in. "They treat her like shit, then try to hit on me. It's baffling."

A growl rattles in Luca's chest, and he advances on the girls. Usually, I try to rein in my brother's violence a bit. Now, however, I'm all for him eliminating anyone who hurts our mate.

Izzy rushes over to him. She grabs his hand and tugs him to a stop. "Cool your jets, wolf boy." I snort at what she calls him. I'm sure it grates on him being called a boy, which just makes me enjoy it even more. "Saying or doing anything to them will only cause problems for me. How about we go somewhere else to talk?"

Luca looks at Izzy for a long moment. Seeming to come to a decision, he turns away from the girls, who have a very short life expectancy if they keep hurting our mate. He intertwines their fingers, not letting go of her hand. I'm jealous that he gets to keep touching her. "Where do you want to go, little mate?"

Her lips part in shock before she turns wide eyes on Luca. "You're going to need a new nickname for me, my dude. That's one thing you can't say here."

After considering her, Luca's lips quirk up in a barely there smile. "I can do that when we're around mages, little one."

Izzy lets out a little growl at the nickname. "I'm not little!" she protests.

"Whatever you say, little one." Luca is purposely antagonizing our mate, if the grin on his face is any indication. He seems to love messing with her. Most people wouldn't dream of sassing Luca the way Izzy does. While he tries to seem annoyed at her attitude, he likes her fire.

Izzy huffs and turns to Bishop. "I'm thinking Annie's Diner."

Bishop chuckles and gazes at our mate with so much emotion that witnessing it makes me feel like a creep. "You want French toast for this conversation?"

"French toast makes everything better," Izzy responds with a nod. She glances over Cain and me. "I refuse to eat French toast anywhere else because it's always an affront to the French toast gods." I manage not to laugh at how serious she is about a breakfast food. I'm getting the sense Izzy lied when she said savory instead of sweet in our game of This or That.

"How'd I know?" Bishop teases her with a fond smile. "You want me to open a portal?"

Before Izzy can chime in, the tall guy says, "I'll create a portal, little raven." He waves us over to him.

When I get closer, I realize he smells…off. While he has the typical peppery scent of mages, it's almost like it's covering up something. Underneath the mage scent is something that smells like smoke, fire, and a hint of sulfur. It's weird.

He waves his hand and mutters gibberish before the most metal portal I've ever seen appears. I'm used to portaling with Bishop, whose rip in space is ringed in blue sparks. Instead of sparks, this guy's portal is rimmed in flames. There's also a yawning black void in his portal, rather than wherever we're supposed to go.

"In you go, wolves, mage, and little raven," he tells us with a sweep of his hand. Izzy eyes the portal warily before stepping through. Bishop looks reluctant but is willing to follow Izzy anywhere.

The fact that the mages are suspicious of the portal doesn't bode well for us. Our mate went through, so I guess we have to. "If this is some trick to hurt my brothers, I'll take great pleasure in ripping out your intestines and strangling you with them," I tell the man in an upbeat voice that's at odds with my words. While Cain isn't related to me by blood, he is my brother in every way that matters.

He lets out a booming laugh. My eyebrows raise in surprise. The man's not even a little intimidated. "It's not a trick, wolf. You're her mates, so I won't hurt you. Hurt her, and you'll be begging for the relief of being strangled when I'm done with you," he says evenly. The only indication that he's bothered by anything is that the red rings around his pupils grow to swallow up his irises.

He's one creepy motherfucker.

Nodding to show I heard him, I walk through the portal. Instead of the typical feeling of slogging through maple syrup, I feel like I'm on a roller coaster. My stomach flips, and I feel like I'm falling for a heartbeat. Then my feet touch the floor outside of a fifties-inspired diner.

Looking side to side, I realize that we're on Hawthorne Grove's main thoroughfare. Red cobblestone sidewalks and a mixture of red brick and colorful clapboard-sided businesses, all squished together, line the paved street. Along with awnings, the businesses also have old-fashioned picture signs hanging out front.

It's a charming downtown for a less than charming town. Hawthorne Grove is known to be hostile toward any supernaturals who aren't mages. Most of us avoid this town. With our mate living here, we'll have to suffer through dealing with the arrogant mages here. Hopefully, we can convince her to move somewhere else, like Lockwood, where our pack is, once she's done with the required mage school.

I had no idea she was young enough to still be in school until Bishop mentioned it. Izzy seems much older than early twenties. Our mate has been through something to force her to grow up fast. I just wish I knew what it was.

I'm so glad wolves aren't required to go to college. School has never really been my thing. Our parents died when I was in my junior year of college, so I never graduated. Even if our entire pack hadn't been thrown into chaos, I probably would have failed out, anyway.

Running our pack is a full-time job for the three of us. We should've had thirty more years to fuck around before we had to assume responsibility. Somehow, the three of us managed not to run the pack into the ground, but none of us were ready for it. Cain handles the administrative work. Luca handles leading the pack. I handle the dirty work that keeps our pack safe. Luca and Cain join in on the hands-on stuff, too, because that's way more fun than pushing papers or resolving disputes.

"That was not a normal portal," Luca gripes as he steps out of the portal. Cain follows him, looking a little seasick. For a man with such a brutal reputation, Cain sure is a wuss about roller coasters and boats.

The man with weird eyes walks out of the portal last. His unnerving gaze immediately finds our mate. It softens with affection before scanning the area around us for threats.

"Who is he, sunshine?" I ask with a nod at the guy. I can't contain my curiosity any longer.

Izzy's stormy-sky eyes flick to the man and back to my face. "That's Levi. He's my combat instructor, and he's like you."

"I don't know what he's told you, but he's definitely not a wolf." If this guy is trying to pass as a wolf shifter, he really needs to work on his scent. It also rubs me the wrong way that he's lied to our mate.

She snorts. "Not a wolf, Archer. I mean, he's like what you are to me," Izzy tells me with a genuine grin.

It takes me a few moments too long to realize what she's saying. "Ohhhh," I draw out when it finally dawns on me that he's also her mate. Luca raises one eyebrow at me, and Cain just shakes his head in exasperation. It's not my fault she was being vague.

Izzy giggles at my confusion, the sound tinkling like bells in a shop door. It's the most carefree sound I've heard from her. My chest puffs up in pride that I was able to make our mate laugh like that.

Making people laugh is something I'm great at, if I do say so myself. With an older brother like Luca, who's perfect at school, sports, and being likable, I needed to find a way to stand out. Being the class clown at least got me noticed growing up.

After our parents died, Luca and Cain needed the reminder to laugh and enjoy life. They were so caught up in running the pack, they forgot to live. It was slowly killing them. I did everything I could to cheer them both up. As the years have gone on, Luca and Cain have both started to be themselves again.

Although, I don't think Luca will ever be the laid-back playboy he was in his early twenties again. The massive amount of responsibility he had to take on has changed Luca forever. In some ways, the responsibility was good. It made him grow up and consider the needs of others. In other ways, it wasn't positive. Dealing with the aftermath of the attack hardened Luca and made him close himself off.

As for Cain, well, his issues started way before the attack. I'm not sure he'll ever be like he was as a boy…before everything. I sigh and rub my hand over the back of my head. Maybe our mate can help him.

Shaking my head to clear it of my worry for Cain, I focus back on our mate. "Ready to get the sustenance of the gods, sunshine?" I ask Izzy as I hold out my hand for her to take. She fights the grin that's trying to cross her full lips as she watches me for a moment. After assessing me, Izzy blows out a breath and puts her hand in mine.

CHAPTER 14

IZZY

*A*rcher tugs me to follow him as he opens the door to the diner. I smile when I see the white-and-black checkered floor and light-blue upholstered booths. The red stools at the bar and the pink-and-blue lights make the diner feel like a time capsule. It's one of my favorite places in Hawthorne Grove.

When Archer hesitates at the empty hostess stand, I pull him along behind me as I head for my favorite booth. It's tucked in the back corner and somewhat hidden from the prying eyes.

Bishop makes it to the booth first, having sat there with me too many times to count. He picks the side with a good view of the front door, and I slide in after him. The vinyl seat creaks as I move across it. Archer sits on my other side and shoots Luca and Cain a smug look.

Cain sits opposite Bishop, followed by Luca, then Levi on the outside. I'm kind of regretting the seating arrangement that has Luca right in front of me. He's staring at me intently, like I'm some puzzle to solve. *I'd like to keep my secrets, wolf boy, thank you very much.*

Before Luca can interrogate me, Lucy sweeps over to our table. In her powder-blue retro diner uniform, perfectly curled and pinned gray hair, and ruby-red lipstick, Lucy looks like she stepped straight out of the fifties. "What can I do for you, sweetness?" she asks me with a wide smile.

I grin back at her. Lucy's a friend of the family, and she runs the diner with her sister Annie. Unlike everyone else here, neither of them gives a rat's ass that I don't have magic. All they care about is if I'm a half-decent person. It's refreshing. "I'd like a berry French toast and a pink lemonade, please."

"You've got it, honey. What can I get the rest of you?" Lucy turns to inspect the rest of the table. I only ever come in here with Bishop or my family, so it's odd that I'm here with a big group of scary-looking dudes.

Bishop orders a burger and a malt. The wolves follow his lead, each ordering a burger and fries. They probably don't know what's good here. The answer is everything. Literally everything these women make is perfection. I'd eat three meals a day here if I could. Alas, my mom insists I eat something at least a little healthy most of the time. Levi orders a country fried steak.

"That'll be right out," Lucy informs us before gliding away. I wish I had as much grace as she does. Unfortunately, I'm like a newborn gazelle most of the time. Inanimate objects love attacking me out of nowhere, so I'm constantly tripping.

Once Lucy is out of sight, the wolves turn their attention to me. I squirm under Luca's intense gaze. He smiles slightly at my discomfort, and I glare at him. Luca asks, "How was school today? Did you behave yourself?"

I grit my teeth at him insinuating I'm the problem. It doesn't matter how I act. I'm going to have a shit day at school, regardless.

"Well, I just had the most fantastic day, Lulu," I start in a sickly sweet voice.

Archer barks out a laugh at the nickname and proceeds to fall over in his seat, he's laughing so hard. Cain cracks a smile, and Bishop hides his face in his hands like I'm embarrassing him. He really should be used to it by now.

"Let's see, I haven't gotten a full night's sleep since Thursday. I fell asleep in my least favorite class and got sent to the dean, who has a hate on for me. I passed out while running laps. Oh, and I got kidnapped by my P.E. teacher and taken to another fucking dimension. So, it was definitely a day filled with sparkles and rainbows. Thanks so much for asking, pookie," I finish with a saccharine smile aimed at a gaping Luca.

Levi groans. "I didn't kidnap you, little raven."

"That's right. You just forcibly relocated me while I was unconscious." The wolves turn as one to glare at Levi. Even with three of the scariest wolves in the country glaring daggers at him, Levi is calm and collected. I envy that ability more than he'll ever know.

He's saved from becoming a chew toy to some very angsty canines by Lucy coming over with our food. She sets down her tray and starts passing out each of our orders. Lucy starts with me and works her way around clockwise. Once everyone has their food, she gives me a take-out box and disposable silverware. "Let me know if you need anything, sweets," she tells me before walking away.

I look around the table and realize Aggie's not here. Tugging on my magic that's connected to her, I wait a moment for her to appear. When she shimmers into existence over the table, her mouth opens to blast me for pulling her to me. Then she sees the food and lights up. "Oh, yes. Come to Mama," she says while making grabby hands at my French toast.

I snort and put half of my French toast in the container. Once I've drowned the toast in syrup, I turn to Bishop. "You going to eat all your fries?"

He shakes his head and pushes his plate toward me. Bishop's used to me giving food to Aggie. As a ghost, she doesn't need to eat. She still enjoys it, though. The only way she can interact with food is if I magic it into the spirit realm.

After I pile a chunk of Bishop's fries in one of the small sections of the to-go box, I hover my hand over the ketchup. "Like you even have to ask, kid. What else would I eat fries with?"

"Europeans eat fries with mayo," Levi answers Aggie. To the rest of the table, it seems like he just announced that factoid at random. All three wolves look at Levi like he's a few screws short of a full crayon box. I snort. He grins at me, and my heart gives a little excited thump.

Nope. Not today, stupid heart. We are not getting attached to another man we can't have.

"That's revolting," Aggie responds with her nose wrinkled in distaste. At least she's not screaming at the mere sight of him. That's progress. I shake my head at her and finish assembling her portion.

"What are you doing?" Luca asks as he watches me box up part of my food before eating anything.

"Secret things," I tell him distractedly.

After putting the disposable utensils on top of the box, I pull on the magic that allows me to go to the spirit realm. Carefully wrapping some around my hand, I grab the food and let the magic slowly crawl over the container. Within a few seconds, the whole thing is in the spirit realm, much to Aggie's delight.

"Holy shit. Where the fuck did the box go?" Archer turns wide eyes to me as I pull my hand back out of the spirit realm. I just shrug and start in on my food.

"You're the best, kid!" Aggie digs into her food excitedly while hovering on top of the table.

As I eat the first bites of my French toast, I whisper, "*Conticescere. Obscurare.*" I throw up a silencing dome and cover it with a cloak to prevent lip reading. I'd rather the entire restaurant not be able to hear my conversation with my mates.

"So, do you guys really kill people for money?" I barely manage to keep the shit-eating grin off my face as Luca and Cain gape at me. Archer chokes on his bite of food at my question. Once he's done coughing, Archer looks at me like he can't believe I just asked that. He scans the restaurant to see if anyone's looking our way.

Bishop sighs. "Stop being a brat, Izzy," he chastises before turning to Luca and Cain. "She put up a silencing dome and cloaked it to obscure our table from prying eyes."

"Party pooper," I grouse as I stick out my tongue at him because I'm super mature.

Luca huffs at me. After debating what to say, he tells me, "Yes. We do. It's a revenue stream for our pack. Does that bother you?"

If he's expecting me to freak out about a little death, he's got the wrong girl. I play with dead people literally every night. "Do you kill innocents? Or do you kill people who deserve it?" There's a huge difference between killing a human trafficker and killing a movie producer who went over budget. For one of them, death is far too easy a punishment. For the other, it's a little extreme.

"We do everything we can to target those who deserve it. We only take contracts for individuals who have committed crimes significant enough to be taken out," Luca explains.

"Then, no, it doesn't bother me."

Luca's brows raise almost to his hairline at my easy acceptance. Death is just as much a part of the natural cycle as life. Sometimes things or people need to die for new life to bloom. It's not something to fear or fight. Without death, life wouldn't be as precious.

"Why not?" Cain asks with his head tilted. His green eyes narrow on me, like he's trying to figure out why I'm so weird. *Good fucking luck, dude.* Experts have been trying to solve that mystery for twenty-one years.

"Death is part of life. People die. Things end. The world keeps on turning. It's nothing to get worked up over. It's also not like you're murdering kids and puppies in cold blood," I try to explain.

"You're pretty nonchalant about death for a sheltered mage," Cain fires back at me. I somehow contain my eye roll. I've seen more death than most people ever will, including him. I haven't been sheltered since I was seven. "Have you ever killed anyone, angel?"

My lips part in shock at his question. That's the one thing I really wasn't prepared for him to ask. I take a deep breath before answering. "Yes."

CHAPTER 15

IZZY

I get the satisfaction of seeing Cain's jade eyes widen a fraction before I look back down to my French toast.

It's not the food I see, though. It's his empty blue eyes staring accusingly at me. His face twisted in a grimace as he lies there, broken, on the rubber chips of the playground. The grass stains on the knees of his pants and the cheery red-and-white stripes on his shirt.

I didn't mean to. It doesn't matter, though. It won't bring him back. It won't give him the peace I stole from him.

He's not the only one I've killed, but he's the one I regret with every fiber of my being. He's the one that haunts my nightmares, and the one I try my hardest to forget.

I try desperately to shove the memories away, not strong enough to deal with them right now.

"You want me to go full poltergeist on his ass?" Aggie asks me. She was there when it happened, so she knows exactly where my mind went. "Juice me up, and I'll haunt the shit out of him."

I let out a small watery chuckle at her offer. Lifting my

gaze from the Formica tabletop, I meet Aggie's concerned one and give a small shake of my head.

My gaze strays to Cain, and I see remorse written on his face. He obviously expected the answer to be no. It should be if I were normal. The green-eyed wolf opens his mouth, probably to apologize, but I cut him off. I can't handle talking about this anymore. "Can we talk about something else? Please?"

The guys exchange glances with each other before Luca asks, "Why haven't you slept since Thursday?"

"I had late nights and early mornings." I'm thankful for the change in topic. I'm also pretty sure Luca asked something he thought would piss me off to take my mind off Cain's question. It's... strangely thoughtful, which makes me uncomfortable. I don't really know what to do with people being nice to me, and I don't like how I'm softening toward Luca.

"Why?" Luca presses.

Sighing, I give him a partial truth. "I work on Saturday mornings, volunteer on Sunday mornings, and have school early on Mondays. With late nights, I had no time to sleep in." My lips tip up in a small smile at the thought of my volunteering. I love working with the kids. The two days a week I volunteer are my absolute favorite days.

"Where do you work?" Archer asks as he turns toward me, throwing his arm along the back of the booth. His warm palm rests on my shoulder, and his fingers play with strands of my wavy, multicolored hair.

"Anya's Apothecary." With the town thinking I'm magic-less, I'm not allowed to participate in most school activities, like sports. All of the clubs at school are run by students who don't want me tainting their activities. I feel a little like Rudolph, never being able to join in on the mage games.

The only way to keep myself busy was to find a job. Anya

was the sole mage who was willing to hire a reject like me. I never had much interest in healing or making potions before working with her. Over the years, Anya has shown me so much, and she sparked a love of healing magic in me. It's nice to be able to do something to heal, instead of being neck-deep in death all the time.

"Where do you volunteer?" Cain asks quietly, like he's not sure I'll talk to him. It would be easier to be mad at him, but I'm not. He didn't ask the question to be malicious, and he had no idea it would pull up bad memories.

"I help with a music program for kids in a human town nearby." Most mages wouldn't waste their time helping normal humans. I love it, though. Around humans, no one's judging me for my magic. All the kids care about is that I can teach them how to play their favorite songs.

Thinking about the kiddos gives me warm fuzzies in my chest. It's disgusting. I hate feeling all gooey on the inside. It makes it hard to keep up my thorny exterior, which I need to maintain around the wolves and Levi. I can't have them liking me or anything. They need to stay away to be safe.

I look around the table and see that everyone's done eating, including Aggie. "Are we ready to go?" I'm more than ready to stop being in such tight quarters with my mates. Everyone nods, so I push on Archer to let me up. He slides out without protest. I ignore the hand he holds out to help me up and hop up on my own. As I stand, I release the threads of my magic. The silencing dome and cloak disappear with a whistle.

Pushing past Archer, I speed walk out of the diner. I don't pause to check if everyone follows. When I step outside, I suck in a huge lungful of air that doesn't smell like my mates. Being wrapped up in their scents is messing with my head.

I pinch my eyes shut as I wait for everyone to catch up. Spending time with the wolves and Levi is definitely a bad idea. If I weren't a stickler about keeping my word, I would definitely renege on the dates with the wolves. The more time I spend with them, the more things I find to like about each of them.

"You okay, sweetheart?" Bishop asks as he steps up behind me. He flattens his hands on my stomach and pulls my back against his front. With my eyes still closed, I enjoy the contact for a second. Once I hear voices behind us, I break away from him.

"As okay as I ever am, St. James." I turn to face the wolves and Levi. All of them are staring at me. Being the center of attention like this makes me uncomfortable.

Noticing my discomfort, Luca turns to my right and starts walking. The wolves follow him. Before I can take off after them, Levi hands me my backpack. He's been lugging the bag around since this morning, and I'm grateful he didn't forget about it. I definitely did.

Taking the backpack, I start after the wolves, Levi and Bishop trailing after me.

Cain drops back behind Archer and Luca to walk side by side with me. "Can I talk to you, Isabel?" he asks softly.

When I turn to look at him, I see him peering down at me. His mossy eyes have a touch of vulnerability that have me agreeing before I think better of it. "Sure. What's up?" Bishop and Levi walk faster to get ahead of us to give us privacy.

"I'm sorry about earlier, angel," Cain starts. I guess he found a nickname for me too. Jokes on him, though. I'm about as far away from an angel as you can get. There's nothing good about me. That's why I have the magic I do. "I didn't think the answer would be yes, or I wouldn't have asked it."

"I figured as much," I tell him. "Why did you ask it, then?"

Cain sighs and shoves his hands in his black suit pant

pockets. With his crisp white button-down and black slacks, he's dressed way fancier than the rest of us. His shirt is rolled up to his elbows, showing off his tanned, muscular forearms.

"I worried you were romanticizing what we do. It's not like it is in movies and games. It's messy and bloody and isn't always clear-cut. Even bad people have spouses, children, parents, and friends who are devastated by their deaths. I didn't want you to think we're the good guys, only to be disgusted when you found out it wasn't glamorous like you thought."

"That's fair. I'm aware of the gritty details of killing people, Cain. I'm not making it out to be sunshine and rainbows, but I also don't think you're the bad guys. I've seen enough evil to know the difference," I add quietly.

Cain doesn't say anything for several moments. When I chance a glance up at him, I see him staring down at me thoughtfully. "If you ever want to talk about it, I'm a good listener. I won't judge you."

My lips tip up into a small smile at his offer. The aloof wolf seems to have a soft center underneath all the gruffness.

"Thanks," I respond, knowing I won't take him up on it. Most of the messed-up shit I've seen that I should probably talk to someone about is magic related. Talking about it puts the other person in danger, so I just keep it all inside. Letting it fester isn't the healthiest option, but I don't really have any other choice.

We walk in companionable silence down the main street for probably ten minutes. When we turn the corner, I spot a seventies Dodge Charger. It has shiny blank paint and white leather seats. With it looking pristine, it's clear someone takes very good care of the muscle car.

"St. James!" I call. When he looks back at me, I point out the Charger excitedly. Bishop smiles at my enthusiasm and looks where I point. When he spots the black car, he knows exactly what I'm fangirling over.

Bishop nudges Luca and nods back to me. When Luca sees me staring at the car, a full-blown grin crosses his face. "You like my car, little one?" My heart skips a beat at his genuine joy. Putting that smile on his normally scowling face makes my insides warm and mushy.

"That's yours?" I squeak without taking my eyes off the coolest car I've ever seen.

"Yeah. I restored it myself." Luca walks over to the Charger, and I follow him. I try not to swoon at seeing my dream car in person.

"That's so cool!" I gush.

"Do you like cars, Izzy?" Luca leans against the hood of the muscle car. He crosses his arms as he watches me with one side of his mouth still kicked up in a smile. Luca's charcoal tee rides above his jeans in this position. I mostly succeed at not drooling over his washboard abs.

"Yeah, I think old cars are cool. But I like Chargers like yours because of my favorite show of all time."

"What show?" Archer asks. He looks like he's trying to smother a laugh at my excitement over Luca's car.

"*Burn Notice*." It's by far the best show ever made. I've watched it so many times, I practically have it memorized. I can recite the opening monologue by heart, at this point.

"Never heard of it. I'll have to watch it sometime." Archer grins down at me as I beam up at him. His golden blond hair falls in front of his aquamarine eyes when he tilts his face down to mine. My eyes flick down to his full lips as I wonder what it'd be like to kiss him.

Fuck. That's not a thought I need to be having. I whip my gaze away from the kissable wolf and back to the car.

"Do you know how to drive stick shift, little one?" Luca asks, dragging my attention to him.

It takes me a moment to realize what he's asking. "You'd let me drive it?" My voice is high pitched with shock. I thought guys were supposed to be super weird about letting other people drive their cars. Luca just nods at me. "That would be so cool! I don't know how to drive at all, though." I've never regretted my inability to drive until now. There's really no need to drive when I can just portal wherever.

"I'll have to teach you, then." Luca grins as I run to him. I wrap him in a quick hug before stepping back. I know I have a stupid smile on my face, but oh well. "Speaking of that, we wanted to talk to you about the dates you promised us. What days work the best for you?"

I'm momentarily stunned speechless. I didn't think the big wolf gave a shit about my schedule. He keeps surprising me by being thoughtful, and I don't like it. It's easier to stay away when he's a major ass.

"Mondays are usually my only free day, so I guess any Monday will work."

"What do you do the rest of the week?" Cain asks me.

"Tuesdays, Thursdays, and Saturdays, I work. Wednesdays and Sundays, I volunteer. Most Fridays are family dinner nights." Keeping busy takes my mind off everything I have to worry about. I try to pack my days full, so I don't have much time to think about all the things that can, and likely will, go wrong in my life.

"We'll take your next three Mondays, little one. I'll meet you after school this coming Monday," Luca informs me. I nod while grimacing at the awful nickname he came up with for me.

Archer surprises me by wrapping me up in a hug. He squeezes me tight and plants a kiss on top of my head. When he lets me go, Archer jogs around to the other side of the Charger.

Cain eyes me like he wants to give me a hug but doesn't

want to get stabbed. Smart wolf. Sighing, I open my arms in invitation. He walks into my arms and gently wraps his muscled arms around me. Cain acts like I'll break if he squeezes me too hard, but I'm made of tougher stuff than that.

"See you around, angel," Cain tells me with a small smile as he follows Archer around to the other side of the muscle car.

Bishop, Levi, and I retreat to the sidewalk as we watch the three wolves drive away. It feels like a chunk of my heart is driving off with them. Part of me cries out for them, hurting with the distance between us. I ruthlessly squash it down.

Even though Luca can be a shithead, I'm already starting to care for the wolves. That's why I won't ever let anything happen between us. Caring about someone means I have to let them go. No matter how much it kills me inside.

CHAPTER 16

IZZY

"**A**re you following me home?" I ask Bishop once the wolves are out of sight.

"Yep." Bishop slings his arm over my shoulders now that the wolves aren't here. He's used to reining in his touchy-feely tendencies with me when other people are around. I guess Levi doesn't count as people.

"I figured as much. What about you, demon boy?" I turn to Levi with a brow raised.

He snorts at his new nickname. "Yes, I'll follow you home, little raven. But I'm not a demon."

"Whatever you say, screech owl." I mutter, "*Aperire.*" A portal *whooshes* into existence in front of us. I reach the portal in a few steps. Even though I know it's coming, I still hate the feeling of getting sucked into sticky quicksand. Luckily, it's over quickly, and I pop out in front of my house.

I live in a two-story, light-blue Victorian house. The porch, columns, and trim are all white, and the roof is dark gray that looks almost black. My favorite part of the house is the turret out front. While the bottom of the turret is a screened-in porch, the upstairs portion is open to the elements. I love lying out there on summer nights, breathing in the warm air and staring at the stars.

Bishop and Levi step out onto the perfectly trimmed green grass of the front yard. It's handy being a mage. Instead of spending an hour mowing weekly, my dad can just use his magic to trim it up. Magic is how I color the ends of my shoulder-blade-length hair blue and purple, too. It would be a lot of upkeep otherwise.

Letting the wisp of magic go, I close the portal behind us. I jog up the front of the white steps and push open the navy door. I shrug my backpack off in the entryway and untie my Converse. My mom prefers no shoes in the house but isn't super strict about it.

Once I'm sans shoes, I pad across the natural antique pine floors toward the kitchen. As an old Queen Anne Victorian, my house doesn't have an open-floor plan. Instead, I have to pass through the foyer, sitting room, and dining room to reach the kitchen where my mom is.

The kitchen is, for the most part, authentic to the time period of the house. Natural wood floors, sage green cabinets, marble countertops, and intricate molding dominate the space. Several large windows keep the space from feeling too dark. A long pine table sits in the middle as an island, which is where my mom is.

When I see her, I break into a run. "Mom!" I say louder than necessary as I crash into her and wrap my arms around her. My mom is a few inches shorter than me. We have the same golden hair, gray eyes, and pointed chins. As I squeeze her tight, I breathe in her familiar rose garden scent.

"Isabel, honey, is something wrong?" my mom asks as she squeezes me tight.

"I just had a nightmare." I pull back when I remember that Bishop and Levi are right behind me. It's probably weird to need reassurance from my mom as a grown adult, but the two of them can get bent if they have a problem with it.

When I step back, my mom smiles at Bishop, who's getting a glass of water, before looking at Levi. She turns her gaze back to me. "Who's this, Izzy?"

"My combat instructor," I tell her as unhelpfully as possible.

"Oh. Why is he here?" my mom asks with the patience of a saint. This woman should get sainthood for putting up with my moody ass for twenty-one years.

"He has a thing for banging students. I agreed to help him live out his fantasy for better grades. What better place to do the deed than my parents' house?" I deadpan. I'm impressed with myself for getting through all of that with a straight face.

My mom gapes at me. I hear coughing and turn to see Bishop choking on his water. Levi is helpfully patting his back. Once Bishop stops hacking up a lung, he glares at me. "Stop being a shit stirrer, Izzy." Bishop turns to my mom and explains, "Levi's another one of her mates, Maggie."

Mom turns to me slowly while glaring. I give her an innocent look and shrug. She shakes her head in exasperation. My mom is used to me being a little shit, though. Turning to Levi, my mom says, "Well, with that stellar introduction from my lovely daughter out of the way, it's nice to meet you, Levi."

Levi is as cool and collected as ever. He doesn't even seem mad at how I introduced him. I'd probably be a little peeved if I were him, but I'd still find it funny. Does anything faze him?

"It's wonderful to meet you," Levi tells my mom, dialing up the charm to eleven. I wish I had that ability, but I don't have any setting other than snarky shit stirrer.

"Why didn't you tell me you found another mate?" My

mom turns back to the lasagna she's making. Yum. Her lasagna is definitely the best out there. I'm lucky my mom is such a good cook. We always eat well in our household.

While my mom likes cooking, I'm the baker of the family. I love the science aspect of baking. Of course, I enjoy the eating sweet treats part of baking too. That's what got me interested in the first place. "Well, I just found out today at school. I didn't have a chance to tell you."

"You have a phone," she points out while turning to place the dish in the oven. Once dinner's in the oven, she takes off her blue apron and smooths down her blue-and-white sundress.

"Fair." I could've texted her, but my day has been crazy.

"Did you hear that Amelia's missing too, now?" my mom asks distractedly as she starts in on the dishes. Bishop, being the thoughtful guy he is, immediately jumps in to help her.

"I didn't. What's that now, three mages missing in as many months?" Mages have been disappearing in Hawthorne Grove on and off for the last year. No one knows what's going on, but I don't have a good feeling about it.

I hope Amelia is all right. She's a few years younger than me and super sweet. I used to babysit her when I was in high school. Since she's from a less influential mage family, she was often the target of bullying too.

We don't have a chance to discuss it further because my oldest brother walks into the kitchen. "What's with all the commotion?" a sleepy Rhys asks. He must have worked late last night to just be getting up. Rhys works in private security. He's powerful enough he could've worked for the mage council, but Rhys wouldn't have done well with all the bureaucracy.

At least he put a shirt on with his blue flannel PJ pants. Rhys loves to wander around shirtless. It's embarrassing when I have people over, which, admittedly, isn't often.

As soon as I see my brother, I run over to him. I slam into him and give him a tight hug. I'm relieved to see that he's all right. My nightmares suck ass. His arms band around me briefly before I pull back. "Tell anyone I hugged you, and I'll slit your throat in your sleep," I whisper-threaten.

He barks out a laugh. "Someone woke up and chose violence today." Rhys ruffles the top of my hair, and I bat his hand away. It's rude to fuck with a lady's hair when two of her mates are watching. Rhys should totally know this.

"Today and every day," I confirm with a grin. Unlike my mom and Aiden, Rhys has always understood my violent side. That's probably why he went into the hands-on aspect of security, while Aiden, as a tech nerd, provides techy support for Elemental Security.

"Izzy found another one of her mates!" my mom interrupts. She's beaming from the other side of the kitchen, and I feel a little guilty I haven't told her about the wolves yet. Mom doesn't understand why I refuse to mate with Bishop. While she respects my decision, she does try to persuade me to change my mind frequently.

Rhys finally notices Levi. His eyes quickly take Levi in, assessing him for strengths and weaknesses. Once he's done giving Levi a once-over, Rhys turns to me. "This him?"

"Yep."

"You're not going to tell him I like to mess around with students, and you're on board for better grades?" Levi asks dryly. He raises one dark eyebrow at me as he talks, and he doesn't sound mad. I don't know him well enough to get a good read on him, though.

"Nope. Rhys wouldn't believe it," I tell Levi, making hesitant eye contact. His black-and-crimson eyes twinkle with mirth when I look at him. Knowing he's not angry at me, I let out a relieved breath.

Rhys snorts. "Yeah, kinda hard to believe when Izzy's a—"

115

He abruptly stops speaking when I jam my elbow into his stomach. Rhys yelps and rubs a hand over his stomach.

"Rhys Matthew Gallagher, don't you dare!" I hiss at him. I will actually murder him if he finishes his statement. That's one thing my mates don't need to know about me.

"Okay, okay! Just don't jab me with your bony ass elbow again. There's nothing to be ashamed of, though, Iz." Rhys's hazel eyes are filled with brotherly affection as he stares down at me. My face heats at the awkward conversation we're having with two of my mates right there.

I need a subject change. Stat. Racking my brain for something, I remember Bishop working for the Nightshade Pack. "Do you even work with Rhys and Aiden full time, St. James? Or was that just another lie?"

Bishop's brows raise practically to his hairline at the abrupt subject change. He's probably wondering how he ended up in the hot seat. "Yes, I work with them as my primary job. I help out the Nightshade Pack on my own time. I never lied to you, sweetheart."

I shrug but don't say anything. I'm feeling suddenly overwhelmed with everything, all the secrets and lies and heartache. As Rhys starts talking to Bishop about some operation they're working on, I quietly slip out of the kitchen. When I'm sure no one's following me, I sprint to my room.

Instead of slamming open my room door like I usually do, I quietly open and close it. I grab my guitar and ease open my window. Stepping through the opening, I stand on the sloped gray roof for a moment. Then I jump off with a grin. I mutter, "*Defensare*." A thick shield forms under my feet, cushioning my body from the fall.

I land in a crouch. Straightening, I wander to my favorite bench in our backyard. It's shaded by a towering elm tree, and the bench faces the forest. I have a beautiful view when I come out here. Lowering onto the stone seat, I lay my guitar across my lap. I also throw up a silencing dome. After a brief debate, I decide to play "Hits Different." I start strumming and belting out the song. Soon, I lose myself to the music.

I pour all of my heartache and sorrow and anger and hopelessness into the song. I'll give myself one song to feel everything I've been trying to avoid. Then I'm pushing the feelings to a dark corner of my mind, never to be seen again.

Why does doing the right thing have to hurt so fucking much?

Bishop is the only one of my mates that I really know. Yet it feels like my heart's cracking in half, thinking about any of them moving on. The thought of them ending up with someone else is worse than anything I've ever felt.

I have to let them go, even though it'll break me.

I'm so tired of hurting. That feels like all life is, jumping from one agonizing moment to another. Just existing feels like walking over a sharp, rocky cliffside, barefoot. It feels like breathing in glass, the jagged shards constantly tearing and ripping. It feels like there's a vise grip squeezing my heart and crushing it with each beat.

Some days, I wonder why I fight so hard to keep going. It would be so easy to heal just one ghost too many and fall headlong into oblivion. My family and mates would be safe, and I wouldn't hurt anymore. I wouldn't have to deal with the taunts, attacks, and memories.

Anytime I consider it, though, I'm bombarded with the vacant faces of all the damaged souls I've healed. I see their relief once I heal them, and I know I can't put my selfish wants and needs above them. Even though it's slowly draining my will to live, I have to keep healing ghosts until it kills me.

As the song ends, so too does my pity party. With tears streaming down my cheeks, I try my hardest to shove everything into a dusty, dark corner of my mind. I have so much I need to do, all of which relies on suppressing my feelings. I can't put one foot in front of the other each day if I think about it all.

A sob rips out of my chest during the process.

"I hate to interrupt, kid, but tall, dark, and scary and Bishop are behind you. They got past the dome," Aggie informs me.

"Fuck," I whisper as I try to wipe the tears from my face. I guess my silencing domes don't keep my mates out. That's inconvenient.

Levi snorts at Aggie's nickname. "I can hear you, ghost."

Aggie's spectral eyes widen as she looks at Levi over my shoulder. "I'm just going to…go elsewhere. Good luck, kid." She fades away. A small smile crosses my face at how wary she is of Levi.

Bishop rounds the bench and sits on my left, and Levi sits on my right. "Come here, sweetheart," Bishop whispers with his arms open. I dive headfirst into his chest. My tears soak his shirt as I cry in his arms for who knows how long.

When I've got my emotions under control, I pull back. "Sorry," I mumble as I stare at the ground, beyond embarrassed they both saw all of that.

"You don't have anything to apologize for, Izzy." Bishop leans forward and rests his arms on his knees as he talks. He turns his head to stare at my hunched-over form. His piercing blue eyes study me, seeing far more than I want him to.

"I do. Feelings are gross, and I got them all over you." I gesture to his tear-soaked shirt.

Bishop and Levi both chuckle.

"Feelings aren't gross," Levi insists. "They're part of the human experience. The ability to feel things so strongly, whether it's joy, sorrow, rage, love, grief, or anything else, is what makes humans, well, human. These feeling are what make life worth living. The hope and love and joy are stolen moments in time you remember to help you get through the moments of grief and sorrow and pain. Without feeling, life would be a bland shadow of what it's supposed to be."

"Jesus, dude. Warn me before you get all philosophical and shit," I say in an attempt to deflect. I don't want either of them to know just how much I do feel. If they knew how hard it was to push them away, then they might push back harder. I don't know if I'm strong enough to resist my mates if they really wanted me. To solve that problem, I just act like a raging asshole.

"Dinner's ready!" my mom calls from the back door, saving me from having to say anything else.

I hop up from the bench and stride to the door, guitar in hand. When I don't hear footsteps behind me, I turn back to Levi and Bishop. "You boys coming inside or what?"

"Anywhere you go, little raven, I'll follow," Levi tells me as he stands.

"Always, sweetheart. I'll always be by your side," Bishop declares.

Why do I get the feeling they're talking about more than heading inside for dinner?

CHAPTER 17

IZZY

I'm walking out of my last class of the day, ready to head to my date with Luca, when I get body-checked into a wall. I hit the wall hip and shoulder first, and I groan when the bony areas make contact with the hard wall. The rough brick scrapes me through my white lacy tank top, though my jeans keep my hip scratch-free.

I totally didn't dress up for my date with Luca. It's just a coincidence that I'm not wearing my usual baggy T-shirt tucked into ripped jeans. Even if I were dressing up for the wolf, I still refuse to don impractical footwear. If I can't sprint in it, I'm not wearing it. So, I'm rocking my trusty white Chucks, as usual.

"Stay away from Bishop St. James, *vilis*," Danielle hisses at me. She's in my personal space and glaring up at me from a few inches away. Madison and Tina stand behind her with matching sneers twisting their faces. "Bishop is mine. He'd never want a disappointment like you, anyway."

I can't contain my snort. Of all of my ninety-nine problems, Bishop not wanting me isn't even remotely one of them. In fact, it would knock off at least three problems from my list if he didn't want me and didn't know I have magic.

"You think this is funny?" Danielle sneers. Her face turns red in anger as she moves even closer to me. "Bishop would never marry a slut like you." Mages aren't big on waiting for fated mates. Instead, most mages marry for power and status. We're the only supernatural race I know of that has zero respect for fated mates.

I choke on my laugh this time, making a weird wheezing sound. I'm many things, but a slut isn't one of them. It's kind of hard to be one when I've never slept with anyone. Bishop came back into my life when I was fourteen. We knew each other as kids, but he moved away when I was seven, right before my magic came in. Even though I won't mate with him, I refuse to fuck around on him.

Banging him or any of my other mates is out of the question because it can trigger a mate bond. Mages bond through a power exchange. Shifters bond through mating bites. Vampires bond through swapping blood. And all the other races have a unique way they bond. While fucking doesn't cause the bond, it can be hard to resist the urge to bond in the heat of the moment.

Not that Danielle should be calling anyone a slut. If a woman wants to sleep around, more fucking power to her. Get it, girl. Tap that shit. Boink that hottie.

I giggle to myself at my thoughts, which only makes Danielle more enraged. She shoves hard on both of my shoulders. My head smacks against the wall painfully. When I stop seeing stars, I straighten and level Danielle with a glare. "Put your hands on me again, and I'll fucking break them. This is your only warning."

Danielle visibly pales at my threat. While she isn't the sharpest bulb in the toolshed, she apparently has enough sense to realize when someone can and will follow through on promised violence.

With one last nasty look, she backs up. Danielle and her minions flounce away as I sag against the wall. I take a few calming breaths as I shove my magic down. It gets really angsty when other mages get physical with me.

After a moment, I straighten, readjust my backpack on my shoulder, and head toward the front of Gallagher Hall. I'm not dreading my date with Luca as much as I thought I would be. Sure, I don't particularly want to spend time with him, but it's because I could actually like him. The big wolf isn't as much of a jerk taco as he seemed at first.

When I step out of the building, I immediately spot Luca in his green tee and dark jeans. He's kind of hard to miss when he towers over everyone and out muscles all the mage guys by at least fifty pounds. Luca's blond hair is cut short and perfectly styled as usual. His aquamarine eyes lock on me as soon as he spots me.

I march over to the colossal man and stop in front of him. I have to crane my neck to make eye contact with him, he's so tall.

"How was your day?" Luca asks, peering down at me with a small smile. His blond stubble highlights his sharp jaw and angular features. He has no right to be that damn attractive. It's cheating.

"Fan-fucking-tastic, wolf boy," I reply as I slap my hands on my hips. "How was yours?" At least he didn't call me a problem this time. That's progress, I guess.

He snorts. "Why do I get the feeling that was sarcasm?" He grabs one of my hands with his massive one and tugs me toward the visitor lot. When I go with him willingly, he looks at me with surprise. I resist the urge to roll my eyes. I don't turn everything into a fight. Just most things.

Luca lets go of my hand briefly, and I feel a flash of disappointment. I don't have time to chastise myself for it before Luca recaptures my hand. He intertwines our fingers, and butterflies riot in my stomach. I'm turning into a major sap if a little hand holding has me twitterpated. "Because that's my default setting, duh."

Luca laughs. I'm momentarily stunned by how young he looks with his head thrown back and face open and unguarded. With his imposing presence, it's easy to forget he isn't much older than me. "What happened?" Luca asks when he gets his laughter under control.

"Oh, nothing out of the ordinary. I just got slammed into a wall and demeaned, while not being able to lay them on their asses." I'd love nothing more than to give Danielle, Madison, and Tina the beat down they deserve.

"Why can't you physically fight them?" Luca's forehead wrinkles in confusion at my restraint. Ah, to be a wolf. What a life. Wolves solve their problems with bloodshed. Mages turn everything into a complicated political chess game. It's exhausting trying to keep up with it.

"I'd probably get kicked out if I broke their stupid noses. My dad keeps the headmaster from expelling me for most things, but I don't know if he could fight it if I fucked them up." Getting expelled means getting sent to the mage council for reformation. With the required magic testing, I wouldn't last an hour. So, I suck up my pride and let them bully me.

"That's a really shitty situation to be in. I'm sorry, little one." As Luca talks, we pass between the final two buildings between campus and the visitor lot.

I scrunch up my nose at his nickname. I'm not small. I'm actually above average in height. It's not my fault his parents were apparently eight-foot-tall giants. "That's a horrible endearment."

Luca sighs. "Would you prefer *baby*?"

I snort. "That's awfully basic of you, wolf boy. Can't come up with anything more creative?"

He growls at me and tugs us to a stop. With his hold on my hand, Luca pulls until I crash into his front. Luca places his warm palm on my back to keep me from moving away. "You drive me fucking crazy, wildcat. You know that?"

"Um," I say, unable to formulate an intelligent response with him this close. I'm drowning in his dark forest scent. Every inch of my body is pressed against his muscular one, and it's short-circuiting my brain.

"I'm trying to be on my best behavior with you. Yet you challenge me at every turn. My wolf is riding me hard. He wants me to make you submit," Luca rasps. He leans down until his lips are inches from mine, and I can't stop thinking about whether his lips are as soft as they look.

"How would you make me submit?" My voice comes out breathless, instead of the steady disinterest I was aiming for.

Luca chuckles, the sound holding a dark promise and threat all in one. "Don't ask questions you don't want the answer to, Isabel."

I like the way my full name sounds on his lips, but I don't show it. Instead, I scowl at him. "Who says I don't want the answer?" Luca has a bad habit of acting like he knows what's best for me. He doesn't. The wolf doesn't know me well enough for that.

Another deep growl rumbles in Luca's chest as he leans even closer, his lips almost touching mine. "I'd force you down on your hands and knees. Then I'd fuck you so hard, you'd be too exhausted to sass me, wildcat."

"Oh," I squeak. My brain is too full of images of Luca fucking me to formulate a full sentence. Most of me screams *sign me up, wolf boy*. The few brain cells that actually have any sense left shout that it's an awful idea. I doubt Luca would be able to stop himself from completing the mate bond if he fucked me. I know I sure wouldn't.

He flashes me a savage grin before pulling back. "Come on, Izzy. Let's go before we give the mages here a show they don't need to see." Luca removes his hand from my back and tugs me along by my hand.

I follow along pliantly until I shake myself out of my lust-induced stupor. Then I hurry up to walk even with Luca. "Wildcat is an aggressively better nickname than *little one* or *baby*. It's not as good as *supreme world overlord*, though."

Luca snorts and shakes his head at me. "I'm glad that's all you got from the conversation."

I just shrug. We walk in silence the rest of the way.

CHAPTER 18

IZZY

*W*hen we walk into the parking lot, I immediately spot his muscle car. "You brought the Charger!"

"I did, wildcat. And I'm going to teach you how to drive it today," Luca tells me as we walk to his car. When we reach it, he leans against the Charger with a half smile.

"What?! No way!" I exclaim as I bounce on my toes in excitement. I'm practically jumping up and down, I'm so stoked. Turning to Luca with a stupid grin on my face, I hug him. One of his arms wraps around my lower back. He cups the back of my neck with his other hand.

After a moment, I step back from the hug I liked way too much. My cheeks are slightly pink with embarrassment at initiating another hug. I don't hug people unless I'm under duress. I don't know what's gotten into me, but I don't like it.

"I haven't seen you like this before."

"Like what?" I ask, peering up at him through my blonde lashes.

"I don't know. Carefree? Happy, maybe?" The earlier

laughter has been wiped from Luca's face. He's staring down at me pensively, seeing way more than I want him to.

"You can thank Michael Westen for it," I tell him flippantly, trying to distract him from thinking about why I don't seem upbeat or relaxed most of the time. I don't need the wolf digging into my life and discovering everything I'm trying to hide to keep him safe.

It works. "Who the fuck is that?" Luca rumbles. He straightens from his perch against the car and advances on me. I stand my ground and refuse to back up. Tilting my chin up, I meet his burning blue eyes. I'm proud of myself that I don't even flinch at the rage I find in his gaze.

"Calm down, wolf boy. He's fictional. He's the main character from the show I like and the reason I think Chargers are super cool."

When Luca realizes that Michael Westen isn't my boyfriend or fuck buddy, he backs up a step. He closes his eyes for a moment. He runs his hands through his short hair before his bright ocean eyes snap open. "Your mouth is going to get you in trouble one of these days, wildcat."

I can't help the laugh that bubbles up at his comment. "It gets me in trouble on the regular."

The corners of Luca's mouth twitch up briefly before he shuts down his grin. Turning away from me, he opens the passenger side car door for me. "Get in."

"I thought I was driving?"

Luca huffs a laugh. "You'll drive when we're somewhere you can't drive the Charger into anything."

"Oh. Good thinking." With how not coordinated I am, there's a huge chance I would drive the muscle car into something else in this parking lot. I climb into the passenger seat and admire the buttery soft leather. Even with it being white, the leather is in pristine condition. It's clear Luca takes great care of this beauty.

Once Luca and I are all buckled up, he pulls out of the parking lot. We drive while listening to his music without speaking for a few minutes before I can't take the awkwardness anymore. "How'd you become alpha so young?" I blurt out.

Luca flicks his gaze to me before darting it back to the road. "My parents were killed five years ago. One of my dads was the previous alpha. When they were killed in a vampire attack, Archer, Cain, and I had to step up to lead the pack."

"Shit, man. I'm sorry." I wince at how sarcastic I sound. While I meant it sincerely, it comes across flippantly. I'm the worst at emotions and dealing with other people having feelings.

He barks out a startled laugh. "Bishop was right, wildcat. You sure do have a way with words."

We're at a stoplight, so I twist in my seat to look at him. "I really am sorry, Luca. On top of losing your parents, which is a pain I can't even begin to imagine, you had to take on so much responsibility. I know how easy it is to be crushed and broken by everything that's expected of you. Taking on leading a whole pack isn't easy, and, from everything I've heard, you do a great job."

"I knew what you meant, Izzy," Luca tells me as he watches me. His eyes soften at what he sees on my face before he has to turn back to driving. "What responsibilities weigh on you?"

"Nice try, wolf boy." I know when someone's fishing for information. Everything that feels like it's trying to bury me under six feet of concrete is exactly what I can't talk to him about. To distract him, I ask him something else. "Is the vampire attack why your pack got into assassination and arms dealing?"

Luca's head whips around to face me before he quickly

jerks his gaze back to the road. "Yes, it is. How do you even know that, wildcat? Our side activities aren't well known."

"Oh. Huh. I thought everyone knew of your shady, back-room, blood-money dealings. I probably heard it from Rhys or Aiden." Luca scowls at me for how I label his pack's illegal activities. I smile at getting a rise out of the serious wolf.

"How do they know?"

"Probably from their work at the security company." Rhys and Bishop are part owners of their mage security and intelligence business. They started it with two other friends straight out of college. Logan and Declan, the other owners, are pretty chill. It's doing decently well, if how many employees they have is any indication.

"Which one?"

"Elemental Security." I think it's a cheeky as hell name because most mages have an affinity for one of the elements. It sounds normal enough not to draw human attention but mage enough to attract the right kind of business.

Luca's eyes widen comically when I tell him the security company name. I manage to hold back my laugh at his shock. "Fucking hell. I didn't realize your brothers worked for them. No wonder they knew."

"They don't work for them. Well, Aiden does, but Bishop and Rhys own it. Are they a big deal or something?"

Luca chokes on his spit. He turns to me with his eyebrows practically at his hairline. "They're the best super-natural security and intelligence operation on the East Coast, wildcat. No wonder Bishop is so good at what he does." He mutters the last part to himself.

"Really? I thought they weren't very good because they have me help out sometimes." My brothers and Bishop hate when I come on their super-secret spy missions, but my skills are sometimes needed. Anya whips me up disguise potions, so no one other than my brothers and Bishop know it's me.

"They let you go on operations?" Luca growls, hands white knuckling the steering wheel. His eyes flash the amber of his wolf as they bounce between the road and my face. "That's dangerous."

I snort. Going on missions with Rhys and Bishop is probably the least dangerous thing I do. Since I'm in disguise, I can use my magic to defend myself. Hell, being at school is more hazardous for my health than the security work I do. "Yes, wolf boy, I go on missions when my particular skills are necessary."

"What skills are those?" Luca pulls into an empty parking lot in front of an abandoned building. He turns to look at me fully as soon as he puts the car in park.

"Ones I can't tell you about." I studiously avoid his eyes that remind me of the sea glass I used to collect as a kid.

"Is your work with Elemental Security why you've killed someone before?" Luca asks gently.

I close my eyes at his question and lean my head against the seat. "I've killed people on missions, but they don't bother me as much." I don't know why I'm shocked when these wolves ask me about it, but I am. I've thought more about that day in the past week than I have in ten years.

"As what?" Luca prods.

I just shake my head in answer, not having the words or will to talk about it with him. I've never talked about it with anyone.

Will what I did ever stop hurting this much? Not that I deserve to escape the pain, but, fuck, do I want to. I throw my arm over my eyes, trying to hide my sorrow. I haven't had the luxury of showing my emotions since I became an outcast. Showing them what hurts me just allows them to hurt me worse.

Maybe being emotional will scare him off, which only makes me feel worse. My shoulders shake from trying to contain my feelings.

Fuck my life. I really can't win today.

Luca is silent for a moment before he gets out of the car. I figure he needs time away from my emotional ass. Only, seconds later, Luca is at my door, opening it.

"Stand up," Luca orders. I'm too busy hating myself to protest, so I do as he tells me to. When I'm out of the car, Luca grabs me under my ass and hauls me up. My arms and legs automatically wrap around the big wolf. I lay my head on his massive shoulder, hiding my face in his neck.

Luca holds me the entire time I try to battle back my emotions. While one of his hands is banded under my thighs as support, his other one is tangled in my hair. He runs his fingers through the strands soothingly. His gentleness surprises me. I didn't know he was capable of tenderness like this, which makes sense. I barely know the guy.

When I no longer feel on the verge of crying and my breathing evens out, Luca murmurs into my hair, "I don't know what you've been through, wildcat, but it's obvious it was traumatic. You don't have to talk to me, but you need to talk to someone about it. You can't keep it inside forever. It'll destroy you, slowly smothering your spark until there's nothing of you left."

I don't know what to say to him, because he's right. It doesn't matter, though. I can't put my well-being above everyone else's. "I have to keep it inside. That's the only way everyone will be safe."

I try to get out of his hold to escape this conversation, but his arms are like iron bands holding me in place. Luca eventually lets me slide down his body.

When I'm on my feet, he stares at me for a long moment. Instead of pushing me to tell him, Luca throws the keys at me. I snatch them out of the air. I'm not sure what surprises me more, me being coordinated enough to catch the keys or Luca not pressing me for answers.

Luca doesn't give me time to dwell on it. "Come on, wild-cat. Time for your driving lesson."

CHAPTER 19

IZZY

"*S*tay behind me. At all times, Mags," Rhys orders as we stare up at a super obvious villain lair. *Like, come on, bad guys. Locate your base of operations somewhere that doesn't scream "I cook up evil plans here that have more holes than a porcupine's sweater."*

It's been a week since my date with Luca. I was supposed to have a date with Cain tonight, but he had to cancel. I'm helping Elemental out tonight. Usually, I don't do work on school nights. With Cain moving our date to tomorrow, I have time to help tonight.

We're looking for a little girl kidnapped by some vampire clan leader. He's angry at his friendly neighborhood bear sleuth for something or other. So, he decided to steal one of the sleuth's kids in retaliation. She's only five, and we're going to get her back to her family.

The abandoned warehouse has seen better days, with most of the formerly red brick cracked, dirty, and falling apart in some places. Despite being dilapidated, it has high-tech cameras, motion sensors, and floodlights surrounding the outside.

That's super stealthy. I'm sure there's nothing nefarious going on here.

"Sir, yes, sir!" I whisper with an exaggerated salute. I hear a few chuckles behind me, but Rhys just rolls his eyes at me. I grin at him in return.

Since my magic is needed, I'm in my typical disguise. With shoulder-length black hair, light brown eyes, and golden tanned skin, I don't look anything like myself. My face is also more rounded, my nose a little longer, and my cheekbones lower. While I'm still the same height, because changing height requires a ton of magic, it'd be hard for anyone to connect Mags O'Sullivan to Isabel Gallagher.

Since Rhys, Bishop, and Aiden are overprotective of me, there's speculation at Elemental that I'm dating one or all of them. We sell it that I'm just an old family friend, but I don't think most people buy that. At least none of them suspect who I am, which is all that really matters.

"No killing unless it's absolutely necessary," Rhys informs me and the five men behind us. Although, I'm pretty sure he's mostly warning me. I may or may not accidentally on purpose kill more bad guys than I'm supposed to on the regular.

David, Max, Finn, Conan, and Cian are with us tonight. They're all good dudes, and none of them are from Hawthorne Grove. I trust them, as much as I trust anyone other than Bishop and my family, to watch my back.

Bishop isn't on this mission with us. He's working on stuff for the Nightshade Pack, so Rhys didn't tell him about our operation tonight. He wouldn't be happy to know I'm working for Elemental without him as backup. Oh, well. I'm not particularly happy he's working for the Nightshades without taking backup, so we're even.

"Sure thing," I agree. Our definitions of "absolutely necessary" might be a smidge different, though. Rhys eyes me suspiciously before turning on his heel. He moves on silent feet toward the warehouse. I follow close behind him with David behind me. The other mages are in a line behind him.

When we reach the back door to the warehouse, Rhys signals for Finn, Conan, and Max to circle around to the front. We're going to go in both entrances at the same time. Rhys hopes we can just get in, find the girl, and get out. But we're prepared for the worst-case scenario.

Along with my disguise, Anya also made us a scent eliminator potion. Vamps have a crazy good sense of smell, along with super duper hearing and vision. Hiding our scent means we're more likely to have the element of surprise, but it's not guaranteed.

After waiting sixty seconds for the others to get into place, Rhys breathes, *"Adflictare."* The padlock on the door shatters as soon as Rhys's magic hits it. The internal deadbolts also break down with quiet clanks.

When Rhys pushes on the door, it swings inside with a loud screech. I wince. There's no way Sparkles and Co. didn't hear that. Rhys hangs his head briefly before shaking it off and leading us inside. I scan the dirty concrete floors, chipped brick walls, and the catwalk above us and see nothing. Our view to the front is blocked by a cinder-block wall dividing the lower portion of the warehouse into multiple sections.

The shouting from upfront has already started. *Sorry, Rhys.* I guess we'll be doing this my preferred way. Get in, kill as many as I can, and get out. Rhys motions me up the stairs as he, David, and Cian make their way to the others. I give him a nod and jog to the staircase that's only still standing through hopes and prayers. A few steps are missing, and the rest are rusted out in spots.

My job on these missions is usually to secure whoever we're rescuing. I'm the most powerful mage Elemental has. By far. I can protect the kidnappee, open up a portal, and fend off attackers, all at the same time. There are very few other mages who can do all of that at once, so it's my job by default.

I take the stairs two at a time, hoping I won't fall through. Leaping to the top, I let out a relieved sigh. That is, until I see the blur of a vampire barreling toward me. One positive about my weird magic is that I have way faster reflexes than the average mage. I'm whipping out a dagger and throwing it at the vampire before I have a chance to think about it.

The downside is it comes out to play more easily when I'm in danger. My magic starts slithering through my veins, leaking out into the surrounding air. I grit my teeth as I waste precious time trying desperately to wrangle it back where it belongs. After a few long moments, I'm able to stuff it back into its prison in my chest.

When the vamp comes to a stop in front of me, he looks in confusion at the dagger protruding from his chest. He then crumples to the floor in a heap, paralyzed by the blade to the heart. Simply stabbing a vampire through the heart won't kill them. Their heads have to be removed and hearts cut out to do that. But it does stun them, which is all I need right now.

Mages, unfortunately for me, are a lot less hearty than vampires. We can be killed by decapitation, ripping our hearts out, piercing our hearts, blood loss, and pretty much anything a normal human can be killed by. It blows being a mage, most of the time.

Shifters are somewhere in the middle, between vampires and mages. Decapitation obviously kills them. Destroying a shifter's heart completely or draining them of most of their blood will also kill them. But they can survive more blood loss and damage than a mage.

I unfortunately have to leave my dagger behind for now. Good thing I'm always carrying extras on missions like these. Glaring at the vamp who is the current proud owner of my favorite knife, I make my way down the hallway. Poking my head into every nook, cranny, and room I pass and finding nothing, I'm starting to think our intelligence that said that Lottie is on the second floor is wrong.

Until I hear a squeak of surprise and fear when I open the third door on the right. I quickly scan the dusty wood floors, crumbling brick walls, and broken furniture. My shoulders slump in relief when I see a small blonde girl huddling in a corner as far from the door as she can get. "Lottie, I'm here to help, honey." She shrinks into herself farther at my voice. Anger for what the vampires put her through bubbles in my chest. I squash it down because the little girl needs me to be calm. Taking a deep breath and unclenching my fists, I try to appear nonthreatening.

Slowly taking off my backpack, so I don't frighten her, I pull out a ragged pink stuffed bunny. "Lottie, it's okay. I won't hurt you, sweetie," I whisper. "Your papa sent us. He thought you might need Benny, so I have him right here for you."

Her wide green eyes finally meet mine when I mention her stuffed animal. She hesitantly unfolds from her protective position and creeps closer to me. When I don't do anything but crouch there patiently, Lottie gains confidence. She darts in to grab her stuffie and backs up against the wall again. Hugging the toy tightly to her chest, Lottie watches me with tears running down her freckled face.

My heart hurts for the little girl plunged into a war she never asked for. I want to give her a hug, but she doesn't know me. What she needs is the people who love her and miss her. "You wanna head home, Lottie?" She nods her head vigorously, her dirt-coated pigtails flopping around as she does so. A small smile tugs at the corners of my mouth. "All right, honey. I'm going to portal you to your papa. You're going to feel magic in the air as I do so. It's nothing to worry about, but it might feel a little ticklish."

Lottie gives me another hesitant nod. Giving her a soft smile, I look away and mutter, *"Defensare."* A light blue dome surrounds us, protecting Lottie and me from any vampires who stumble in.

When I'm sure the defensive shield is sturdy enough, I whisper, *"Aperire."* I open a portal to one of Elemental's conference rooms. Through it, I spot a large blond man paces around the oval wooden table, his brown boots silent on the navy carpet tiles. With his red flannel shirt, full blond beard, and barrel chest, Lottie's dad, Chuck, looks like a lumberjack.

Aiden is sitting in a mesh chair pulled up to the table with three computers and a bunch of papers strewn across the oak tabletop. He's so absorbed in providing mission support that he doesn't see us at first. Chuck rips his gaze from the warm taupe walls and calm landscape pictures to stare at me. I give him a small nod to let him know we found her. He lets out a harsh exhale as tears fill his green eyes that are a copy of Lottie's.

It takes Lottie a moment to open her eyes. She squeezed them shut as soon as I started using my magic. When she sees her dad, she runs straight toward him. I quickly step in front of the portal before she can go through. Lottie stops just short of crashing into me. I reach out to steady her, but she flinches away from my touch.

"You can go through the portal, Lottie. It's going to feel sticky and heavy and pretty weird, okay? I just wanted you to be prepared, but you can go to your Papa whenever you're ready." I move away from the portal to allow her to go through.

Her eyes dart around the room before she searches my face intently for a moment. Deciding I'm not trying to trick her, Lottie rushes through my portal. When she pops out on the other side, her dad is there to scoop her up into a massive hug.

"Oh, Lottie, I'm so sorry, baby. You're safe now. We won't let anyone hurt you again." Chuck rubs her back gently as her little shoulders shake with quiet sobs. While she's physically safe, Lottie's got a long road ahead of her. The things she's seen and experienced over the last few days will take more than being rescued to heal.

Chuck looks up from his daughter to lock eyes with me. He sounds seconds from breaking down. "Thank you. Thank you so much for finding her and bringing her back. We've all been sick with worry for her. None of us would've ever been the same without Lottie."

A lump forms in my throat, and a few tears trail down my cheeks. I swipe them away with the backs of my hands and clear my throat. "Yeah, no problem." I hear shouting and realize I've spent too long already on getting her out. The team needs me to help with the rest of the vampires. "I've gotta go. Just, give her some extra love and attention for a little while? She's going to need it."

After getting a nod from Chuck, I close the portal. I cover my eyes with my hands as I take a moment to get myself together. Stuffing down all the anguish and heartache for Lottie, I pull on the anger that's simmering just below the surface. I let it rush through me like a prairie fire. It burns away the softer emotions.

Dropping my hands from my face, I straighten and grasp a knife in each hand. I can't fix anything for Lottie, but I can damn well get her a little revenge. I bare my teeth in a savage grin before rushing out of the room to rejoin the others.

∼

"You LOOK EXHAUSTED TODAY, DEARIE," Anya observes. Her raspy voice breaks my concentration. I stop stirring the potion I'm working on to rub my hands over my tired eyes.

Leaning back against the front counter, I look at the small Russian woman who's become a surrogate grandmother to me. My dad's parents want nothing to do with a magicless disappointment, and my mom's parents aren't around much. Anya gives me all the grandmotherly love I never knew I was missing.

At barely five-feet tall, with white hair permanently in a French twist, Anya shouldn't be intimidating. But her sharp brown eyes, no-nonsense personality, and potent magical abilities make her a force to be reckoned with.

"Yeah. I stayed out late last night helping with Rhys's operation." It was totally worth it, but I only got two hours of sleep. I can function pretty well while sleep deprived, but the tiredness really hit me after school today. My date with Cain is tonight, so I've been drinking energy potions to try to perk up.

"Did you need a disguise potion?" Anya walks around me to peer into the cauldron housing my potion.

"Yep. I had an extra one. Thanks for those, by the way. They're super helpful." While I've worked with Anya for years, I'm still not good enough at potion making to make them myself.

Anya hums before turning her too insightful gaze on me. "And what would Rhys need his magicless sister to be disguised for?"

"Oh, you know, a little this and that." I look away from

140

Anya as I lie. While I'm lying to protect her, it still makes me feel slimy. Anya is one of the few people I like in Hawthorne Grove. She gave me a chance when no one else would, and she deserves honestly. Knowing my secret will only get her killed, so I have to do what's necessary to protect her.

Anya hums in disbelief but doesn't push it. "And you're working on your special project again."

It's not a question, but I answer, anyway. "Yeah."

She sighs and places one wrinkled hand on my forearm. "It won't work, dearie. I've been around for one hundred and forty years, and this type of magic cannot be done."

Panic coils around and tightens my airways until I'm gasping for breath. Failing isn't an option with this potion. Making it is the only way everyone will be safe. I have to make it work.

"There's a first time for everything, Anya." I try to keep my voice light, but it comes out choked up instead.

Anya turns away to study the potion once more. Moving surprisingly quickly for her age, Anya hurries to the back room. She comes back with a few ceramic jars and puts them on the counter in front of me. Grabbing one, she opens it and walks over to my potion. "Have you tried dried marigold?"

"No, I haven't. The recipes I've seen haven't suggested it."

"Well, we'll need to go off recipe if we want a result the recipe doesn't promise, now, won't we?" She waits for my nod before moving closer to the potion. Anya meticulously measures the marigold powder before adding it in stages to the potion. Chanting something I can't make out, Anya's signature forest green magic flares in the mixture for a moment before fading.

"You think it will do anything?" I can't keep the hope out of my voice, even though I've tried so many different ingredients to get it to work.

141

"I don't know. The only way to find out is to try. We tried, and now we have to wait." As Anya finishes speaking, the bell on the shop's front door tinkles. Anya walks out front to greet the customer.

I stare at the potion a moment longer, willing it to work. Blowing out a breath, I settle in for an afternoon of waiting for the potion to work and Cain to pick me up for our rescheduled date.

CHAPTER 20

CAIN

"*Y*ou said we were just going to talk to them!" Bishop shouts in exasperation at Archer. It's hard to make out his voice over the bursts of automatic gunfire from the approximately twenty men across the warehouse from us. Due to Bishop's shield encasing the three of us, we're relatively safe. At least for now.

"It's not my fault they didn't want to talk to us!" Archer counters with a grin. Pausing to reload his M4 carbine, Archer fires at the men protecting the weapons crates once more. He's enjoying himself much more than Bishop is.

"Considering you stole from them last month, I would say it is your fault," I chime in.

Bishop glares at Archer, who just rolls his eyes. Archer frequently drags the mage into chaotic situations without warning him beforehand. It's only Bishop's quick thinking that has kept him alive this long while working with Archer.

Shaking my head at the two of them, I slip out from behind Bishop's shield. I keep close to the wall and use the various crates scattered throughout the open industrial space as cover. While Bishop is fairly strong, he can't hold the shield indefinitely. Archer keeps the men distracted, so it's my job to incapacitate them.

Sneaking behind one of the shooters at the back, I lunge toward him and slap one hand over his mouth. With the other, I sink my blade into his vulnerable throat and sever his windpipe to prevent screaming. I tear through his carotid artery and jugular vein as well. A rare smile crosses my lips as I watch him choke on his own blood. When he finally goes limp, I drop his corpse to the dirty warehouse floor and stab him through the heart a few times.

I feel no remorse as I slowly work through the remaining men the same way. Instead of doing anything to help others, these panther shifters are content to sell automatic rifles and machine pistols to cartels, human traffickers, and the occasional dictator. Their deaths only make the world a better place.

When only five shifters remain, they start to realize something is wrong. Fools. I roll my eyes as they frantically search for whoever killed their associates. As they're searching for me, Archer manages to pick off four of them. I glare at Archer when I step behind the last one and slit his throat. His warm blood sprays onto my forearms, already dripping with blood from the others.

"I had them handled, Archer." I drop the last panther's body to the ground and walk to one of the largest crates. Pulling off the top of it, I see the M4s and MAC 10s we were looking for. At least today wasn't a bust like last night. We've been looking for these weapons for a week. I had to cancel my date with Isabel yesterday to go on another wild goose chase. She agreed to move our date to today, so we need to wrap this up quickly.

"Sorry for stealing your kills, man." The shit-eating grin on Archer's face tells a different story. He isn't sorry in the least. Sighing, I ignore him to start inventorying the other crates. Bishop, Archer, and I split up to tackle three to four crates each.

"Where are these weapons going?" Bishop asks.

"To a handful of packs, clans, and mage towns in the south. The small groups of supernaturals are getting hit hard by the Knights of Aeneas right now. We'll see how those fuckers like being subject to automatic weapons." Archer bares his teeth at the thought of the Knights. They're a human organization dedicated to wiping out anyone with magic. The Knights want to steal the magic for themselves, which usually means killing anyone who has it.

Since they have no honor, the Knights often use automatic weapons on unarmed shifters, mages, vampires, and others. While magic users all have their own inherent weapons, they're not always enough when it comes to the Knights. We try to even the playing field by smuggling weapons to supernaturals across the country. The wealthier packs, clans, or towns will buy them from us, while the poorer ones get the guns for free. It's not the most lucrative of our revenue streams, but it does arguably the most good.

"Can you two handle the rest of the inventory and clean up?" I ask as I finish with my last crate. "I need to get to my date with Isabel."

"You might want to clean up first," Bishop informs me. "You have blood splatter on your face, your arms are covered in it, and your gray shirt is now red. You can't go out with Izzy looking like that."

Glancing down, I see that he's right. My arms are painted with drying rust-colored blood, and my shirt is stained with the same substance. Even my pants are splattered with it, but my shiny black derby shoes are relatively clean. A quick check of my watch shows that I'm already late. "I don't have time to change, Bishop."

Bishop mutters something under his breath about me being a psychotic wolf before mumbling a spell. I'd be offended if it weren't the truth. My skin tingles where his magic brushes against me. I close my eyes at the unnerving sensation. When I don't feel his magic anymore, I open my eyes to see that I'm completely clean.

"You need a portal too?" Bishop asks while continuing to inventory one of his crates.

I nod at him. "Yes."

Bishop whispers another spell before a portal to Isabel opens. I check to make sure no one is waiting to ambush me before stepping through.

"Thank you," I tell him. Bishop portaled me straight to Hawthorne Grove's downtown, which saved me thirty minutes of driving each way. We're across the street from Anya's Apothecary. The shop is on one end of the main street, so there aren't as many people milling about in front of it.

"I would say no problem, but this whole afternoon has been a problem. If you or Izzy need anything, just let me know." Bishop gives me a distracted wave before turning back to the warehouse and shutting the portal.

My fingers drum a steady beat on my thigh as I regard the shop. It's a whitewashed brick building with a greenery-filled sign hanging out front. The sign matches the dark green awning. A variety of bottles and plants fill the shop windows. I can't see Isabel from where I'm standing. While she goes by Izzy, the nickname doesn't seem to fit my mate. Isabel matches her much better.

I'm surprised to realize I'm nervous. I haven't been nervous since I was a child. The memories try to flee their boxes in my mind, but I slam the lid shut on them before they can. Nothing good comes from remembering that which is best forgotten.

Smoothing my hand over my light gray button-down shirt, I make my way across the street to the shop. When I pull open the door to the apothecary, I'm hit with the overwhelming scent of medicinal herbs. I can barely smell the berry and sunshine scent of my mate.

Isabel glances up when I walk in. She's standing behind the counter with an old woman. The woman is much shorter than her and has her white hair twisted up. The old woman's brown eyes twinkle when she sees me, which is odd, as I've never met her before.

A shy smile crosses Isabel's pink lips when she sees that it's me. "I'll be right over, Cain. Just give me one minute."

I dip my chin in answer and take the time to study my mate. Her tongue darts out as she focuses on something. Isabel's blonde hair with purple and blue ends falls into her face as she glances down at the thick book she's writing in. She bats the wavy strands away with an impatient hand.

When she's done writing, Isabel turns to the old woman. "Are you sure it's okay for me to skedaddle early, Anya? I can stay later to help if you need."

Anya huffs. "Go on your date, dearie. Be a young woman for once. Have fun. Make bad decisions. Live a little."

Isabel snorts and grins at Anya. "Shouldn't you be encouraging me to be safe and make good decisions?"

"You're too responsible for your age, so no." Anya's brown eyes fill with sadness as she considers Isabel. I wonder if Anya knows what Isabel can't or won't tell us.

"Me, responsible? I think you have the wrong girl, Anya. I've turned in at least three assignments late this week, my mom still cooks my meals, and I've converted six of my fellow students today alone to lives of debauchery." Isabel grins at Anya as she talks. The sadness in the old woman's eyes lifts at Isabel's teasing. It's impressive how well my mate uses humor to ward off any serious conversations.

147

Anya shakes her head at Isabel and shoos her away. Isabel holds her hands up in surrender. "Okay. Okay. I'm going!"

When Isabel walks around the counter, I take in her light purple dress dotted with small white flowers that's so different from anything I've seen her wear. The A-line dress has cap sleeves and flows around her pale thighs. It accentuates her narrow waist and flared hips. A grin wants to break out across my face at the sight of her white high-tops with the dress. It seems very Isabel to pair sneakers with a dress.

"What?" Isabel questions as she notices me staring. "I got something on my dress, didn't I?" She groans as she looks down, trying to find what I'm looking at.

"You don't have anything on it, angel. I was just surprised by the dress. I haven't seen you in one before. You look beautiful."

Isabel blushes at my compliment, her cheeks turning an enticing shade of pink. I wonder what else I could do to make her flush like that. My dick perks up at my thoughts, and I will it to go down before I tent my pants.

"Oh. Well, you always dress up, so I wanted to be at least a little dressy. I wasn't sure if we were going somewhere super fancy or something." Isabel fidgets with her dress as she talks, and I find her nervousness endearing.

I do dress up more than my peers. One of my fathers instilled in me the importance of first impressions. He always told me that dressing sharply is essential to being taken seriously and earning respect. While I don't think there's anything wrong with a T-shirt and jeans, I can't shake the feeling of being underdressed when I leave the house dressed like that.

"We're not going anywhere fancy. Thank you for going out with me this afternoon instead of yesterday. I got caught up unexpectedly." I don't elaborate on what held me up. She doesn't need to know all the gritty details of our less-than-legal businesses.

"No worries, quiet boy." My lips twitch again at her nickname for me. I haven't been a boy in a long time, but I don't mind her endearment. "Where are we going?"

"I wanted to take you to meet some of the pack." I offer her my hand. Her storm cloud gray eyes bounce between mine briefly before she places her hand in mine. Isabel's hand is so small compared to mine. I have the urge to wrap her up to keep her safe from the world. I highly doubt she'd let me do that, otherwise I would.

"That's an intense first date, dude." Isabel worries her lip between her teeth, and I resist the urge to pull it free with my thumb. While she's visibly nervous, she still follows me out of the shop. Her trust in me makes me puff up in pride.

"You mentioned volunteering with music and children. The pack provides after-school programs for children whose parents work late. I thought you might enjoy playing music with the pups." We reached the secluded alley that should work for portaling, so I turn to face my mate as I talk.

Her delicate face lights up with pure joy at the mention of working with children. "I take back my first judgment. That totally sounds like fun."

"I'm glad you think so. The music room has guitars and pianos. Do you need anything else?" My hands itch to settle on my mate's waist, so I shove them into my pockets. I'm not sure what she's comfortable with touch wise. After how she reacted when sparring with Luca, I want to be extra careful when touching her.

"Nope. The only instruments I can play are guitar and piano. I prefer guitar, though."

"Perfect. If I show you a picture of the music room, can you portal us there?" I drag my phone out of my pocket as I wait for her answer. Mages can portal anywhere they've seen before. If a mage hasn't been to a location, then a picture of the place will often work instead.

"I can do that, quiet boy."

I show her a picture of the music room at our pack house. It has warm, dark wood floors, matching paneling, and a thick oriental carpet at the center of the room. The sizable room is dominated by four pianos and racks of guitars. Maria Nightshade, Luca and Archer's mother, loved music, so we have her to thank for this room.

After taking in the picture, Isabel mutters something, likely in Latin, under her breath. I feel her magic burst out into the air. The electric currents of her magic ghost over my skin, causing my hair to stand straight up. While the sensation is eerie, it's not entirely unpleasant.

A portal snaps to life on the brick wall in front of us. I don't see any of the pups yet, but I'm sure they'll be excited to see a portal for the first time. Offering Isabel my hand, I wait for her to take it before stepping through the portal.

"Cain!" a chorus of young voices cheer when I walk through the portal. I release my mate's hand as Noah crashes into me. I lift up the small boy and am rewarded with peals of laughter. As soon as I set the blond pup down, I have four more clinging to my legs and arms. I pretend to struggle to lift my arms or walk. The pups giggle at my antics, and a rare smile crosses my lips.

When I look over to my mate, I see her lips stretched in a wide grin as she watches me with the children.

"What's a mage doing here?" Addison, one of the teenagers in the program, sneers. Her navy eyes are glaring at my mate. It's understandable that Addie is wary of strangers, after what happened to one of her dads, but I still don't like her talking to my mate like that.

"She's my mate, Addie. Treat her respectfully, please." At my proclamation, the entire room freezes. Almost as one, all the pups turn to look at Isabel with wide eyes. She stares back at them with similarly wide eyes, unsure what to do as the center of attention to twenty pups.

"Does that mean—" Addie begins to ask. I give her a nod, telling her that Isabel is also Luca and Archer's mate. She squeals so loud, I have the urge to slap my hands over my ears. "Oh my God! Finally!" The other teen girls join Addie in squealing and jumping around.

Isabel's confused gaze meets mine. I suppose, with having to pretend to be magicless, my mate isn't used to anyone being excited to see her. An ache forms behind my sternum at that thought.

"I didn't bring Isabel just to introduce you to my mate. She also plays guitar and piano, and she's here to teach you to play some songs."

"Can you play Taylor Swift?" Mia, a brunette pre-teen pup, asks. Addie and her other friends nod frantically next to Mia, excited at the prospect of learning some of their favorite songs.

"Yeah, I can play quite a few of her songs. What song do you wanna learn first?" Isabel gives her full attention to the girls as she talks. I can tell that the pups are already smitten with our pack's future luna. As the mate to the pack's alpha, Isabel is automatically considered as highly ranking as Luca, even though she's not a wolf.

Addie and her friends look at each other before all shouting at the same time, "'You Belong with Me'!"

Isabel's lips kick up in a smile before she nods. "Yep. I can totally play that. Come on, let's all get guitars. I'll play it through for you once before I teach it to you." The girls stare up at my mate with stars in their eyes as they all trail her.

My mate goes to the racks of guitars and starts passing them out. She makes sure every pup who wants one gets it before taking a guitar for herself. I'm surprised that some of the boys grabbed an instrument as well.

Isabel sits on the ground with her legs tucked under her. She rests the guitar on her lap as she waits for the pups to get settled. The kids fan out around her as Isabel plays a few notes to get a feel for the instrument. Once she's sure everyone is ready, Isabel starts playing the song. She has a lovely alto voice. Her delicate fingers expertly play the guitar. It's clear she's very experienced with the instrument.

As Isabel sings the song, Prue walks up beside me. "This her?"

"Yes." I glance at my sister, who's the spitting image of one of our fathers. With her auburn curls and hazel eyes, she looks just like him. I look like our mother, with the same black hair and green eyes. Any time I look in the mirror, she's all I see. As such, I try to avoid my reflection.

"She's really pretty. Your mate also has a way with the kiddos. She's much better than the vipers you like to fuck." Prue smiles sweetly at me as I gape at her. Leave it to her to bring that up.

"Prudence! You're lucky she's not a wolf and can't hear you." My little sister just grins at me chastising her. Prue's mischievous and loves causing chaos. I don't have the heart to rein her in most of the time.

"Relax, Si. She seems chill. I doubt she'd claw my eyes out just for mentioning you've screwed women before." Isabel might seem calm now, but I've seen the rage burning in her eyes at times. With what Bishop said about her power, she could easily take Prue. My mate doesn't seem prone to fighting for small slights, thankfully.

I just shake my head at her. Much like the pups, Prue and I are both transfixed with my mate singing. Even the pups who didn't grab a guitar have gravitated closer to her.

Once she's done with her play through, Isabel patiently

teaches the whole group how to play the song. Never once does she get frustrated with the constant questions. Instead, she lights up each time she's asked something.

I've never seen my mate like this. She's so relaxed and open. Instead of her usual thorniness, she wears like armor, Isabel is sweet and gentle with the pups. Her laughter frequently rings out across the room, and Isabel has a perpetual smile on her graceful face.

Prue leaves sometime during the song, having to get back to her many tasks she does to keep the pack running.

Once Isabel teaches the pups the first song, she asks if anyone else has a song they want to learn. "Can you teach us something that's not girly shit?" Jake calls from his spot near the back. At thirteen, Jake is all long limbs and awkwardness. He's at the age where he thinks it's manly to put down things girls like.

Isabel doesn't get upset at Jake's rude request. She just rolls her eyes at him. "I can teach you to play 'Gasoline.' Let me know if it's too 'girly' after the play through."

As Isabel plays the catchy song, Jake can help but bop his head, making his brown curls bounce everywhere. When she finishes the song, Isabel looks to Jake to see if he wants to learn the song. "That was dope. Will you teach it to us?" Jake asks shyly, his earlier bravado gone.

"Sure thing, my dude." Isabel looks down at her guitar to begin teaching the pups. I watch her teach song after song to the kids. She happily stays until the last pup is picked up. Our date that I meant to be an hour or so turns into three hours of her working with the children. Every single pup makes her promise to come back again.

Once all of the kids are gone, Isabel stands up and puts away her guitar. She stretches her arms and her skirt rides even higher on her toned thighs. I'm a bastard for continuing to look rather than turning away, but I do it anyway. When she turns to walk toward me, I drag my eyes up her alluring form. I meet gray eyes and pink cheeks as she watches me watch her.

"Thanks for bringing me here, quiet boy. I really enjoyed it. The kids or, um, pups? Whatever you call them, they were adorable. I had a ton of fun." Isabel gifts me with one of her rare genuine smiles, and I know at that moment that she holds all the fragile shards of my heart in her small hand.

After my childhood, I dreaded finding a mate. Even in the short time I've known Isabel, she's proven herself to be compassionate, kind, caring, thoughtful, and the complete opposite of my mother. Watching Isabel with the pups has only nurtured the growing trust I have in my mate.

"Both pups and kids work. I'm very glad you enjoyed spending time with them. I know it's late. Would you like to have dinner with me before going home, angel?"

"I'd love to, Cain. I'd enjoy spending time with just the two of us."

I offer her my hand again, and she takes it. I walk out of the music room, excited for what the future holds for the first time in a long time.

CHAPTER 21

IZZY

I can't believe it's already October, my birthday month. Unfortunately for me, my birthday is on Halloween. Yep. A witch born on Halloween. Cliché as fuck, and I hate it. My family and Bishop always insist on throwing a stupid party, but I'd prefer if everyone just forgot it happened.

With it being October, I've known the wolves for almost a month. Today's my date with Archer. I'm looking forward to what he has planned. It'll probably be lots of fun.

Surprisingly, I've enjoyed both of my dates so far. Luca and Cain took me on very different dates, but I had a blast with both of them. I'm trying not to think about what happens after my date with Archer. Once the dates I promised are over, I have to stay away from the wolves. I already like the three of them too much for their own good.

I walk toward the front of the building with a dopey smile on my face. It drops the second I hear a familiar voice call out from behind me. "Isabel Gallagher, just the girl I'm looking for." I'd know Tyler Giles's voice anywhere. It's so similar to his brother's voice.

My heart sinks as I scan the deserted hallway. I close my eyes, already knowing how this will go. "Go get Levi," I tell Aggie under my breath as I open my lids. Her wide eyes meet mine, and she frantically nods. "Quickly, please."

Once Aggie poofs away, I reluctantly turn to Tyler. He's tall, with light blond hair and washed-out blue eyes. With his football player physique, he really nails the all-American look. It's not until you really look at his eyes that you see the cold, unfeeling psychopath he tries to hide. It must be a family trait because his brother is the same way. "Funny. I was definitely trying to avoid you."

"Oh, don't be like that. I know about all the fun Mason and Rich had with you. Now that they've gone, it's my turn." Mason Giles and Richard Whelan were two of my biggest tormentors my first three years here. When they graduated last year, I thought I'd be safe. I guess that was wishful thinking.

"Leave me alone, Tyler." My voice is shaky, betraying just how scared I am. Being alone with Tyler brings all the memories I try not to think about to the surface. I feel like I'm being suffocated by them, and I can't take a full breath.

My fear makes Tyler's sleazy grin grow. He advances on me, and I back up. I chance a glance over my shoulder and see that I only have a few feet until I hit the wall.

Hopefully, I can stall him until Levi gets here. If not, well, then I just make it through this. Whatever happens, I can handle it. To keep my family and mates safe, I can endure anything. Maybe not with the last pieces of my already damaged soul intact. But that's beside the point.

It's a fight to push the memories aside so I can think of everyone I love and care about. All the people I need to keep safe by not letting my magic out right now. I focus on locking down my magic even tighter than normal as I see who I'm fighting for in my mind. I refuse to put them in danger to save myself.

When my back hits the rough brick wall, I know my time is up. I look up at Tyler's predatory grin and fight the urge to throw up. I'm shaking like a leaf, but there's nothing I can do about it. When his strong forearm presses into my throat, limiting my oxygen and keeping me in place, I close my eyes. I'm not strong enough to look at him while he hurts me.

I can do this. I can do this. I can do this, I chant in my mind. Maybe if I repeat it often enough, I can make it true.

Tyler uses his other hand to roughly yank my deep purple blouse out of my jeans. As he puts his hand on the waistband of my dark pants, a portal sizzles into existence behind him.

Levi steps through, and his obsidian eyes find me. I've never been so relieved to see someone in my entire life. His dark eyes turn blood red as he takes in the situation. Fury lines every inch of his face. At his strong emotions, the spooky skull flickers in and out over his face. This is probably the closest I've ever seen the normally unflappable man to losing control.

"What the fuck is going on here?" Levi demands, his deep voice booming in the empty hallway.

Levi's voice startles Tyler, who has the situational awareness of a goldfish. Tyler turns toward him. "Sorry, teach. Me and my girl were just getting frisky. You know how it is." I'm glad Levi knows that's not the case, because Tyler's charming grin is damn believable. I'd never be his girl, though, and Tyler would never want me for that. Being magicless, I'm apparently not good enough to be a girlfriend but good enough to screw. I really don't understand the logic.

"Do girls always cry when you touch them, Giles? Do you always have to hold them down to get 'frisky' with them?" I didn't even realize I was crying. Now that Levi mentions it, I can feel cool air blowing over the wet tracks on my cheeks.

Tyler lets go of me to face Levi, and I sag against the wall in relief. I don't ever want to feel his dirty hands on me again. "She likes it rough. I'm just trying to keep her happy." Tyler shrugs while keeping the disarming smile on his disgusting face.

"Stop lying, boy, before I have a talk with Elder Gallagher about your behavior. You know he won't stand for anyone hurting his daughter." That's extremely true. My dad is super protective of me. If he had any idea of what went on at school, the bullying or this, he'd raise hell. Standing up for his magicless daughter would make my dad deeply unpopular, though. He does so much good on the council that I don't want to get in the way of.

Tyler's face mottles with rage as he looks between Levi and me. He's at least smart enough to realize when he's been outmaneuvered. "This isn't over," he hisses at me before he takes off back down the hallway.

Once I can't see him anymore, my legs collapse underneath me, no longer capable of holding me up. The strength I was trying to find to get through what Tyler wanted to do evaporates. All that remains in its place is fear, shame, and a deep well of despair.

Levi manages to reach me before my knees can crack on the dingy tile. He wraps his strong arms around me. His touch is so different from Tyler's. Whereas Tyler's touch aimed to break me, Levi's tries to hold me together. I'm not sure even Levi's muscular arms are strong enough to keep me from shattering right now.

"I have you, little raven. You're safe now," Levi whispers against my hair. He picks me up like I weigh nothing and carries me to a secluded alcove toward the back of the building. Once there, he sits down with me still clinging to him. Levi sits cross-legged and arranges me so I'm sitting on his lap. My legs wrap around his trim waist, and I bury my face in his broad chest.

The tears that've been running down my face nonstop turn into loud, hitching sobs once I finally feel safe. Tucked away from prying eyes and in my mate's arms is about as safe as it gets. As I cry out all of my heartache and terror and self-loathing, Levi holds me and rubs his hand over my back. I appreciate him not forcing me to talk or do anything other than cry more than he'll ever know.

Nothing happened. Levi got here in time, and I'm physically fine. Yet I feel so far from fine on the inside, I could laugh. That is, if I weren't busy trying not to break so badly, I can never put myself back together again.

I don't know how long I cry before Levi's phone dings. He digs it out of his pocket without stopping his soothing rubbing on my back. "Hey, little raven," Levi begins gently. "You have your date with Archer today, don't you?"

Fuck. With everything that happened, I totally forgot about Archer. What a mate I am. The wolves are definitely better off without me. I nod my head, not able to stem the tears long enough to talk to him.

"Do you mind if I tell him where we are? He's worried about you."

"As long... as you don't... tell him... what happened," I agree through hiccuping sobs. My breath catches after every few words, making the sentence take a lot of effort to get out. I don't want Archer to view me differently or think I'm weak.

"I can do that. I won't tell any of your other mates, but I'm going to need you to talk to me about this soon. I have a feeling no one knows what's been going on at school, do they?" Levi asks in the same gentle tone. I shake my head because he's absolutely correct. Aggie is the only one that knows. "Always so strong, my little raven. Always trying to protect everyone else. Do you think, maybe, it's time to let us protect you for a change?"

"I don't know," I whisper into his chest, voice scratchy. Everything I do is to protect everyone else. How do I let people protect me? It feels like, if I let others help me, I won't have the strength to do everything I need to.

If I'm going to talk to anyone about what happened, it would be Levi. He's so calm and levelheaded. I don't have to worry about him flying off the handle or acting rashly once he hears about it all.

"You don't have to know right now. You don't have to do anything right now." Levi moves his hand up from my back to play with my thick hair as he types on his phone. I close my eyes as he runs his hands through my hair, the motion calming me.

We stay like that until I hear footsteps heading toward us. I stiffen in Levi's arms, worried it's Tyler coming back to finish what he started. Even though I know Levi won't let him hurt me, my nervous system is still trained to fear both Giles brothers.

"It's just Archer."

All of my muscles loosen briefly when I realize that it's Archer. Then everything coils tightly again as I realize I must look a mess. I probably have red-rimmed, puffy eyes, a snotty nose, and a paler-than-usual complexion. Not to mention, I'm still crying. Archer will know something's up the second he sees me.

I hear Archer kneel to my left. "Hey, sunshine." When he doesn't ask me anything, I hesitantly turn my head to look at him. Archer is smiling gently at me as he kneels in his dark jeans and plain blue tee that matches his eyes. "There they are. There are those beautiful gray eyes."

My cheeks flush at his compliment, but I don't know what to say. I just stare at him silently with tears still running down my cheeks. Archer doesn't get mad at my silence, and his warm smile never drops. "May I hold your hand, sunshine? If not, that's A-OK. You're in control here."

I close my eyes briefly at Archer somehow knowing exactly what to say. After a run-in with Mason, Richard, or now Tyler, I feel like I'm so out of control. Like life just happens to me. Taking back control, even in a small way, helps.

Blowing out a shaky breath and opening my eyes, I slowly stretch my hand out to Archer. He tenderly captures it between both of his hands. I soak up the warmth radiating from him. It slowly starts to thaw my insides.

"How do mice floss their teeth?" Archer asks me out of nowhere. I look at him in confusion, and his lips inch their way a little higher on his handsome face. "They say laughter's the best medicine. Since I'm not a doctor, that's the only medicine I can prescribe. The answer is string cheese, if you were wondering."

A ghost of a smile crosses my lips at his corny joke. Archer rewards me with a blinding grin, like I just gave him the best gift possible. "What do you call a happy cowboy?" I give him a small shrug in response. "A jolly rancher. What did one wall say to the other? I'll meet you at the corner."

Archer keeps telling me cheesy dad jokes.

As I listen to him, my tears slow, my breathing evens out, and my shaking subsides. His silly jokes take my mind off what just happened. Thanks to his humor, I'm slowly able to cobble myself back together. Sure, there are some new cracks and missing bits. Eventually, though, I'm able to wade through all the jagged edges and aching pieces to find myself again.

Archer never tries to rush me. He just kneels on the hard tile, holds my hand, and keeps telling jokes as long as I need. I don't think I'll ever be able to express to Archer how grateful I am for what he's doing or how much it means to me.

"What kind of bagel can travel?"

Since I don't have the right words to tell Archer how much I appreciate him, I do the only thing I can. I finish his joke. "A plain bagel."

Archer beams at my hoarse answer, and I feel like maybe, just maybe, things will be okay.

CHAPTER 22

IZZY

"There you are, sunshine." Archer gazes at me with emotion swirling in his aquamarine eyes. "I'm happy staying here and telling you jokes for as long as you need. For our date, I planned to take you to my favorite arcade, but we can do whatever you want to. If you want to go get ice cream, watch a movie, be dropped off at home for alone time, I'll make it happen."

My eyes burn with unshed tears for a different reason this time. Archer's offer is crazy thoughtful. He's putting what I need ahead of what he wanted to do. "Is the arcade in Hawthorne Grove?" I whisper past the lump in my throat.

Archer winces slightly. "No. It's not. I can try to find one here if you want?"

I shake my head at him. "I want to get out of Hawthorne Grove for a little while. I fucking hate this town."

"Oh, thank God. Hawthorne Grove is fucking awful. I'd do anything you want, but I'm glad you wanna split." Archer's face is twisted in distaste, and I can't help the giggle that slips out. He's not wrong about how much Hawthorne Grove sucks ass. When he hears my quiet laugh, Archer's face splits into a smile so wide, a dimple I never noticed before appears.

"I want to go to the arcade, if that's okay." I'm not sure he still wants to take me, but I don't want to let Tyler ruin my only date with Archer.

"That's good with me. Are we taking demon eyes over here with us? He's welcome if you want him." I snort at Archer's nickname for Levi.

Archer's question makes me realize I'm still sitting on Levi. I kind of forgot about him for a moment with all of Archer's jokes. My cheeks burn slightly from using him as basically a pillow and a tissue. I peer up at Levi through my lashes. He looks down at me with a soft smile on his face. Now that Tyler's gone, his eyes are back to their usual black with a small red ring.

"I'm happy to go with you or stay behind. It's up to you. If you want me to come with you, I can also hang back and let you and Archer have your one-on-one time." Levi has continued to play with my hair this whole time. I don't ever want him to stop running his fingers through the strands, but I know I need to get up eventually.

Honestly, I need both of them right now. I'd love to see Luca, Cain, and Bishop, too, but there's no way I'm dragging that many people on Archer's date.

I don't want to examine why, exactly, I have the urge to see my other mates. Surely, I haven't forgotten the ending I knew from the very beginning. None of my mates are mine to keep. I'm just borrowing them for a heartbeat in time. Only, my heart doesn't understand that. It's already starting to sync with theirs, leaving me wondering how it'll remember how to beat once they're gone.

"You sure that's okay with you?" I bite my bottom lip nervously, feeling bad for hijacking the date.

"Yep. Demon eyes can open one of his freaky-ass portals

for us too. Then I can show you how much fun it is to lose at bumper cars and Skee-Ball." Archer waggles his eyebrows at me, and I crack another smile.

"You think you can beat me at arcade games, sunny boy?" Unlike his nickname for me, calling Archer sunny isn't ironic. He's like sunshine after a lifetime of darkness. You can't help but stretch toward him to bask in his uplifting personality.

"Ooh, I get a nickname too. I can't wait to rub this in Cain's face."

"I already gave Cain a nickname. Sorry to ruin your fun." I shrug apologetically, not wanting to let the happy wolf down.

"What's Cain's nickname?" Archer tilts his head in curiosity as he regards me.

"Quiet boy."

"What nickname did you give demon eyes?"

"Screech owl or demon boy." Levi chuckles at his nicknames. I can feel the sound rumbling in his chest, since I'm still pressed against him. I should probably get off him, but I'm just so comfortable in his arms.

Archer laughs. "All solid choices, sunshine. You ready to blow this joint?" He waits for my nod before standing up and offering me his hand. I grab it, and he hauls me to my feet with surprising ease. The only problem is that standing over Levi puts my crotch right in his face. I scramble back and almost fall over when I try to get away. Archer's grip on my hand and Levi's almost burning hands on my thighs stop me from falling on my ass.

Once I'm steadied and no longer over Levi, Archer asks, "You coming, demon eyes?"

"Yes. I'm not a demon, wolf." Levi stands up and brushes off the back of his black jeans. He's wearing a red long-sleeve tee today. His outfit matches his eyes. It's strangely adorable.

"Sure, you're not." Archer gives me a conspiratorial wink, so I know he's just messing with Levi. He doesn't know that Levi's not a mage, though. Levi never did tell me what he is. That's a problem for another time because I'm at my limit of dealing with shit today.

Levi shakes his head and opens his fire-ringed portal. "Ready to go?"

"How do you know where we're going? I haven't told you the name of the arcade." Archer eyes Levi and his black hole portal suspiciously. If I didn't already know Levi's abilities were definitely not normal, I'd probably be skeptical too.

"I know because of my non-demonic powers, wolf. It's the Power Play Arcade in Lockwood, isn't it?" Levi raises one black brow at Archer, daring him to disagree.

Archer turns wide eyes to Levi. He opens and closes his mouth a few times, trying to figure out what to say. "It is. Holy fuck. That's some creepy-ass shit right there, demon eyes."

I also turn to Levi and see him fighting a grin. "Why do I have the feeling you like fucking with people, demon boy?"

Levi's eyes dance with mirth, and he gives me a shrug. "If you're done with your dramatics, wolf, shall we go to the arcade?"

Archer sputters at being called dramatic, but he can't help his smile at the banter. Without another backward glance, Archer walks into the portal and disappears.

"Why are your portals different than normal, screech owl?"

"That's a conversation better had when we're not at school, little raven." He offers me his hand, and I take it. We walk through the portal together. Only, this time, I don't feel like I'm falling. I don't feel the normal sticky air surrounding and coating me, either. Instead, I just feel like I'm walking in the hallway. It's only the bright, flashing lights and games galore that let me know we're no longer at school.

Before I can ask Levi about that wild portal experience, Archer snags my free hand and pulls me along after him. He animatedly talks to me about the music playing and every game we pass until we reach the bumper cars. Even Levi joins us. I laugh so hard while we're in the bumper cars that it feels like I'm going to puke and cry at the same time.

The crazy laughter doesn't end for the entire time we're at the arcade. Archer delights in showing me his favorite games, playing laser tag, and racing go-karts. He's happy to include Levi. Laughing and playing silly arcade games and gorging myself on junk food for hours straight with two of my mates heals something in me I never thought would be whole again.

Before I know it, the arcade closes, and we're kicked out. I don't how we managed to spend so much time just goofing around, but I enjoyed the time not thinking about everything that happened earlier. I know it's all going to hit me when I'm alone in my room, trying—and failing—to fall asleep.

Maybe Bishop will let me sleep over tonight. I've spent the night with him every time Mason and Richard tried something. Bishop wrapping me up in his protective embrace all night allows me to sleep without being bombarded by the memories. I'm sure Bishop has noticed that I cry myself to sleep every time I sleep over, but he never pushes me to talk about it. Bishop always knows exactly what I need even before I do.

"Is it okay if we head to Bishop's place?" I ask Levi as he prepares to open a portal to take me home. He gives me a questioning look. "I don't think I can sleep alone tonight."

Levi's eyes soften in understanding. "I can do that, little raven." When he opens the portal, he reaches out his hand for me. I grab his with one hand and Archer's with the other.

Hopefully, Archer won't feel like he's tumbling from the top of a roller coaster if he holds on to me while I hold on to Levi.

We step out of the portal in front of a three-story, red-brick building. The bottom floor houses several small businesses, like a candle shop, a specialty grocer, and a boutique. Bishop converted the top two floors to apartments. Although there are four lofts available, Bishop is the only one who lives there. He doesn't need the income from renting the other spaces, so Bishop would rather have the peace and quiet of living alone.

I guide Archer and Levi around the back to the stairs that lead up to the second floor. Once we're at the top, I knock on Bishop's door.

CHAPTER 23

BISHOP

*J*collapse onto my bed, not caring about my damp hair getting my pillow wet. I'm exhausted from yet another day at Elemental, followed by working for the Nightshade Pack all evening. At least I don't have an operation tonight. Though I'm drained from the long days and nights, I would do this for the rest of my life to protect Izzy.

If only the stubborn woman would mate with me, it would be ten times easier to protect her. When mages merge power to complete the mate bond, it allows mages to know where their mate is at all times. Plus, it would allow me to send her extra magic remotely if she ever drains herself, which, knowing Izzy, is always a possibility. She's incredibly reckless with her own safety.

I'm only lying on my bed for a minute before I hear a knock on my front door. Groaning, I want to ignore it. It's probably work related. Knowing I have to answer, I mutter, *"Circumspicere,"* to bring up the mage camera at the front door. I like to know what I'm walking into before actually answering.

A live image of Izzy, Archer, and Levi standing there causes me to bolt upright in bed. If Izzy is here this late, something happened. Izzy hasn't asked to sleep over in probably six months.

She won't talk to me about what happens to make her spend the night when she's usually so against sleeping over. She won't tell me what makes her cry herself to sleep. She won't let me in, and I hate it.

Grabbing my jeans from the floor, I pull them on as fast as possible. I don't bother with the button as I'm rushing to the door to see what she needs.

When I unlock and pull open my front door, I'm greeted with Izzy's gray eyes haunted with sadness and pain. Rage simmers in my chest at whoever put that anguish in her gaze. When she finally tells me who it is, I'm going to enjoy slowly and agonizingly killing them.

"Can I spend the night, St. James?" Izzy's voice is small and unsure as she meets my eyes hesitantly.

I stuff down all the rage and plaster a non-threatening smile on my face. Izzy doesn't need to know about that violent part of me. She needs me to be calm and stable for her. "Of course, sweetheart. You want Arch and Levi to stay?"

Izzy bites her lip in indecision. She flicks her gaze between her other two men before landing on Levi. "It's up to you, little raven. Whatever you need."

Then she looks to Archer. "Yeah, sunshine. I'm happy to stay or go. It's your choice."

She meets my eyes again. "You really don't mind?"

"Not at all, sweetheart." I open the door wider and let her, Archer, and Levi in. While I've gotten to know Archer pretty well over the years, Levi is a wild card. There's something about him that's not quite right. As long as he treats Izzy well, I won't dig into whatever Levi is hiding.

Turning around, I lead them farther into my apartment. The exposed brick walls, dark wood floor, and bare rafters give the former warehouse an industrial feel. It wasn't an aesthetic choice. I just couldn't be bothered with finishing it any further when I desperately needed somewhere to live that wasn't with my aunt. I'm going on seven years without seeing her, and I hope to extend that streak to my entire life.

"You always answer the door like that, St. James?" I turn back to Izzy, who is glaring at my bare chest and unbuttoned jeans riding low on my hips. I hold in my laugh at her possessiveness.

"Does it bother you if other people see me like this?" While I shouldn't antagonize her, a fucked-up part of me loves when she claims me. Knowing she's my mate but not being able to complete the mate bond for the past seven years has been torture. I'll take whatever scraps of claiming I can get.

Izzy scoffs. "No." Her cheeks flush and she won't meet my eyes, so I know she's lying.

"I knew it was you, sweetheart. That's the only reason I didn't bother to get dressed." Izzy lets out a cute little sigh of relief she probably thinks I can't hear. "Do you want something to eat or drink? Or do you just want to go up to bed?"

"Bed. I'm fucking wiped." Izzy tiredly walks over to the coat closet near the kitchen. With concrete countertops, espresso wood cabinets, and plain subway tile backsplash, it is simple but functional. When she reaches the coat closet, Izzy plops on the floor to untie her Chucks. Pulling the door open, Izzy puts her shoes on the shoe rack I only have there for her. She can't stand shoes or clothing scattered everywhere.

Archer and Levi follow her example. Once everyone is ready to head upstairs to my room, I hold out my hand for

Izzy. She places her tiny, soft hand in mine. Whenever I hold her, I'm painfully aware of how easily I could break her slight frame. My protective urges come roaring to the surface, but I stuff them down. Izzy doesn't need to see that right now.

We walk up the curving wrought-iron staircase together. I lead her down the hallway to my room. Pushing open the door, I'm glad I have a king-size bed. It's still going to be a tight fit with Levi. He's an inch taller than Luca and almost as bulky. I'm the same height as Cain but slightly more muscular. Archer is the shortest and leanest of us, but he still towers over Izzy.

I head to my dark wood dresser to grab one of my shirts for Izzy to sleep in. She likes to steal my clothes, and I pretend not to notice. Seeing her wearing one of my shirts and nothing else gives me an instant fucking hard-on. Izzy pretends not to notice it when I hold her.

Riffling through my drawer, I pull out one of my faded System of a Down tees that Izzy has told me is especially comfortable. "Here you go, sweetheart. You can change in my bathroom." I nod toward my en suite. Izzy takes the shirt and heads to the bathroom, closing the door behind her.

When I hear the shower turn on, I look at Levi and Archer. "What the fuck happened?" I try to talk quietly enough so Izzy won't hear us discussing it.

Levi clenches his jaw. "I promised her I wouldn't tell you." He scrubs his hands over his face. When he drops his hands, his eyes are almost entirely red with just a black pupil in the middle. It's eerie. "When I find that disgusting piece of shit, he's going to beg for a death I can ensure is much worse than living."

"Fuck!" Archer hisses, his eyes burning with rage and torment. I turn to him and raise an eyebrow to wordlessly ask what's going on. "The front of her shirt was haphazardly untucked when I found her with Levi. Combined with demon eyes mentioning a guy and how she reacted to Luca pinning her, I really fucking hope I'm wrong about what I think happened."

It takes a moment for me to put together what Archer is implying. My stomach bottoms out, and pure fury like nothing I've ever felt before rages through my veins. I'd like to say Izzy would tell me about guys at school hurting her, but I'd be lying. I don't think Izzy knows about the other side of me, the one that revels in torturing anyone who even looks at her wrong. But I do think she knows I would kill anyone who touched her against her will.

The sound of the shower turning off breaks through my rage-induced haze. Taking in a shaky breath, I force down all of the anger, devastation, and thirst for vengeance on her behalf. I pull out the tame Bishop she knows and needs right now. Tomorrow, when she's not here, I can lose it. Right now, she needs someone to comfort her, not kill for her.

Izzy comes padding out of the bathroom in just my shirt, and my boxers get uncomfortably tight. With the bathroom light shining behind her, Izzy looks ethereal. Her pale skin and blonde hair contrast the dark gray tee I gave her.

I have the urge to push my shirt up her thighs to see if she's wearing any panties or just my tee. With a small shake of my head, I shut those thoughts down fast. Izzy isn't ready for what I want to do to her, especially if she's been hurt before.

Fuck! I need to be thinking about something other than murder or fucking. What a weird combination.

While I try to pull myself together for what feels like the eighth time tonight, Izzy shuffles over to my bed. She climbs up and goes to the middle of it. On her knees, Izzy looks over at the three of us by the door. "You boys coming or what?"

"For you? I'll always come," Archer purrs.

Izzy's eyes widen when she realizes her unintentional

innuendo. Her cheeks turn pink in embarrassment, but she doesn't say anything. Archer strips off his shirt and jeans before walking over to the bed and climbing in. Izzy admires the wolf's bare chest as he walks toward her.

Levi eyes Izzy for a moment before blowing out a breath and moving closer to the bed. Seeming to come to a decision, he takes off his shirt. Izzy sucks in a breath at all of Levi's tattoos. They're all black and gray designs. From where I'm standing, I can see that he has full sleeves on both arms and a pair of dark angel wings covering his whole back. One sleeve looks like a massive snake winding around his arm. I can't see the other arm.

"Do they bother you?" Levi asks, misinterpreting Izzy's gasp. She wasn't horrified by them. Tattoos fascinate her.

I have a large Saint James cross on my right side and hip for my parents and baby brother. Izzy loves looking at it. Anytime we're watching movies or hanging out, she'll idly trace my tattoo with her dainty fingers. Having her hands on me, dancing up my side, does not help my self-control, but I like it too much to ever tell her to stop.

My heart squeezes uncomfortably thinking about my family. I know my parents would be thrilled that Izzy is my mate. They always loved her and her whole family. Deacon, who was three years younger than me, would tease me about how much of a sap I am. I clench my fists as the pain of everything they're missing tries to overwhelm me. Now's not the time. Izzy needs me.

Shaking my head, I try to focus back on the present.

"What? No. I think they're cool!" Izzy knee walks toward the end of the bed to get a better look at Levi's tattoos. She waves him closer so she can inspect the art better. After a moment, Izzy gasps again. "You dirty fucking liar! When were you going to tell me you had a screech owl tattoo? I've been trying to annoy you, not call you an animal name you liked."

Levi huffs a laugh. "I didn't think it was relevant, little raven."

"Not relevant, my ass. No wonder you grin every time I call you that." Izzy shakes her head at him but continues her perusal. She reaches out to touch his chest before stopping and looking at him in question. Levi gently grasps her wrist and brings her fingers to his pec.

While Izzy is checking out Levi's tattoos, I move to my side of the bed and sit down. I dig my elbows into my knees and rest my head in my hands. It's only a few minutes until I hear her shuffling across the bed to me. Izzy's arms wrap around me, and she presses her front to my bare back. "You okay, St. James?" she whispers into my neck.

"That's my line, sweetheart. How are you?" I dodge her question because I'm not fucking okay. How can I be anything other than destroyed when Izzy has been hurting for years, and I haven't fixed it yet?

She shrugs behind me. "I don't know. I just want to feel safe." Her quiet admission completely undoes me and shatters my heart. Izzy is so reluctant to admit when she's hurting or needs something. For her to tell me that, things must be worse than I thought. I would give anything to protect her, to wrap her up, to keep her safe. But I can't when I don't even know what I need to protect her from.

Rather than dwell on all the ways I can't help Izzy, I try to think of ways to make her feel better. "Would having your other mates here help you feel safer?"

Her breath hitches, and I already know her answer. "Yes," she breathes so quietly I can barely hear her.

"I'll go get them." Izzy's hands are clasped in front of my throat. I bring them up to kiss them tenderly before I unwind her arms from my neck. Standing, I pull on my shirt from earlier and shove my feet into boots.

"What if they're busy?" Izzy bites her lip in worry.

I barely contain my snort. Even if Luca and Cain were in an important meeting, they'd drop it in a heartbeat if Izzy needed them. Izzy doesn't know it, but she already has the wolves wrapped around her finger. "They're not. I'll get them and be right back."

When I get a nod from Izzy, I open a portal to Luca's bedroom. I step through and close it behind me.

"Can I help you, Bishop?" Luca questions sarcastically from the mahogany desk in the corner of his room. I'm relieved to see he's at least wearing pants. Wolves are weird about nudity. They walk around naked more often than I'd like.

"Izzy needs you and Cain."

"What fucking happened? Where is she? Is she hurt?" Luca jumps up from his desk and storms over to me.

I clench my jaw, wishing I had more answers to give him. "I don't know what happened. She's at my loft with Arch and Levi. She's physically fine."

"But?" Luca perceptively realizes I'm leaving something out.

I sigh. "Arch thinks someone tried to sexually assault her. I'm inclined to agree. Levi's the only one who knows anything, but he promised not to tell us."

Luca's eyes turn the amber of his wolf, and he lets out a wordless howl, full of anger and pain. His eyes flicker between amber and blue as he gets in my face. "How did this fucking happen?"

I'm used to dealing with his temperamental alpha wolf, so I don't even flinch. As an alpha, Luca's wolf is stronger than average and has its own personality. While it's helpful for leading the pack, it makes managing strong emotions a challenge. "I don't know, Luca. I get what you're feeling, man. I really fucking do, but you need to rein it in. Izzy needs all of us to help her feel safe right now. What she doesn't need is a rampaging alpha."

"What's going on?" Cain asks from Luca's doorway. He must've heard his alpha howling and came running. Scrubbing my hands over my face, I tell him the same thing I told Luca. Cain grips the doorframe so hard, a chunk of it crumbles in his hand. The normally stoic wolf's eyes are also flickering amber as he fights the urge to shift. His lips lift into a snarl, but he stays by the door as he struggles to regain control.

It takes ten minutes to calm the wolves enough so we can get back to Izzy. I'm drained from trying to keep my own seething rage in control and help the wolves with control too. When I open another portal and step through it, my steps are dragging.

I wake up when I see a massive bed in my room that definitely wasn't there before. Izzy is spooned by Levi and facing Archer. Luca and Cain bump into me as I stop in my tracks. I turn to look at Levi, my brows raised in a question.

"Your bed barely fit us. It wouldn't fit the other wolves too. I expanded it." Levi looks at me from over Izzy's shoulder, his tattooed arm curled protectively over our mate.

"How?" Mage magic doesn't work like that. It can't create things out of thin air. Our magic relies on manipulating what's already there.

"I have my ways, wolf." Levi doesn't say any more, and I decide to leave it for now.

I toe off my boots and shuck my pants and shirt. As I approach the bed, I tell Archer, "Move." The perks of having my mate sleep in my bed is that I get to sleep next to her. Archer rolls his eyes but scoots over. I climb in next to Izzy. Luca gets into bed on the other side of Archer, and Cain takes Levi's opposite side. I brush a lock of golden hair out of Izzy's face. "Feeling safer now, sweetheart?"

"Yeah. Thanks, St. James. You always know what I need." Her words are soft and laced with sleepiness. With one last look at me, Izzy closes her eyes and succumbs to sleep.

As I watch her peaceful face and even breaths, I vow to do whatever it takes to protect her and provide her that peace when she's awake too.

CHAPTER 24

IZZY

*I*t's been over a week since I've seen the wolves. I've been avoiding Bishop and Levi, too, after last Monday night.

Everything was just too much. My mates made me feel too much. I don't know how to get back all the pieces of me they stole when they dropped everything to hold me and make me feel safe again.

The feeling of safety evaporated when I returned to school on Tuesday. Tyler glares at me and bodychecks me any chance he gets. I can tell that he's biding his time to try something again.

I'm honestly just so tired of the bullshit at school. It probably doesn't help my exhaustion that I've been avoiding sleeping. Every time I close my eyes, I see memories I'm not strong enough to deal with. It's just easier not to sleep and handle problems my favorite way: ignoring them.

That's part of why I'm avoiding Bishop. He'd be able to take one look at me and know how much of a broken mess I am on the inside. For now, at least, he's buying the excuse that I have extra work and volunteering. Bishop is also crazy busy essentially working two jobs, so it's easier to evade him than it used to be. He's running himself into the ground to try to keep me safe, which is yet another way I'm fucking up his life.

I sigh at my thoughts and rub my hands over my gritty eyes. My lids are drooping the longer I wait for Aggie to bring the latest round of ghosts. She's even been on my case to sleep more, but I can't. I just can't.

I debate sitting on the ground because standing is draining, but I'm worried I'll fall asleep if I do. I'm so exhausted and lost in my mind that I don't see Aggie until she's right in front of me. "Holy shit! You scared the crap out of me, Aggie!"

Aggie's forehead is pinched in worry as she looks between me and the abnormally large herd of fucked-up ghosts. "We're going to have a talk about what's going on with you, kid. But, first, we have a problem. There are a lot of ghosts tonight, and they all look the same."

Swinging my tired gaze to the mob of ghosts, I startle when I recognize quite a few of the empty, blank faces. They're the young mages that have been going missing in Hawthorne Grove. My heart develops another crack in it when I see Amelia. Her normally sweet, happy face is marred by jagged cuts and hollow eyes.

"Amelia!" I call, even knowing she won't understand me. I turn to Aggie. "Can you bring Lia to me? I'll heal her first."

Aggie strides toward the crowd, cutting through the middle to snag Amelia by the hand. It's always a little jarring seeing Aggie walk. In the spirit plane, she's as real as she was in the normal plane when she was alive. Instead of floating around like she usually does, Aggie has to walk.

Amelia follows Aggie docilely, nothing behind her light

brown eyes. I gasp when Aggie brings Amelia to me. Her clothes are shredded, with bloody slashes covering her almost head to toe. Some of the cuts are long and wide, and others are thin and short.

What the actual fuck happened to her?

With how much blood stains her clothes, I wonder if she bled to death. That won't be fun to heal. Then again, it was infinitely worse for Amelia to experience in the first place.

Amelia stands still as I pull on my spirit magic. My hands glow ice blue before I direct the magic to her. It arcs to and slams into her. She stumbles back a step but, otherwise, doesn't react. Slowly, my magic starts mending her wounds, fixing the tears in her clothes and wiping the blood from her pale skin.

When her cheeks are flushed, eyes are clear, and my magic can't find anything else to heal, I pull back on it. Amelia blinks a few times before she focuses on me. "Izzy? Where am I?"

"Hey, Lia." A lump forms in my throat as I stare into her confused gaze. This is always the hardest part. Most damaged ghosts don't know they're dead, so I have to break the news. "You're dead, honey."

"What?" Amelia's light brown eyes widen as she processes what I said. "I can't be dead! I was just at the council for their mage development program."

"Their what?" My dad is on the council. I've never heard of a mage development program, and that's something my dad would mention. He's been pushing for the council to devote more resources to helping the average mage, instead of pandering to the wealthy.

"Mage development program. I got an invitation at the beginning of the school year for a program for lower mages. It's supposed to help us get better jobs." Amelia's lower lip trembles as she takes in the almost alien landscape of the spirit realm. How strange it is compared to the realm of the living is what convinces most ghosts they're dead. "Are you sure I'm dead, Izzy? What if this is just a weird dream?"

"I'm sure, honey. This isn't a dream. It's the spirit realm, where people end up when they die." I give her a minute to process that she's dead. It's the hardest for ghosts who die unexpectedly, like a sixteen-year-old newly awakened mage. When Amelia bursts into tears, I pull her into my arms and rub her back.

After crying for a moment, Amelia wipes away her tears. "What am I supposed to do now? Will I see my family again?"

"Now, you cross over. You will see your parents and sisters, eventually. Do you have any relatives who have died?"

"Yeah. Grammy died a few years ago, and Gramps died this summer." Amelia looks close to tears again, and I feel awful. I've crossed over thousands of ghosts, but it never gets easier to deal with the questions. It never gets easier to tell them they won't see their loved ones for a while. It never gets easier to watch them grieve for a life they should've had.

"You'll be able to see them when you cross over," I lie and don't feel even a little guilty about it. The truth is, I have no idea what happens when ghosts cross. The spirits could end up in heaven, hell, purgatory, or even just vanish forever. I don't know, but I don't want to scare Amelia with that.

She sniffles a few times before nodding at me. "Okay. How do I cross over?"

"You'll follow the yellow brick road to cross over, but I wanted to ask you something first. What's the last thing you remember?"

Amelia tilts her head in thought. "The last thing I remember is being taken to the basement of the council building. I was hooked up to something that was supposed to measure my magic. It felt like it was sucking out all of my magic, though. Then I was overwhelmed with pain, and everything went black." She's shaking by the time she finishes.

I hug her again before stepping back. "Thanks for telling me, honey. Do you want me to go with you to cross over?"

She shakes her head. "No, but thanks. Thank you for everything, Izzy. I always loved when you hung out with me. You and your family were the only high mages that didn't treat me like dirt. It meant a lot."

Now I'm the one who's choked up. She was such a good kid. It's not fair that this happened to her. None of the lives cut short are ever fair. It just hits harder since I knew her.

I dart in for one more hug before Amelia wanders down the yellow brick road. Aggie and I wait for the telltale flash of purple light before turning back to the hoard. "What the hell is going on?"

"I don't know, kid. Am I the only one who gets shady vibes from the council?"

I snort. "No, Aggie. Literally everyone knows they're corrupt, but it's hard to change a nearly millennium-old system." The council is... a problem I really don't have energy to deal with. Hopefully it's just a coincidence that all the ghosts have the same injuries.

It's not a coincidence.

Spirit after spirit tells me the same story as Amelia. They were offered a spot in the prestigious new mage development program. They're from lower mage families in Hawthorne Grove and other mage cities on the East Coast. Every single one of them remembers being in the council basement for testing before blacking out from pain.

My stomach sinks as I realize the council is a bigger problem than I thought. They're clearly preying on lower mage families, but why? What are they getting out of it? None of the ghosts have the answer.

I don't bother to pause between ghosts to heal my injuries. When I don't heal myself between spirits, I have to heal all the injuries at once. It sucks ass. But I'm so caught up in the mystery that I lose track of how many ghost I heal.

"Kid! You have to stop!" Aggie shouts from beside me, pulling me out of my thoughts.

"What?" I look around for the first time in a while. The gaggle of ghosts is a lot smaller than it was when I started, which isn't good news for me.

"You've healed twenty ghosts! Your power is growing, but that's too many, kid!" Aggie is frantically gesturing as she speaks, and she's worn down the grass underfoot with her pacing. "I've tried to get your attention, but you've been in a trance for the last five ghosts."

Fuck. Aggie is definitely right. That's way more ghosts than I can heal in a night. I can already feel the land of the living trying to yank me back to pay my penance for all the healing. My form is flickering in and out as I stand here.

"You need to get Bishop, Aggie. I don't have enough magic for this. Go to Levi, and he can get Bishop for you. Only get Rhys or Aiden as a last resort, okay?" Without enough magic to heal all the wounds, I'm going to die. While that's more appealing than it should be some nights, tonight is not one of them. I can't die until I figure out what the council is up to.

"I can do that, kid. Can you stay here until I get back?" Aggie's blue eyes are wrinkled in concern. She's wringing her hands as she watches me struggle to stay in the spirit realm.

I'm unable to answer her question as I'm forcibly pulled back into my body. I stare up at the clear night sky for a single moment of peace. Then it feels like my skin splits open all over my body. Blood gushes out of what feels like thousands of burning cuts as I scream and scream. My hands claw at the soft dirt underneath me, and my back arches in agony.

I can do nothing but ride the waves of never-ending pain and hope Aggie gets back soon. If she doesn't, well, then at least my mates and family will be safe.

Hurry, Aggie. Please, is the last thought I have before I'm dragged under the swells of excruciating pain, unsure if I'll ever surface again.

CHAPTER 25

LEVI

"*T*all, dark, and scary! Wake up!" someone shouts over me. I jackknife in my bed and launch a throwing knife I keep under my pillow at the noise. I see a very startled ghost looking between me and the knife embedded in the wall behind her. "Well, that was terrifying, but we need to go. Izzy needs Bishop!"

"What's the problem, ghost?" I get out of bed and hunt around for my clothes. I'm still confused by how the spirit is able to come and leave this plane at will. It must have something to do with her spending time around my very powerful mate. It baffles me how those mages are unaware of the staggering amount of power she possesses. I almost think she could take my brother in a power fight, which is unheard of.

"There's no time! The kid's dying. We need to get to Bishop, now." The ghost's eyes are frantic and pleading with me. It's clear the spirit cares deeply for my mate.

My blood runs cold when I process what she said. While I want to know what exactly is happening, I care about my mate's well-being more. "Then, hold on to me, ghost. We won't waste time with portaling."

When her spectral hand hesitantly touches my shoulder, I pull on the blood-red flames of magic in my chest. I transport both of us to Bishop St. James's room. The moonlight streaming in from one of his large windows gives me enough illumination to see the mage. He bolts up in bed much like I did, but he aims a gun at my head. Interesting. It seems the pretty boy mage has more to him than I first thought. A gun won't do anything to me if I did want to harm the mage, however.

"What the fuck are you doing here, Levi? It's two in the goddamn morning." The mage drops his hand holding the gun when he realizes it's me. He scrubs his hands over his face and seems like he could fall back asleep sitting up.

"The ghost says Izzy's in trouble and needs you." My voice remains steady, but the worry for my little raven is like acid crawling through my veins.

"Or Aiden and Rhys, but that's only as an absolute last choice. The kid doesn't want her family knowing what she does." I nod to show I heard the spirit.

"What type of trouble?" Bishop throws off the covers and rushes around his room to get dressed.

"I don't know. The ghost just said she's dying and needs you."

Bishop pales. "She's still healing them, isn't she, Aggie? Does Izzy need my magic because she overdid it tonight?"

"Yeah, she is. The kid never stopped, Bishop. She doesn't have enough magic to make it through tonight." The spirit's eyes soften in sympathy as she gazes at the mage.

I relay what she said to Bishop.

"Goddamn it, Izzy," Bishop rasps brokenly. He shoves one hand through his hair before seeming to shake himself. "She and I are having a talk once she's better, and she will get through this. There's no other option. We need to go get the wolves. Their touch can help her heal."

187

I dip my chin in acknowledgment. "Hold on to me, mage and ghost. I can get us there faster than using a portal." Once both the mage and spirit are holding on to my arms, I call on my magic again. As soon as I picture the alpha wolf, all three of us are standing in his room.

Unlike Bishop and me, he's not asleep. Instead, the wolf is bent over his desk, working on something. He turns to face us, not startled in the least to see the mage and me. "What is it this time, Bishop?"

"Izzy's hurt. She needs you, Archer, and Cain." The wolf's relaxed demeanor evaporates as Bishop talks.

He stands up and stalks over to us. As with most shifters, the wolf is wearing the bare minimum, with only a pair of faded jeans on. "What's going on?"

"I'll explain later, but we need to go. She likely doesn't have much time." The wolf's eyes flash amber at the threat to his mate. I'm mildly impressed the young alpha is able to keep his wolf from taking over. At his age, I had decidedly less control over myself. My brother loves to remind me what a menace I was, even though it was so long ago.

"Archer! Cain!" the wolf bellows. My ears ring from the sound. The wolf gives my brother's hounds a run for their money on sheer volume. I hear the thuds of footsteps rushing toward us before the other wolves come into view. While the youngest wolf is dressed similarly to his brother, the middle wolf is fully dressed in a suit.

"Fucking what, bro?" Archer leans against the doorframe, seeming fairly relaxed, at least compared to the mage, alpha, and me. While he tries to appear easygoing, I can spot a predator far too easily for him to fool me. It's the sharpness in his gaze and how he always scans rooms for threats that give him away.

"Izzy's injured." Both of the other wolves' eyes turn fully amber. Fur ripples up the youngest wolf's arms, but he's able to stop the shift a moment later. Good. We don't have time for wolf temper tantrums if what Bishop says is correct.

"If we're done stalling, everyone needs to hold on to me. I'll get us there faster," I explain for the third time. I could transport them there without touching them, but it can be draining. Since I don't know exactly what's wrong with my little raven, I don't want to waste any of my magic.

"Before we go, all of you need to prepare to see Izzy in rough shape," Bishop warns. "She'll have what looks like fatal injuries, but as long as I can give her enough magic, she won't die."

While the mage meant that to be reassuring, it's not. With how much power Izzy has, I'm doubtful the mage has enough to sustain her. I may find out tonight whether my mate can absorb my power or not. No one from this realm should be able to, but nothing about my mate's magic is normal.

When the wolves nod at the mage, he places his hand on my shoulder. The wolves and ghost follow suit. As soon as I think about my mate, the six of us are transported to a clearing in the forest that surrounds Hawthorne Grove.

With the moon shining brightly, I can see every heart-wrenching detail of my mate. She's writhing on the forest floor in only a bra and shorts. Although it's hard to tell exactly what she's wearing through the blood painting every inch of her paler-than-normal skin. My mate has ragged slashes marring most of her normally smooth skin. Her mouth is open, but only a hoarse whisper of a scream comes out.

As I'm taking in my mate, the mage rushes to her right side and grabs her bloody hand. Izzy's nails are ragged and broken, like she's been clawing at something. The mage's hands glow blue as he starts funneling his magic into her.

"What the fuck happened?" the alpha wolf demands as he

falls to his knees on my mate's other side. He grabs her other hand, uncaring of the blood smearing on his hands and pants. The other two wolves move to the alpha's side and also place their hands on my mate's bare skin. Shifters of this realm can help their mates heal through physical touch.

Bishop clenches his jaw as he stares at my mate's face twisted in agony. He's reluctant to betray her secrets, which I can respect.

Izzy never told me not to divulge the fact she can see spirits, so I feel comfortable turning to the ghost. "What happened, ghost?"

"Ghost?" the youngest wolf echoes, but I don't pay attention to him.

"The kid can heal ghosts with soul wounds. By healing them, the ghosts can cross over. When the kid heals these wounds, she has to experience the same injury as some sort of consequence for it. Normally, the kid heals, at most, eight to ten ghosts a night and rests in between each one. Tonight, she healed twenty without any breaks. I tried to stop her, but I couldn't get through to her." The spirit's voice breaks, and a lone tear trails down her translucent cheek.

I repeat what she said word-for-word to the mage and wolves. While I'm repeating it, I come to a conclusion that shouldn't be so startling, given how much power she has. "Izzy isn't just a spirit mage. Healing ghosts isn't possible for spirit mages."

Spirit mages have an affinity for death, unlike the typical mage that has an affinity for a natural element. Their unique magic allows them to see ghosts and access the spirit plane. Spirit mages are often exceptionally powerful, which is probably why they were outlawed centuries ago. However, spirit mages cannot physically influence the dead, and no spirit mage I've ever met comes close to matching Izzy's power.

"Spirit mage?" the alpha wolf breathes. "Oh, fuck. No wonder she wouldn't tell us what she could do."

As Bishop's magic flows into my little raven, her cuts heal fully, only to split back open. It happens over and over and over. The youngest wolf looks a little green watching this happen. If I didn't have the extensive experience I do, I'd probably be a little sick seeing it, too.

"Your magic isn't working, Bishop!" The normally calm and collected suited wolf glares at the mage, and a low-pitched growl vibrates in his throat.

"It is working, Cain. Izzy's trying to heal the mortal wounds of twenty different people all at once. They all died from something similar, which is why her injuries keep healing and reforming. I don't know what drove her to think she could heal twenty fucking people, though." The mage continues to funnel his magic into my mate. He surprises me by not looking as drained as I thought he would. The mage has been hiding the extent of his true power, which is curious. Most mages love flashing their power.

"It was a group of young mages, including Amelia, who were killed at the council headquarters. She was trying to figure out what happened," the ghost tells me. I, again, pass on the spirit's message.

"Fuck. Izzy must've been devastated to have to heal Amelia. What the hell is going on at the council?" The mage mutters the last part to himself.

"If she's passed out from the cuts, why does she keep moving around?" The young wolf is staring at my mate with his brows furrowed, and his lips that are usually smiling are now downturned.

"She's not passed out, Arch. Whatever allows her to heal ghosts also ensures she stays awake while she experiences the same wounds. Izzy is lost to the pain right now but not unconscious." The mage gazes at my mate with sorrow and anguish swimming in his eyes.

I'm sure the same pain is reflected in my own eyes. I would rather spend a year being tortured in the pits than watch my mate go through this for even a minute.

Without knowing exactly what she is, there's nothing I can do to help. The helplessness causes my magic to roar in my chest, demanding we burn down this plane for hurting our mate. If I thought my mate would enjoy that, I'd do it in an instant. However, I doubt she would be pleased with me razing her home.

We watch my mate suffer for more than two hours. By the time her struggles cease, and the wounds no longer reopen, Izzy has lost her voice. She's been screaming silently for the last hour, which is somehow worse than the pitiful hoarse whimpers she was making.

The mage releases her hand and slumps over on the forest floor. He must've given my mate everything he had. I begrudgingly respect him more for sacrificing himself for her. Since his chest is still rising and falling steadily, I know that the mage will wake up eventually.

The wolves bounce their gazes between my mate and the mage. They look like they don't know who to be more worried about. "The mage will be fine, wolves. It also appears that little raven's done healing. Is there a place in this realm we can take her to recover?"

"We'll circle back around to your realm comment, demon eyes," the youngest wolf says, "but Bishop and sunshine can recover in our pack house. They'll be safe there."

With a nod, I bend down and gently pick up my mate. I resist the urge to roll my eyes at the youngest wolf. "I'm far worse than a demon, pup. Can one of you grab the mage?"

"That's… not reassuring." He turns to watch his brother

easily pick up the mage. While the mage is large for his species, the alpha is a fair amount bigger than him.

"It wasn't meant to be, wolf." I wait until all the wolves and the spirit place their hands on me before transporting us to the alpha wolf's bedroom.

Once we're in the pack keep, I pull on my magic to cleanse my mate of her blood, sweat, tears, and forest debris. She'll feel much better when she wakes up if she's clean. I stride over to lay my little raven gently in the wolf's bed. I place the blanket at the end of the bed over both my mate and the mage.

Then I settle in to wait for her to wake up.

CHAPTER 26

IZZY

*W*aking up feels like I'm wading through miles of dense fog. I keep trying to fight through the heavy air. Every time I feel like I've made progress, all I continue to see is the same damn fog. After what feels like years of wandering around lost, I'm finally able to grab on to consciousness. I yank it toward me with both hands.

Blinking open my eyes, I slam them shut again when the light feels like a barrage of stinging needles stabbing into my eyeballs. My head is pounding, and I feel like I'm going to throw up.

Fucking shit. "What the hell did I do last night?" It feels like I have the worst hangover I've ever had, but I know I didn't drink my weight in tequila. I had ghosts to heal and no time to drown myself in alcohol.

"You healed twenty ghosts," Luca tells me from somewhere to my right.

"That explains why I feel like I got run over by a herd of angry llamas. Wait… what?" I struggle to sit up as I realize Luca fucking Nightshade just told me about healing ghosts.

When I'm able to push myself up onto my elbows, I look

over at Luca. He's sitting in a wooden chair in front of a reddish wood desk. Luca looks rough, like he hasn't slept in a while. His stubble is approaching a short beard instead of the normal five o'clock shadow, and he's wearing only a pair of jeans. My eyes linger a moment too long on his six-pack, but can you really blame me? His abs are drool-worthy.

"The secret's out, wildcat. We know you're a spirit mage." Luca's aquamarine eyes assess me as I process what he said.

My stomach sinks and twirls. Since I'm already feeling nauseated, the strong emotions are enough to make me puke. I barely have enough time to sprint to the open bathroom door and drop to my knees before I empty my stomach into the toilet bowl. Gentle hands brush my hair out of my face and hold it behind me to keep it clean.

When I'm done heaving, I flush the toilet, wipe my mouth with the back of my hand, and mutter *"Purgare"* to rinse out the taste of vomit. I turn to face Luca, who's kneeling on the bathroom floor in front of me. "How'd you find out?" My voice is hoarse, and talking scratches my throat.

"Your ghost friend told Levi, who told us." Luca's eyes flick between mine, filling with worry at whatever he sees on my face.

I don't respond, instead, sinking down onto the white-and-black penny-tile floor. Lying on my side, I hug myself and pull my knees up to my chest. My cheek is absorbing the chill from the cold tile while hot tears run down it. My bare midsection and legs are also freezing from the floor, and I start shivering.

It's funny what your mind chooses to focus on when everything is falling apart. As I lie on the bathroom floor, I can't help but admire the precise grout lines and wonder how Luca keeps his bathroom so clean. He must have someone clean it for him. Perks of being the alpha, I guess.

Luca lies down on his side on the floor across from me. I

get lost in his tropical ocean eyes for a moment. "What's going on in your mind, wildcat?"

"I shouldn't have asked Aggie to get Levi." My voice is flat and monotone. Although I'm crying, I don't really feel much of anything. It probably has to do with my heart shattering the second I realized I failed to keep the wolves safe. I tried so hard, but it didn't work.

Simply being around me will get the wolves killed. The council doesn't just murder spirit mages. They execute anyone who knew about the spirit mage and didn't tell them. I've been working on a potion to give Bishop and my family to make them forget what I am. That way, even the memory readers won't know they knew.

Even after trying for years, I still haven't had any success making a potion that actually works. Now, I have to figure out a potion not just for mages but for the wolves too. I'm starting to lose hope that I'll be able to find a solution.

"You would've died," Luca grits out. Anger and heartbreak war for dominance in his eyes.

"I know. Everyone would be safe if I had." The council can't find out I'm a spirit mage if I'm dead.

"You think we care more about being safe than having you?" Luca asks incredulously.

"I know you will, eventually. You'll get to know me, the shininess will wear off, and you'll realize you could do so much better than me. By then, it'll be too late." I close my eyes as some of the numbness starts wearing off. I don't want to feel. It hurts too much. A whimper gets trapped in my throat, but I press my lips tightly together to stop it from coming out. I'm on the verge of begging Luca to make everything stop hurting, but I refuse to be that weak.

"The mages really did a number on you, wildcat, didn't they?" Luca brushes a strand of my multicolored hair out of my face. He cups my face with one warm hand, and his breath fans over my lips. It wouldn't take much to close the distance between us to kiss him.

"It's not just the other mages. There's clearly something wrong with me, or I wouldn't have been born a spirit mage. I'm rotten on the inside, and my magic reflects it." My voice is barely a whisper as I tell Luca something I've never shared with anyone before. I know my family would try to deny it if I told them, because that's what family does. They ignore all the bad in you and love you, anyway.

"That's... fuck. I don't even know if I have the words to tell you how fucking wrong that is. Just because something's illegal doesn't mean it's immoral. There's nothing wrong with being a spirit mage. Your powers are neutral, just like every other affinity out there. What you do with it is what matters. From what I've seen, you sacrifice everything to help others with your magic."

He's wrong, but I don't have the words right now to tell him how defective I am. Instead, I lean in and press my lips against his to distract him. Since it's my first kiss, I freeze once our lips touch, unsure what to do.

I don't have time to worry about it before Luca takes control of the kiss. With his hand cupping my face, he angles my head the way he wants. Luca's tongue swipes along the seam of my lips, and I part them for him. His tongue darts in to tangle with mine, and we spend who knows how long kissing on his bathroom floor.

Eventually, Luca pulls away. I bite my cheek to keep from asking him to fuck me on the floor right now. Kissing him made all the fear and anger and heartache go away for a little while. I would give almost anything to escape again, even if it's just for a moment. The one thing I'm not willing to risk is forming a mate bond with him.

"As much as I enjoy kissing you, wildcat, you're not in the right headspace for that right now. When I fuck you, it's going to be because you want me. Not because you need a distraction." I gape at Luca, wondering how he knows exactly what I was thinking. Luca chuckles, the deep sound rumbling through me. "You're like an open book, Izzy. Every thought you have flits across your beautiful face. I also did exactly what you're doing when I lost my parents. I tried to fuck the pain away. It didn't work for me, and it's not going to work for you."

"I'm sorry about your parents," I whisper. There's no point in denying anything he said because he's absolutely correct about what I was considering. "What helped the pain go away?"

Luca sighs and briefly closes his eyes. When he opens them again, I see an ocean of suffering and sadness in the aquamarine orbs. "Honestly? Nothing's helped the pain go away completely. There are still random moments when thinking about my parents absolutely guts me, but I'm also able to remember some of the happy moments without it hurting now. Archer, Cain, and my pack helped me get through the worst of it. Leaning on them when it felt like I could barely get out of bed, much less lead hundreds of people, is what helped the most."

My heart clenches at the pain in Luca's voice. The big wolf is normally closed off and exudes confidence. I had no idea he was hurting so much, but I guess the same could be said for me. No one really knows how much I feel like I'm dying inside on the daily. I wish Luca's solution would work for me, but there's one flaw. "I can't lean on anyone. It just puts them in danger."

"You think I give a fuck about the danger? All I care about is you. All I want to do is help you, if you'd just let me in." Luca cups my face in his hand again, tenderly rubbing his thumb over my cheekbone.

"But I'm not worth it," I tell him in a small voice. The

tears that stopped with the kiss start dripping down my cheeks again as I tell him what I know he'll figure out eventually. The good parts of me will never outweigh all the bad. Nothing I do will ever balance out all the danger that's always one wrong move away.

"Oh, wildcat. You are worth it and so much more. If I have to spend every day for the rest of my life showing you how worthwhile you are, I will. Happily." Luca's voice is sincere, and it makes me cry harder. He pulls me into his arms as sobs rack my frame, smooshing my face against his chest. Despite our rocky first interaction, Luca seems like a genuinely good guy. He doesn't deserve getting stuck with me.

I so very badly want to let Luca and the rest of my mates in. I'm so fucking tired of trying to do everything alone. It's been getting harder and harder to keep putting one foot in front of the other lately. I don't know how much longer I can fight, but I do know that I refuse to drag anyone else down with me. I'd rather die in a thousand excruciating ways than see any one of my mates or family hurt.

When things get so much that it feels like I'm being strangled by it all, I just need to remember why I'm doing this. Why I claw my way through each day. Why I take the bullying and taunts. It's because of them. My parents and brothers. Bishop. The wolves. Levi. Every fucking thing I do is for them. When I do die, I want to do it knowing I did everything possible to keep them all safe.

Inhaling Luca's dark, woodsy scent, I shove all of my longing and exhaustion and devastation and agony behind a reinforced door in my mind. I secure it with multiple padlocks and thick chains to make sure the feelings don't get loose again. My tears come to a stop as I stuff down my softer emotions. In their place is an aching hollowness in my chest, but I can deal with it to protect everyone.

When my crying stops, Luca pulls back and looks down at me. His lips tip up on one side as he asks, "How are you feeling?"

"Like I've been lying on a tile floor for who knows how long after almost dying." While my snark isn't back in full force, it's better than it was.

Luca snorts. "Then, how about we get up and get you somewhere more comfortable?" I nod at him, and he untangles himself from me. Pushing to his feet, Luca holds out a hand for me. I grab it, knowing this is the last time I can let the big wolf help me. No matter how much I might need it in the future.

CHAPTER 27

IZZY

I freeze when I step out of the bathroom. All of my mates are waiting for us in what I assume is Luca's room. His room has dark wood floors and mossy green walls. Luca's massive bed, desk, nightstands, and bench at the foot of his bed are all mahogany. Breaking up all the dark wood is his sage comforter, light tan sofa, and the nature paintings hanging on the walls.

Before I have a chance to ask Luca about the beautiful paintings, Archer comes bounding over. He stops just short of crashing into me. "Can I hug you?" At my nod, he wraps his arms around me and squeezes tight. Anywhere his skin comes into contact with mine lights up like a firework. The mate bond jumps and dances over my skin. "Don't ever do that again, sunshine. I was so worried when we found you."

"I'm sorry, sunny boy," I murmur against his chest. I hate the way the normally happy wolf's voice wobbles. It feels like bringing people down is all I do. Archer doesn't say anything more. He just holds on to me for a moment longer before stepping back.

In his place is Bishop. Instead of greeting me with his

usual easygoing smile, Bishop is glaring down at me. "Did you do it on purpose?"

"What?"

Bishop leans down until we're nose to nose. "Did you heal too many ghosts on purpose?" I've never seen Bishop this angry, and it makes my heart hurt. I feel like I've failed him and disappointed the one person who's always there for me. I just want my Bishop back.

Seeing how furious he is with me makes me feel like I'm going to cry. Somehow, I manage to shove the feelings down. "No," I whisper while looking away. I don't need him to see in my eyes that I've considered it before.

Bishop captures my chin with his thumb and finger and turns my head toward him, forcing me to meet his gaze. "But you've thought about it, haven't you?" I close my eyes, so I don't have to look at him. I'm not strong enough right now to see hatred in his gaze. "Fucking answer me!"

At his roar, my eyes pop open. "Yes," I breathe.

"Goddamn it, Isabel!" he shouts. He lets go of my face like I burned him. Bishop opens his mouth to yell at me some more before snapping it closed. All at once, every emotion drains from his face. He stares at me with the same empty eyes from my nightmares. "I can't fucking do this with you right now."

After his declaration in the coldest voice I've ever heard from him before, Bishop turns around and storms out. He doesn't spare me a glance before he leaves, probably for good. I know I should feel relief about Bishop giving up on me. I've been trying to push him away since my parents told me we were mates when I was fourteen.

But I don't feel even a hint of relief. All I feel is someone shoving a hot knife into my chest. With each searing stab of the blade, my heart is split, and I wonder how it's even still beating in my chest. Looking down, I almost expect to see a bloody wound, but there's nothing. There's not even a single outward display of the how utterly and completely destroyed I feel inside.

"Hey," someone says in front of me. I robotically lift my gaze from the floor to look at Cain. Whatever he sees on my face has his forehead wrinkling in concern. He holds out a gray sweatshirt for me. When I just blink at it, Cain sighs. "Arms up, angel."

I do as he says without protest, which just makes the lines in his forehead more pronounced. It's hard to be snarky when I'm desperately trying not to drown in my despair.

Cain carefully slips the sweatshirt onto my arms and over my head.

Once the sweatshirt is on, I lower my arms. I don't have the strength to hold them up any longer. I'm usually weaker for half a day after healing ghosts. When I use up all of my magic, I can be sore for up to a week after.

Cain gently untucks my hair from the collar of the warm top. I was getting pretty chilly in my ghost healer outfit of a sports bra and shorts. From the dark forest scent, I know the sweatshirt is Luca's. That explains why it comes down to mid-thigh on me.

He then kneels and holds out my white Chucks for me. I mechanically lift each foot, and he slips them on, not bothering to tie them. "Can I pick you up?" Cain asks softly.

A fizzle of surprise at his question breaks through the pain trying to choke me. Cain isn't as physically affectionate as the other wolves, so I didn't expect him to want to pick me up. When I nod my head, Cain places his large hands on my waist to hoist me up. I wind my arms around his neck and wrap my legs around his narrow waist.

"Can I take you somewhere?" Cain rasps. Since my head is on his shoulder, his warm breath tickles my ear. I give him a small nod, and he starts walking. Instead of paying attention to where he's taking me, I just soak up his warmth.

A few minutes later, Cain comes to a stop. Figuring we reached our destination, I unwrap my legs and slide down him. He keeps his warm hands on my waist until he's sure I'm steady. When I step back and look around, I realize we're in the music room.

"I thought playing something would take your mind off everything." Cain stares down at me with concern shining in his forest-green eyes.

"Thanks," I manage past the lump in my throat at his thoughtfulness.

I always break out my guitar when I'm feeling overwhelmed, which is often. While I usually gravitate toward guitar, seeing the four grand pianos makes me want to play one of my favorite sad bops. I'm a sucker for sad songs that sound upbeat.

I wander over to the piano tucked into a corner. Sitting at the bench, I play a few keys to get a feel for the instrument. After a moment, I start playing "Numb Little Bug" and singing along. While playing the song, I can't help but wish I felt numb. Instead, I feel too much, but that's the story of my life. I'm always feeling too much, and I wish it would just stop.

When I finish the song, I don't feel any better.

Before I can dwell on it, Cain asks, "Is that your favorite song?"

Turning around, I see him standing only a foot or two behind me. I was so lost in the music that I didn't hear him approach.

For a moment, I admire his broad shoulders and strong forearms. My mind wanders back to seeing him shirtless last week. The boy is ripped, and it's a shame he hides it under his dress clothes.

I shake my head to clear my thoughts and answer his question. "Nope. My favorite is 'The Albatross.' Have you heard it?"

"No."

"I can play it for you if you want."

"I'd love to listen to you play another song." Cain's earnestness makes me blush.

Except for when I volunteer, I don't play in front of anyone. At least, not intentionally. Bishop and Levi were the last people I accidentally played in front of, but thinking about Bishop will make me cry right now.

Pushing the thought out of my mind, I hurry over to the guitars. Once I grab one, I start tuning the guitar. "What's your favorite song?" I ask as I get the instrument ready.

"'Granite' by Sleep Token," Cain answers after thinking for a moment.

My lips tip up at him sharing a part of him, no matter how small. He can be pretty closed off. "I'll have to listen to it sometime." I glance up and see his half smile. Butterflies flutter in my stomach at his joy, and I duck my head, so he doesn't see my blush.

After I get the strings tuned properly, I move over to sit on the piano bench again. Cain sits next to me. Closing my eyes, I start playing and singing "The Albatross."

As I sing, my mind wanders to all the ways I bring danger and hold back those I care about. Bishop has been stuck waiting for a mate he can't have. My family has to deal with the judgment of the whole town for a magicless daughter. And now the wolves have to worry about the mage council.

When I'm done with the song, I open my eyes and turn to Cain to see what he thought about it. "I liked it. What makes it your favorite song?" Cain tilts his head and rubs his jaw with one hand as he watches me.

Throwing a leg over the piano bench, so I'm straddling it,

I turn to Cain. "Well, I love the sound of it. I think it's my favorite because I can relate to feeling like an albatross."

"You're not a burden." I scoff at Cain, and he sighs. "Do you think I'm a burden?"

"What? No! Of course not." I'm appalled that he would ever think he's a burden.

"As a child, I was constantly told what a burden I was and how worthless I am. Just because someone tells you that you're a danger or bad or wrong doesn't make it true."

"I'm sorry, quiet boy. That sounds like a really rough environment to grow up in. Do you want me to kill whoever told you that?"

Cain barks out a startled laugh. It's the first time I've heard the quiet wolf laugh. His deep, slightly rough, chuckle rumbles through the room and tugs the corners of my lips up in a smile. "My mother's dead, but thank you, angel."

"Oh. I'm sorry? Or I'm glad?" I'm not really sure which one to go with. When in doubt, do both. That's my life motto.

His mouth twitches up in a smile at me. "Thank you."

Seeing him smiling and laughing makes my heart skip a beat. The serious wolf needs more joy in his life. All three of the wolves do, really. They don't laugh nearly enough.

I open my mouth to respond when a voice from the doorway cuts me off. "Can I talk to you, Izzy?"

Looking over, I see it's Bishop. My stomach sinks, knowing exactly what he wants to talk about.

CHAPTER 28

IZZY

"You ou don't have to talk to him, angel." Cain glances between Bishop and me with a frown.

"I know, but it's better to get this conversation out of the way. Thanks for bringing me here. It helped." It wasn't playing music that's made me feel better. It was Cain and his thoughtfulness.

These damn wolves are dangerous to my heart. They're considerate, sweet, and funny. Luca can still be demanding at times, but he's grown on me. Unfortunately.

Standing up, I put the guitar away before walking to Bishop. My steps drag as I desperately want to avoid this conversation. I know he's going to tell me I'm too much trouble and he's done dealing with me. It's the last thing my heart wants to hear while being exactly what my brain knows is necessary.

When I reach Bishop, he turns around and starts striding away. Walking away without a word is a great start to the conversation. Not.

Sighing, I follow Bishop as we wind through the wolves' ridiculous palace. There's no way this counts as a house. I knew they were wealthy, but this is just absurd. They have multiple ballrooms, dining rooms, and from what I can see, an absolutely colossal kitchen.

Bishop finally slows when we reach a room that has its door closed. He pushes the dark wood door open to a moderately sized sitting room. Three comfy-looking gray couches dominate the center of the room. Dark wood floors, light blue walls, and a massive TV give the room a casual vibe.

A wall of windows to my right overlooks the forest behind the house. From here, I can see a hint of a lake. I'm transfixed by the rippling surface for a moment. I wonder if the wolves will take me to their lake sometime.

I shake myself out of my perusal of the water and wander over to where Bishop is sitting down on one of the sofas. I stop a step away from his muscular legs.

He shoves one of his hands through his hair and blows out a breath. Bishop then looks up at me with his arresting baby blues. "I'm sorry," he tells me gruffly.

My stomach drops like I jumped off a cliff, and my heart feels like it splattered on the canyon floor after the fall. "It's okay. I understand." I do understand why he's done with me, but it still feels like someone is putting my heart through a shredder.

"You understand what?" Bishop stares at me with confusion in his gaze.

"That you're done with my shit. You lasted longer than I thought you would," I say, trying to joke. It falls flat as my voice cracks on the last word. I close my eyes, so I don't have to see the rejection in his.

"Fuck." Bishop surprises me by placing his warm hands on my waist and tugging me down onto his lap. My eyes pop open when my knees land on the plush sofa on either side of him. "I'm not fucking done with you, Isabel. Jesus, sweetheart. I'm sorry I lost my cool that badly that you thought I was leaving for good. Yelling at you was what I was trying to apologize for."

"You're not leaving?" I ask through the lump in my throat. My voice wobbles as I hesitantly meet his gaze with mine.

"No, sweetheart. I'm never fucking leaving you. You're it for me." Bishop crushes me to his hard chest. I always feel so safe in his strong arms.

"But you were so angry," I mumble into his neck.

"Yes, I was. I was and still am fucking livid that it's gotten so bad you've considered dying to escape it." This time, it's Bishop's voice that breaks. He clears his throat before continuing. "But I'm not mad at you. I'm just... fuck, I don't know what I am. Heartbroken? Terrified? Wanting to burn the world down because it hurt you?"

"Why are you terrified?" I know I shouldn't be snuggling him like this, but I don't want to stop. After feeling the utter heartbreak of thinking I was losing him, I need this comfort more than I need oxygen in my lungs or blood in my veins.

"Because I need you, Izzy. I won't survive losing you. Do you not understand how much you mean to me? You're my entire world, sweetheart. You have been since you crashed into me outside of Anya's shop eight years ago." I can hear the smile in Bishop's voice.

My mind briefly wanders to the day when I plowed straight into Bishop on my way to my first day of work. I was distracted with something and not looking where I was going. My arms tingled like crazy where Bishop gripped them to keep them steady. But I didn't know what that meant then. All I knew was that my heart was trying to beat its way out of my chest in excitement from seeing Bishop again after so long.

Pulling back, I sit upright so I can look at him. Bishop's

eyes shine with so much emotion that I feel a little choked up. "You could do so much better than me."

Bishop growls at me, and I raise my eyebrows in surprise. He must be spending too much time with the canines. "No, Isabel, I couldn't do better than you, because there simply isn't anyone better. You're smart, kind, caring, incredibly funny, and the most gorgeous woman I've ever laid eyes on. Please, tell me, how I could ever do better than my amazing mate?"

It feels like I blush from the top of my head to my toes at Bishop's sweet declarations. I'm not used to getting compliments from people, and I don't know what to do with all the mushy feelings it stirs up. So, I just ignore them.

"You could find someone who doesn't put you in danger," I remind him.

"Jesus fucking Christ, woman. What don't you understand? I don't want to be safe if it means not having you!" Bishop tangles one hand in my hair and tugs me to him. His soft lips crash against mine, and his tongue demands entrance. When I part my lips, his tongue darts in to twirl with mine. I twine my arms around his neck and shove my fingers through his short hair.

Kissing Bishop is even better than I imagined. I've been thinking about kissing the boy for eight years, and the real thing somehow manages to top every fantasy I've had about it. His lips are softer, warmer, and more skilled than I dreamed they would be.

As we kiss, my hips start moving back and forth on his lap, grinding my center over his hard-on. While Bishop leaves one hand gripping my hair, he moves his other to my hip. He helps me move back and forth on him, driving me closer and closer to climaxing.

Before I can, Bishop rips his mouth from mine and stills my hips with his hand. "If you don't want your first time to be hard and fast on this couch, we need to stop, sweet-heart." Bishop pants like he just ran a marathon. His chest rises and falls rapidly as he stares at me with hunger in his eyes.

My horny self is all for the hard and fast part. I'll take Bishop any way I can get him. The two brain cells that are still online shriek about how horrible of an idea it is. Fucking Bishop is almost guaranteed to form the mate bond.

"Stopping's probably a good idea." My voice comes out breathy as I try to slow my heart rate and even out my breathing. The rest of what Bishop said eventually registers. "Wait. How do you know it would be my first time?"

Bishop chuckles, the sound vibrating through where we touch. "I knew you hadn't slept with anyone before we reconnected. I also know exactly the type of person you are, Iz, so I know you haven't fucked anyone since, either."

"I guess I won't have to kill Aiden or Rhys for telling you." Aiden loves to tease me about still being a virgin, so I wouldn't put it past him to tell Bishop about it. With Aiden's loud mouth, Rhys knows, too, as much as I wish he didn't.

"Your brothers didn't spill your secrets. Speaking of secrets, we need to talk about what's been going on, Izzy. You're so focused on making sure everyone else is safe that you forget how much we all need you.

"You think your mom would ever mend her broken heart from losing her only daughter? You think your dad, who only took the council position to abolish the spirit mage law, would get over your death? You think your older brothers, one of whom started an entire security company to keep you safe, would simply move on if you died? If you think your death wouldn't shatter your family, you don't know them very well, Izzy."

By the time Bishop finishes speaking, my mouth is hanging open in surprise. "I didn't know any of that. I thought Dad wanted to be on the council like his dad, and I thought you and Rhys just liked security work."

I guess I never really thought about how it would impact my family if I died. That makes me sound really selfish, but all I've been able to see is the ways I put them in danger. In my head, I figured that my family would just go on about their lives. It never occurred to me that they'd miss me or anything. After all, I'm a little shit, so I kind of thought they'd be glad to get rid of me.

"Sweetheart, your dad hates the council. He never wanted to be on it. Neither Rhys nor I really had any idea what we wanted to do. We bonded our last year in college over our worry for you. That's what led us to start Elemental with Logan and Dec. Aiden learned everything he could about technology to protect you too."

I lean my forehead on Bishop's shoulder as I take a moment to process everything. My thoughts are whirling frantically in my head as I realize a flaw in my plan. All I want is for everyone I care about to be happy. If I lost any one of my family or my mates, I don't know that I'd ever be truly happy again. But I expect them not to give a rat's ass about losing me.

"What am I supposed to do?" I ask him quietly. I've spent so long focused on keeping everyone else safe, I don't have the first clue how to survive this.

My five-year plan has always been simple. Step one: keep my family safe. Step two: die healing ghosts. It's easy and mess free, other than the whole dying part. Without step two, my whole plan has gone to shit, and I don't know how to make a new one.

"I don't have all the answers right now, Izzy, but I know we need to work together. I know we'll figure out something. You can't be running off, trying to handle everything your-self, sweetheart. Let us help you. Please." Bishop's blue eyes glisten with unshed tears as he begs me to let him help, and it guts me. He's so strong and unyielding. Nothing should be able to make Bishop cry, certainly not me.

"I can try," I breathe, willing to do anything to make my mage feel better.

"That's a start for now." Bishop glances at my watch before looking back at me. "Your family is going to be here soon. As much as I enjoy holding you, we need to get up."

"What? Why is my family coming here? How do they even know I'm here?"

"I called Rhys once I woke up after giving you magic. Before anyone could freak out that you were missing, I let them know where you were and what you had been doing." One of Bishop's hands is still in my hair, running gently through the strands. All of my mates seem to love playing with my hair, and I'm here for it. I'll take free head massages any day of the week.

"You snitch," I tell Bishop, without any real heat behind it.

Bishop calling Rhys is better than my mom and dad launching a city-wide manhunt for me. Although, they're still going to be absolutely furious with me, especially my mom. The thought makes me wilt against Bishop. My mom is a force of nature when she wants to be.

"I wouldn't have had to snitch if you told them in the first place or didn't overdo it." Bishop makes logical points. I hate it when he's all sensible and shit. It makes it hard to argue with him.

"But my mom's gonna be sooo mad at me," I whine. Bishop snorts and has zero sympathy for me, the asshole.

"Damn right, I am, Isabel Magnolia Gallagher."

CHAPTER 29

IZZY

t my mom's voice, I close my eyes briefly before opening them to glare at Bishop. He just smirks at me.

I turn to look over my shoulder at my mom. Her long blonde hair is free to float over her shoulders and down her back. Mom's gray eyes are narrowed at me as she puts her hands on her green-sundress-clad hips.

"Mother of my heart! It's just lovely to see you. Whatever are you doing here?" I ask as I bat my eyelashes at my mom.

She rolls her eyes at me. "Nice try, Izzy. I had to learn from Bishop that my daughter almost died after lying to me that she wasn't healing ghosts for—" She breaks off and turns to Bishop. "How long was it?"

"Six years," Bishop helpfully supplies.

"Traitor," I hiss under my breath. He just smiles at me. Frustrated with him, I move to get off his lap, but Bishop's hold on my hips prevents me. When he doesn't make a move to release me, I sigh and slump back down. I guess I'm having this conversation with my mom while on one of my mates' lap.

Awesome. I love awkward situations. That's clearly why I always find myself in them.

"Oh yes, six years. Six entire years, Isabel! I can't believe you lied to me, your father, your brothers, and Bishop for that long. What on earth were you thinking?" My mom's voice raises as she finishes until she's almost shouting at me. For my very even-tempered mom, raising her voice at all is a big deal.

I sigh. "I was thinking about the ghosts. They need to be healed, and no one else can do it. I knew you'd try to stop me."

"Yes, I would. You almost died! Again, Izzy!" Tears slip down my mom's cheeks as she tries to gather herself. My mom is the most put together person I know, so it's rare to see her cry. "I just don't know why it has to be you."

My heart hurts from seeing my mom so upset. "There's no one else who can, Mom."

"I know that! I just don't know why it always has to be you. Why can't it be someone else's daughter who's always in danger?" Mom's voice breaks on the last word. She presses her lips together and closes her eyes for a moment.

This time, when I push on Bishop, he lets me up. I stand from the couch and walk over to my mom. "I'm sorry."

She shakes her head at me and opens her eyes that are so similar to mine. "It's not your fault, Izzy. I just... We can't lose you, baby. You're supposed to outlive your dad and me by at least fifty years. You're supposed to annoy your brothers for centuries." My lips briefly twitch up. "You can't keep going like this."

"I know." My mom's eyebrows raise practically to her hairline at my easy acceptance. I snort. "Bishop already talked to me, Mom. I'll try to be more careful. I just wanted to keep everyone safe." It kills me that I put everyone I care about in so much danger. I just want them to be happy and safe, and I don't know how to make it happen.

"Oh, honey. That's not your job." My mom wraps her arms around me and squeezes me with a surprising amount of strength for her slight frame. She rubs my back for a long moment. "You're always thinking about everyone else, but it doesn't all fall to you. We can help you if you tell us what's going on."

"Yeah," I mumble into her shoulder.

With one last squeeze, my mom releases me and steps back. She smooths down her sundress before glancing at her dainty gold watch. It's a gold chain of interlocking crescent moons with a small watch face. It was originally my grandmother's. We don't see her often, but she's always been nice to me, unlike my paternal grandparents. "We're late for dinner. Your father and brothers portaled here with me and are anxious to see you. They're waiting in the dining room."

"Oh good, more people to yell at me," I grumble.

My mom rolls her eyes at me—again—before looking over my shoulder. "Do you know the way, Bishop?"

"Yep, I do." Bishop gets up from his perch on the sofa and walks over to me. He tunnels one of his hands through my hair and tilts my face up to his. He slams his lips on mine for a hard, fast kiss. After just a few seconds, Bishop pulls away and walks out the door, leaving me reeling.

Mom grins at me before clasping my hand in hers and pulling me after Bishop. "So, you're kissing Bishop now? Does that mean you're going to mate him?"

"No, it definitely doesn't mean that, Mother." We walk down a maze of winding hallways. I have no clue how Bishop knows his way around this place. I have zero idea how to even get back to the room we were just in.

"Whatever you need to tell yourself, Izzy." My mom gives me a wide grin before we follow Bishop along dark wood doors into a huge dining room. The dark wood continues onto the floor and through the trim in the elegant room. She nods toward Luca, Archer, and Cain standing on the other side of the massive table. Levi is standing near the wolves and gives my mom a charming smile. "Are these your other mates?"

I'm momentarily distracted by the absolutely massive white oak table that dominates the space. It's big enough to sit around twenty-five people. With the light table and cream walls, the dining room feels airy. The bank of windows behind the wolves also helps brighten up the space.

I shrug at my mom's question. "I dunno. All wolves look the same to me. It's especially hard to tell the two blond meatheads apart." I can't say the whole thing with a straight face. A small grin crosses my lips as I stare at my wolf mates.

Archer laughs at my comment, Luca rolls his eyes at me, and Cain smiles slightly.

Before my mom gets a chance to scold me, a voice pipes in from behind us. "How dare you talk about the alpha like that!"

"Oh, boy." Sighing, I turn to face the wolf dude behind me who feels the need to make an already shitty day worse. He's taller than me but shorter than any of my mates. He has pale skin, dark hair, and brown eyes. Overall, he's pretty unremarkable. "Who the fuck are you?"

"I'm—" he starts to say.

I cut him off. "No, I actually don't give a shit." Dismissing the wolf, I turn around.

As I'm facing forward, I hear steps behind me right before a large hand lands hard on my shoulder. Before he has a chance to yank me back, I grab his hand and pull it with both of mine. When he's off-balance, I squat and shove my hips back into his before straightening and throwing him over my shoulder. He lands with a satisfying thud.

I conjure my favorite blade without a thought as I straddle the wolf. This is exactly why I have to lock down my magic at school. If I'm unexpectedly under attack, my magic pours out of me before I have a chance to react. And I turn into a knife-toting wack job who reacts with excessive violence, apparently.

Pressing the dagger to the terrified wolf's throat, I lean in and snarl, "Touch me again, and I'll fucking break every one of your fingers. Then I'll heal them, break them again, and heal them in the wrong position. Do you understand me?"

"That was hot," Archer whispers to someone to the right of me. I'm too distracted with the rando wolf to see who he's talking to.

"Y-y-yes." The wolf I'm kneeling on widens his eyes at whatever he sees on my face. Fucking great. I'm sure my eyes are glowing the same light blue as my magic, since my blade is shining blue too.

My hair starts floating in a non-existent breeze, and I know I'm in trouble. The wolf senses the same thing and starts thrashing under me. Unfortunately for both of us, that only encourages my magic to keep flowing out to put an end to the threat.

"Stop! Stop fucking moving, you dumbass! Do you want me to slowly and painfully kill you? You're antagonizing something more powerful than you can even comprehend, wolf. You need to be still, so I can put it back in its cage. Understood?" The wolf stills at my warning and looks up at me with abject terror on his face. I would feel bad for him if he weren't running around grabbing women he doesn't know.

"Izzy. Rein it in." Bishop strides toward me until he's standing a foot in front of me. His eyebrows knit together with concern.

I roll my eyes before glancing up at Bishop. "What the

fuck do you think I'm trying to do here, St. James? Fuck. Should I just kill him? Has he seen too much?" The wolf whimpers under me. I look down at him. "You got yourself into this situation by touching a woman without consent, my dude. We don't fucking do that from now on, do we?"

The wolf frantically shakes his head, his wide eyes darting around the room. No one's making a move to help him. Sucks to be him.

"That'd be awfully messy, honey," my mom chimes in while frowning down at the wolf.

The wolf's eyes widen even farther, like he expected someone in my family to try to stop me. He clearly doesn't know the Gallaghers, because we're all a bit unhinged. I'm actually surprised my dad and brothers are letting me handle this myself. They like to swoop in and steal my kills. It's super rude.

"I mean, it doesn't have to be. I could just do the... um, thing," I finish lamely to avoid telling my mates what I can do. While my family knows about that aspect of my magic, my mates don't need to. Even for a spirit mage, I'm unusual. Aggie couldn't do most of what I could when she was alive. I don't want my mates to think I'm even more of a freak.

Levi chimes in before my mom can say anything. "I can erase his memories."

I whip my head up to look at Levi, who's watching the encounter from the other side of the table with the wolves. His red irises are the only thing that gives away that he's not as calm as he seems. "You're a memory reader?"

Levi's lips twitch up in a small smile. "Still not a mage, little raven."

"He's apparently not a demon, either," Archer grumbles while giving Levi an epic side-eye. A small smile crosses my face at Archer's antics.

My magic also starts pulling back when it realizes the

wolf under me isn't a serious threat and my mates would help if he were. I let out a long sigh of relief when my hair lays back against my shoulders and the knife stops glowing. It's weird as fuck that my magic receded without a fight, but I'm not going to question it right now.

"Can you leave the memories of me flipping him and the general feeling of being about to shit his pants when he thinks about me?"

Levi snorts. "I can."

"Cool. Have at 'im, then." When Levi reaches me, I get off the wolf while still holding my blade to his throat. Levi straddles him, and the wolf looks even more scared. I step back to give Levi room to work.

"This will probably hurt. A lot." Levi takes great delight in telling him that before a black mist completely covers the wolf.

Yet again, I wonder what the actual fuck Levi is.

CHAPTER 30

IZZY

"What is he?" Rhys whispers from behind me as we watch Levi remove the wolf's memories with morbid fascination.

Mage memory reading is an invisible process that's pretty quick. It certainly doesn't involve a black mist and the person getting their memories removed writhing on the ground.

I shrug and realize I'm still holding my favorite blade. Her name's Olga, and she's beautiful. The knife has a wicked-looking curved blade, with a silver skull on a torch as the hilt. The dagger has apparently been in my mom's family for a while. When I started going on super-secret spy missions with Rhys and Bishop, Mom gifted her to me.

How do I get my blade back home? Conjuring is definitely not a mage skill. Mages can't just pull things from other places. While mages can shape their raw magic more than, say, shifters or vampires, we're still limited in what our magic can do. Every mage, other than me, can't make something out of nothing or transport anything without a portal.

That's the problem with my weird magic. It does things on its own that I have no idea how to do when it goes away.

Shaking my head, because I always have more questions than answers when it comes to my magic, I open a portal to my room behind me. As I step through, I hear Luca call, "Where are you going?"

My lips twitch up into a smirk at riling up Luca as I walk through the portal without answering him. I let it close behind me as I walk over to my desk to put Olga in her drawer. Why, yes, she does have her own drawer. She's special like that.

Being alone for the first time since I woke up, everything is trying to slam into me like a five-mile-long freight train. But I definitely don't have time to panic about everything that's gone horribly wrong since last night. Or what I assume was last night. I'm not actually sure how long I was out.

Shoving all my feelings into a dark corner of my mind, I try to blank my face as I open a portal back to the dining room. When I step through the rip in time, I come face-to-face with a very angry alpha wolf. Luca has crossed around the table to stand where I was before I portaled back to my room.

Peering around Luca, I don't see the wolf who tried his luck with me. Levi must've dealt with him while I was in my room.

"Where the fuck did you go?" Luca hisses at me as he steps into my space. He leans down until his lips are inches from mine, and his aquamarine eyes try to stare into my soul. *Good fucking luck finding it, my dude.* I'm pretty sure I was born without a soul. In its place is a pit of pure snark.

"To my room, wolf boy. Calm the fuck down." Does saying *calm down* actually make anyone calmer? Probably not, but Luca getting up in my space is pissing me off. Or it could be all the feelings I refuse to deal with coming out, but who knows, really.

"How am I supposed to be calm when you disappear to who knows where? What if you got hurt or needed us?"

Ah, shit. Now I know exactly why Luca is upset, and I feel a little bad. I did just almost die on him. I'd be pretty anxious if the roles were reversed, and he disappeared without a word.

Rubbing my hands over my face, I blow out a breath. "I'm sorry." Luca's blond brows jump at my apology, and I resist the urge to roll my eyes at him. "I am capable of apologizing and admitting when I'm wrong, wolf boy."

"I know. I guess I just expected more of a fight." Luca settles his hands on my waist as we talk. I want to lean into his touch, but I'm still not on board with the whole mating thing. It's still more likely than not that I'll die. I don't want to take them down with me.

"I can argue with you if you want."

Luca lets out a rare laugh, and I fight the smile that's trying to break out at his joy. "I'm good, wildcat."

"Are you two lovebirds done over there? 'Cause I'd really like to eat sometime in this century," Aiden calls. I peer around Luca to glare at my annoying brother. Aiden just grins at me.

Stepping out of Luca's hold, I walk over to my brother and flick him in the pec. He yelps, and I smile sweetly at him. "You're such a dick, Aiden."

Aiden snorts and gives me a quick hug. "I'm glad you're okay, Izzy." He sounds a little choked up, which is rare for my goofy brother. I squeeze him back hard to reassure him that I'm fine.

After I pull out of Aiden's hug, I go over to Rhys next. He ruffles my hair and then hugs me tight. "You scared us, Iz."

"I'm sorry," I say for what feels like the millionth time. It comes out a little muffled because my face is smooshed into Rhys's chest.

"Just take one of us with you next time, okay?" Rhys peers down at me with hazel eyes that shine with concern.

Seeing how worried my family was makes a lump form in my throat. "I can do that." Rhys holds me for another moment before thoroughly messing up my hair. I glare daggers at him, and he laughs at me.

Brothers are the worst.

I walk over to my dad next. He's the same height as Rhys, with brown hair just a touch darker and hazel eyes a bit greener. My dad is also a little more muscular than my oldest brother. He can be super intimidating when he wants to be. Right now, my dad is just watching me with worry in his gaze.

I walk up to him hesitantly, unsure whether he's mad at me. "Hi, Dad." I stare at his shiny black dress shoes that match his slacks to avoid meeting his gaze.

My dad is silent for a beat at my hesitation before pulling me into his arms. I lay my head on his gray dress shirt and soak up the comfort. "Hey, sweetie. I hope you know you can always come to me if you need help. I'll help you, no questions asked. I'll even handle your mom for you."

"Sean!" my mom says in exasperation. A small giggle slips out at their dynamic.

"I know, Dad. I just didn't want to bother you. You have so much on your plate." My dad works around the clock at the council. He's always trying to help the lower mages, and I don't want to take his attention away from that.

"You're never a bother, Izzy. I always have time for my favorite daughter."

I snort. "I'm your only daughter."

Dad grins down at me. He hugs me tight for a moment before stepping back. "Be that as it may, I'll always have time for you. My job will never be more important than my family," my dad finishes seriously.

I nod at my dad before changing the subject because I don't do well with mushy feelings. "We should probably sit down for dinner before not-your-favorite son expires of hunger."

"Hey! I'm totally the favorite. I'm fucking delightful, unlike you two losers," Aiden informs me and Rhys with a huff.

"Language, Aiden Michael," my mom chastises, like he hasn't been swearing since he could talk.

I chuckle as I take a seat at the absurdly large table. My mom sits to my left and Levi sits to my right. The wolves, Bishop, and Rhys are on the other side, with Luca directly opposite me. Dad sits next to Mom, and Aiden sits next to Levi.

When everyone's seated, I take in the bone china plates, expensive linen napkins, and probably real silver cutlery. Combined with the huge wood table, tufted cream high-back chairs, and the gold chandelier dripping with what I hope are crystals and not diamonds, the whole room screams money.

"This is a fancy-ass dining room you've got, wolf boy." Luca's lips twitch, but he shuts his smile down and narrows his eyes at me. I grin at him because I've got his number. He totally finds me funny, even if he doesn't want to show it.

"Izzy!" my mom hisses as she nudges me with a bony elbow.

"What?"

"Be polite! You want to make a good impression."

I can't contain my laugh. "Oh, come on, Mom. Have you met me? I don't make a good impression on anyone. Wolf boy over there knows exactly what to expect when it comes to me. For some unknown reason, he's not running for the hills yet. There's still time for him to change his mind, though."

I try to be flippant about the possibility of any of my

mates deciding I'm not worth it. But the thought feels like a dagger ripping through my heart.

"I won't ever change my mind, wildcat," Luca tells me seriously.

"Bold words for a wolf who has no idea what he's getting into with me." I still don't think the wolves quite grasp just how dangerous being with me is. They also don't know about all of my freaky extra abilities.

"You could drag me to the depths of hell, and I'd happily follow, Izzy. I don't care where we are or what we're doing, I just want to be with you." The conviction in Luca's tropical ocean gaze never wavers as he stares me down.

Fuck me, man. Who the hell let Luca be so damn sweet, my teeth ache? I'd like the raging asshole I first met back, please. He's much less dangerous to my secretly sappy little heart than this version of Luca.

I look away first and stare down at the cream-and-gold napkins like they're the most interesting thing ever.

I'm saved from any more conversation by a few wolves striding into the room with huge platters of food. There's a gigantic ham, gravy, a variety of salads, mashed potatoes, rolls, green beans, and more. They set the mouthwatering spread on the table before leaving back the way they came.

We all serve ourselves from the communal food dishes. I've just shoved a delicious bite of ham, smothered in gravy, into my mouth when Bishop asks, "So, when are we breaking into the council headquarters?"

CHAPTER 31

IZZY

I choke on my bite of food at Bishop's question. After hacking super attractively for a moment, I've cleared my airway enough to ask, "What the hell are you talking about, St. James?"

Bishop smirks at me, enjoying my predicament. I flip him off with my right hand, hoping my mom doesn't see. When she doesn't comment on it, I resist the urge to fist-pump in victory.

"Aggie told us about the council killing young mages. I figured you'd want to investigate." Bishop shrugs as he drops that bomb on my family.

"What are you talking about, Bishop?" my dad asks him.

I can't focus on that as I realize I haven't seen Aggie since I woke up. Trying not to worry that something has happened to the ghost who has become one of my best friends, I pull on the thread of magic that connects us.

Aggie materializes over the table. She looks around, confused, for a second before spotting me. "Kid!" She zooms over to me and wraps me in a spectral hug I can't feel. "How are you feeling? Are you okay? Is your magic okay?"

I smile at her rapid-fire questions as she backs up to float over the table in front of me. "I'm fine, Aggie. I'll be back to full strength in a few days."

"You scared the shit out of me! Don't do that again, kid!" Aggie yells at me now that she's assured that I'm not dying.

"I'm sorry, Aggie. I really am." Worrying everyone is the last thing I was trying to do.

"You better be. I'm too old for this shit." Aggie huffs.

I laugh, and she glares at me. When I take my focus off Aggie, I realize the whole table is staring at me. That's not awkward or anything.

"Are you talking to a ghost?" Archer asks while bouncing a little in his seat.

"Um, yeah. Sorry if it's creeping you out. I can stop." I cringe as I wait for him to tell me I'm too weird for him.

Archer surprises me by becoming even more enthusiastic. "It's not creepy. It's seriously the coolest thing I've ever seen! Can the ghost see us?"

Aggie gives him a droll look. "I can indeed, wolf. I can even hear you. Crazy how that works."

I snort at her sarcastic reply. Archer's question is reasonable for someone who knows nothing about ghosts, though. "Yep, she can."

"Oh, man. That's awesome!" Archer gives me a wide grin, and his eyes dance with delight. At my small smile from his enthusiasm, Archer's face lights up even more. It's clear how much joy he gets from making others happy.

I wonder who makes sure he's happy. A small voice in my mind whispers that I could be that person. I shut it down really fucking fast. Happiness and I don't go hand in hand. All I do is drag people down. Someone like Archer deserves a delightful ray of sunshine, which I certainly am not.

Before I can get bogged down by my thoughts of how

Archer deserves better, my dad asks me, "Can you tell me what's going on with the ghosts and the council?"

I groan as I remember what led to this whole debacle. It's yet another problem I have no idea how to solve. "Young mages from less powerful families are being recruited by the council. All the ghosts could tell me was that they were in the mage development program, were taken for testing in the council basement, and then nothing. There were about forty to fifty ghosts. The twenty I healed all told me the same story."

"That's Doyle's pet project," my dad informs me. I shudder at the thought of that awful mage. Something about him always gives me the heebie-jeebies. "I thought it was strange he suddenly wanted to help less advantaged mages and didn't want my input at all."

"I don't know what they're doing, but it's not good. All the ghosts were really messed up, including Amelia. They were all killed by a bunch of cuts that resulted in losing too much blood, I think." I try to swallow around the lump in my throat at the thought of Lia. She didn't deserve what happened to her.

"Oh, honey. I'm so sorry." My mom wraps one of her arms around me and pulls me into a comforting hug. I linger for a few moments before pulling back.

When I straighten, I see the wolves and Bishop staring at me with concern. I avoid their gazes because I don't need them to know how much I'm hurting inside over Lia dying. They're already worried enough about me as it is.

I'm a mess.

Dad's expression has become increasingly thunderous as he listens to me. "That conniving little fucker! I knew he didn't want to help them out of the goodness of his cold, dead heart."

"Why is he killing them?" I ask him.

"I don't know, Iz. I have no idea what Doyle stands to gain from murdering children."

"I thought Izzy, Levi, and I could go with you to the next council meeting," Bishop tells my dad. "We can poke around while everyone's occupied. Hopefully, we'll be able to get a better idea of what's happening."

"Absolutely fucking not. Izzy isn't going with you," Luca growls at Bishop.

My brows raise in disbelief at him thinking he gets to dictate what I do and don't do. "That's cute, wolf boy, that you think you have any say in whether I go or not."

Luca narrows his eyes on me and opens his mouth to say something. Bishop starts talking before he can. "Okay, you two. How about everyone just dials it down a notch or five? Luca, she's the only one who knows what the ghosts looked like. She needs to come with us. Izzy, how about you not rile the alpha wolf who almost lost his mate, yeah?"

I deflate in my seat. Bishop makes a good point, the jerk. Luca's wolf is probably riding him hard after he found me half dead. Alpha wolves are notoriously temperamental and psychotically protective of their mates. When I think about it, I'm actually impressed Luca has been this levelheaded thus far.

"You won't be safe there," Luca rumbles.

"I hate to break it to you, but I'm not really safe anywhere, wolf boy," I tell him without my usual attitude. "Bishop and Levi are more than enough to ensure nothing happens to me. I'd invite you along, but mages hate wolves. You'd stand out."

"I don't like it."

"That's fair."

Luca blows out a breath and rubs one of his hands over his too handsome face. He closes his eyes briefly before snapping them open and fixing his gaze on me. "Will you be careful and not take any unnecessary risks?"

He stares at me with so much raw emotion in his eyes that I'm temporarily at a loss for words. "Yeah," I croak, feeling like a fly caught in a trap while unable to look away from his gaze.

"That's a solid plan, Bishop. The next council meeting is a week from today. Does next Friday afternoon work for everyone?" At my dad's voice, I'm able to break eye contact with the big wolf. I shake my head to clear the Luca haze from my mind.

When I do, I realize what my dad said. "Today's Friday?" I could've sworn I passed out from ghost healing on Wednesday night.

"Yes, it is, little raven. You've been out since late Wednesday." Levi twists in his seat to face me. His eyes flick between mine in worry as I process what he said.

"Oh," is all I say. That hasn't happened before. Even when I almost died when I was younger, I was out for a few hours. Not an entire day.

"I'm free Friday afternoon." Levi sits back in his seat after staring at me for a beat.

"I'm free for some B&E then too." I'm always available for messing with the council.

"I'll get council passes for the three of you. If anyone does catch you, that'll help." Anger at the council and worry for us war in my dad's eyes. I'm sure he'd rather someone else investigate what's going on, but we can't let anyone else know what I can do.

We all turn back to our food now that we have a plan in place. I'm almost done with my food when an auburn-haired woman bursts through the doors to my left. She jogs over to Cain with her curls bouncing and gives him a hug from behind. After wrapping her tanned arms around his neck, she leans her cheek on his shoulder.

Jealousy sparks in my chest, tempting my magic to slither

out of its prison. I'm able to lock it down, but the jealousy burns like acid through my veins as I watch another woman put her hands on my mate. I'm not touching the reason for the jealousy with a ten-foot pole, though.

"I'm glad you're finally out and about, Si. I've been worried about you holed up in Luca's room." She looks up at me from where her head rests on Cain's shoulder. By the way her hazel eyes twinkle with mirth, she's putting on a show to provoke me on purpose. Rather than react, I simply grind my teeth and hope to incinerate her with my gaze alone. Now, that would be a nifty power to have. It sounds way more useful than seeing ghosts.

"Prue. Is this really necessary?" Cain asks with exasperation. It grates on me that he doesn't remove her arms from his shoulders. Is he into her? Not that it should matter to me whether he is. Yet, here I am, ready to kill someone just for touching him.

"Absolutely. I wouldn't have to annoy you if you'd just introduce me to your mate." Prue gives Cain a kiss on the cheek. I have to grip the edge of my seat hard enough to hurt to stop myself from marching over there and punching her.

Fucking hell. I guess the mate bond makes me a bit psycho too. I can't find a shred of regret for my violent thoughts when she's still touching Cain.

Cain sighs heavily and side-eyes the woman before looking at me. His eyes widen at whatever he sees on my face. "Isabel, this is my little sister, Prue. Prudence, this is Isabel, my mate," he hurries to explain.

My anger evaporates when I hear that it's just his sister.

"Wow, using the full name. You must be really ticked off, Silence." Prue notices the confusion on my face, and her grin gets bigger. "Ooh, you haven't told her your full name, have you? This is great. His full name is Silence Cain Blackthorne.

He goes by Cain most of the time, for obvious reasons." Prue grins at me like I wasn't just planning to murder her.

Wow. That's certainly a name. I can see why he prefers Cain. His parents must've really disliked him to give him that mouthful of a name.

Because I don't have anything nice to say about his full name, I skip over that tidbit of information. Instead, I glare at Prue. "I'd say it's nice to meet you, but you're kind of an asshole."

Prue looks at me for a second before throwing her head back and cackling. When she gets her laughter under control, she tells Cain, "I like her."

"Of course, you do, Prudence Luisa. Isabel enjoys stirring the pot almost as much as you do." I'd be offended if what Cain said weren't true.

Prue's name is almost as bad as Cain's. Their parents really shouldn't be allowed to name children.

"I mean, you're not wrong about me," I mutter under my breath. Cain gives me a half smile, and butterflies swarm in my stomach. I love seeing the serious wolf smile, even if it's not a full one.

"We're going to get along great. I would come around and hug you, new sis, but you definitely look like you'd stab me with a rusty spork right now. I'll let you marinate in my awesomeness before we hang out. Luca. Archer. Mage randoms," she says with a dip of her head at everyone. Prue then strides back the way she came, leaving me confused about what just happened.

CHAPTER 32

IZZY

*C*ain covers his face with his hands and groans. When he drops his arms, his eyes reluctantly meet mine. "I am so sorry about Prue, angel."

"It's not your fault, quiet boy. Your sister's lucky I didn't have any rusty silverware to stab her with, though." I'm not sure whether I'm joking or not. Good thing Prue ran off or we'd find out. Cain smiles at my disgruntled tone, and I give him a small one back.

"Like you're one to judge, Izzy. If anyone knows a thing or two about annoying little sisters, it's you." Aiden grins at me from the other side of Levi. I resist the urge to chuck my napkin at him. Instead, I roll my eyes at my currently least favorite brother.

With Prue gone, everyone returns to their food. When we're all done eating, the wolves, Bishop, and my brothers come over to our side of the table. Everyone breaks into groups and talks for a little while.

When it's time for my family to go, my dad shakes hands with each of my mates. My mom gives them all a motherly hug. Rhys does the bro hug with Bishop, and Aiden fist-bumps each of them.

My dad and brothers each hug me tight before it's my mom's turn. While she's squeezing me, my mom whispers, "I love you, Izzy. We all do. I know I can't stop you from healing spirits. But please be careful. I don't know what I'd do if I lost you, baby." Mom's voice breaks, and I hold her a little tighter.

Eventually, she pulls away and gives me a watery smile. Dad wraps his arms around Mom and kisses the top of her head before they go through a portal with my brothers. Aggie gives me a wave before disappearing to wherever she goes when she's not bugging me.

Now that my family is gone, it's just my mates and me. All of my mates are staring at me, and none of them says anything. Like the awkward person I am, I shift from foot to foot and avoid eye contact with any of them.

Levi is the one to finally break the silence. "Will you take a walk outside with me, little raven?"

"Yep!" I say way too quickly and a little too loudly. I'm just stoked to have an out from the awkwardness.

Bishop chuckles at me. I narrow my eyes at him. Rather than be intimidated, he widens his grin. Levi grabs my hand and tugs me after him before I have time to flip off Bishop. There's always later, though.

Levi leads me out of the grand dining room, down a white wood-paneled hallway. At the end of the hallway is an unassuming dark wood door. When Levi pushes through it, we walk out into an absolutely gorgeous backyard. Lush grass surrounds a gray brick paver patio. Trees and shrubs line the patio on the sides. In front of it is a dense forest, full of stunning yellow, red, and orange leafed trees.

We head over to a gray stone wall at the edge of the patio. I chance a look behind me and almost swallow my tongue.

Holy fuck. That's a gargantuan house. Pack houses tend to be large because they need to house the entire pack in an emergency. With the Nightshade Pack having almost a thousand shifters, that's a lot of wolves to lodge.

I probably should have expected the sprawling U-shaped house to be this big. Even though it's large, the red brick exterior with white trim, matching shutters, and a gray roof is elegant. The dormers that pop up every five feet or so add interest to the long roof line. Green ivy creeps up the house in several places, breaking up the brick.

When I turn back around, I see Levi sitting on the low wall. He pulls me until I'm between his legs with my back to his front. Levi wraps his arms loosely around me and settles his hands on my stomach. "How are you doing, little raven?"

"I'm fine," I respond automatically. I never want Bishop or my family to worry about me, so my default setting is insisting that I'm all good.

Am I fine?

I really don't know at this point. Too much has happened for my exhausted brain to process right now. So, it's future Izzy's problem to deal with.

Levi hums, like he doesn't believe me, but doesn't push. "How long have you been able to heal ghosts?"

"Since I got my magic." That was not a fun discovery. Little me was freaked out by the gory ghosts that wandered into my room at all hours of the night. Only healing them ever made them go away, so that's when I found out I could do that.

Luckily, Aggie found me within six months of me developing my magic. She was able to keep the spirits at bay better than I did.

"How old were you when you got it?"

"Seven." When Levi doesn't say anything, I get defensive.

"I know I'm weird, okay? I don't need any comments about it. I'd change it if I could, trust me."

The only time I've ever prayed to any being that would listen is when I found out what would happen to my family if anyone discovered my magic. I've spent so long wishing, praying, and hoping for my magic to disappear.

It never works.

"That's not what I was going to say, little raven," Levi tells me sternly. He flattens his palms on my stomach and presses me tightly against him as reassurance. I feel something hard nudge my back, but I'm distracted by what Levi says next. "I was just pondering what you are because it's clear you're not just a spirit mage. I wondered if your magic could've come from my realm."

"What do you mean, I'm not a spirit mage? I'm a mage and can see ghosts. Ergo, I'm a spirit mage." It would sure make my life easier if I weren't, but no other mage type can see ghosts.

"I didn't say you weren't a spirit mage. I said you're not *just* a spirit mage. You know healing ghosts isn't a typical spirit mage power. And I'm betting you have other abilities that aren't typical for spirit mages too." With my back against Levi's front, I can feel his deep voice rumbling through me. It makes me shiver a little.

I really don't need him knowing the full extent of my magic. I'm already enough of an abomination as it is. In an attempt to redirect the conversation, I ask, "What is your realm?"

"That's… difficult to explain."

"Can you tell me what you are, then?" I know he's not a mage, but he hasn't told me what he is yet. I'm dying of curiosity.

"I'd need to show you, and we don't have space for that here."

I huff at his evasive answer. "What about how old you are?"

"I'm far older than you can comprehend, little raven."

"So, you're hundreds of years old?" I guess.

Levi chuckles. "No. Much older."

My eyes widen. Supernaturals typically live hundreds of years. It's longer than humans but apparently shorter than Levi's lifespan. "Thousands? Millions?"

"Mm, getting closer."

"Billions?" I squeak.

"Somewhere around there."

My jaw drops, and my poor little mind can't quite comprehend that one of my mates is billions of years old. "Holy shit. Do you remember the beginning of the universe?"

Levi barks out a laugh. "I'm not quite that old, little raven. I know the same thing you do about the beginning of the universes. Something caused magic to explode into all the universes. Everything in each universe is just a remnant of this explosion."

"There's more than one universe?"

"Of course. There are many other universes out there, like mine."

"You're super casual about dropping that bomb, screech owl. Most people on Earth don't know that there are other populated universes."

"That's awfully self-centered of you Earth dwellers."

I snort. "That about sums up most people's attitudes here. Do you remember the Earth forming?"

Levi tilts his head in thought. "I'm not sure. I've seen many planets form in my lifetime. Earth may or may not have been one of them. All of the ones that can support life form basically the same way. Balls of pure magic attract rocks and other debris. The weight of these rocks eventually causes the whole mass to heat up, forming a molten surface that cools over time.

"Then the tectonic plates shift and change the crust until the magic at the core starts seeping to the surface. This magic escaping is what allows all life to begin, like the microbes, plants, animals, and eventually people on this planet."

"I did pay attention in mage geology class, demon boy." I may not be as old as him, but I'm not completely clueless. "I even know that, when anything dies, the magic that sustained it returns to the core."

Levi misses my teasing tone and continues on with his history lesson. It's cute how excited he is to discuss all of this. "Exactly. Earth, however, is unique in the number of creatures with the bare minimum magic. Humans and their technology have altered magic availability in a way I've never seen before."

Before five or six thousand years ago, all people had magic. They were all mages, shifters, fae, vampires, and others. Once people started messing with technology to master nature and wage war on others, their access to magic declined.

This magical decay created the magicless humans that dominate the planet today. While most of them don't know about magic or how it powers the world, some do. Those who know, like the Knights of Aeneas, are obsessed with finding a way to have magic again. They also want to drain anyone who does have magic, so we try to avoid those crazies.

I didn't know that the gradual decrease of magic was an Earth specific thing, though. "That doesn't sound good."

"It probably doesn't bode well for the future of humanity, but it likely won't affect the planet itself in the long term." Levi is tracing patterns on my stomach with one of his fingers. I can't decide if I like it or if it tickles.

It's crazy that he can talk about the extinction of everyone here so casually. Then again, he's lived far longer than I can really understand. One planet's worth of creatures being wiped out probably isn't a big deal to him. I'm sure he's seen far worse.

That does beg the question, though. Why is he here?

"Why'd you come to Earth, screech owl?"

Levi blows out a breath that ruffles the top of my hair. "I came to check in on someone for my brother's wife, but I had trouble locating her."

I try to tamp down my jealousy that Levi was looking for another girl. Since he was on an errand for his sister-in-law, he's probably related to whoever he's searching for. No need to hunt the random lady down and kill her. Yet. "Oh. Did you find her?"

"No. I'm still searching."

"Is that why you work for the university?"

"No."

Getting Levi to answer questions is like pulling teeth. I huff in frustration. "Why, then?"

Levi sighs. "As soon as I came to this realm, I realized my mate was here. I found a position at HGU to get to know you while keeping an eye on you."

My eyes widen in surprise. "Why didn't you tell me?"

"Would you really have been receptive to it?"

I shake my head instead of saying anything because we both know the answer. If I knew he was my mate, I'd have dropped his class and avoided him at all costs. Even though he's right, I still don't like being lied to for an entire semester.

Before I can grouse about him lying to me, I realize something else. Levi was probably pretty disappointed to find out his mate was posing as a magicless loser. "I'm sure I wasn't what you imagined your mate would be," I say in a light tone to try to mask how much it hurts. He was probably majorly let down to get stuck with me, of all people.

"No, you weren't." My stomach drops, and my eyes burn. "You're so much better than I ever could've imagined."

My throat constricts, and I fight to stuff all my sappy emotions down. He can't honestly mean that. Levi is probably just being sweet because that's what mates do. They lie and say they're happy to have you. Even when they'd be better off if they never met you.

"But I'm just a twenty-one-year-old bumbling her way through life." I am so not suited to be the mate to a dude from another universe. Hell, I'm not even suited to being an alpha mate, if we're being real here.

What the fuck was the universe thinking when it chose my mates?

It wasn't, obviously. Or the universe was high. Or wasted. Or having a midlife crisis.

"We're all bumbling our way through life. That never changes, even when you're as old as I am. But you, little raven, are wise beyond your years. You're also kind, empathetic, fiercely protective of your loved ones, have a great sense of humor, and a strength that's far beyond anyone I've ever met."

Levi hears my quiet sniffles at his sweet words and turns me around to face him. His forehead wrinkles in concern as he takes in my drawn expression. After cupping my face with both hands, Levi swipes his thumbs comfortingly over my cheeks.

I lean into his touch while keeping my eyes locked on his. He leans down slightly, and my gaze flicks to his lips. My lids start drifting closed as I lift up to press my lips to his. Before I reach him, a loud bang sounds from behind Levi, startling both of us.

CHAPTER 33

IZZY

"*S*unshine! Just the woman I was looking for!" Archer grins at me over Levi's shoulder as he saunters over to us.

Levi sighs deeply before pressing a kiss to the top of my head. "I'll let you have your time with the pup, little raven. But we will be finishing this later."

My eyes widen at the heat I see in his gaze. At his promise, arousal snakes up my spine and pools in my core. Before I have a chance to respond, Levi is striding back to the house.

When I shake myself out of my horny fog, I see Archer standing right in front of me. "Hey, sunny boy."

He gives me a wide smile that lights up his eyes at the nickname. "Wanna come to the lake with me?"

I can't help my grin at his question. "Abso-fucking-lutely!"

Archer chuckles at my enthusiasm. He grabs one of my hands and leads me into the forest. We don't talk as we walk through the trees. I'm too busy admiring the pretty fall leaves and the cute wildlife to say anything.

After around ten minutes of walking in companionable

silence, we reach the end of the wooded area. A sparkling blue lake stretches as far as I can see in all directions. I can just make out the bank on the other side. The lake is way bigger than I thought from my peek of it earlier.

We veer to the left toward a wooden dock. Archer walks us to the end of the dock, then drops my hand to kneel down and unlace his black skate shoes. Once he peels off his matching black socks and rolls up his jeans, Archer sits on the edge of the dock and dips his feet into the water.

"Isn't it cold?" I ask. It is October. While the days can be warm enough, the nights get chilly. I'd imagine the water isn't balmy, like it would be in the summer.

He tilts his head back to grin at me. "Shifters run hot, so it's not cold to me. If you're not too much of a scaredy-cat, you can try dipping your feet in to see."

I glare at the frustrating wolf because he knows exactly what he's doing. I have a really hard time backing down when I'm challenged. While I'd like to blame that personality flaw on my magic, I'm pretty sure most of it's just me.

After I toe off my unlaced white Chucks, I pull my white ankle socks off and hesitantly approach Archer. Sitting down on the edge, I reluctantly lower my legs until my toes dip into the chilly water. "Fuck me, that's cold!"

Archer snorts at my reaction. "It's not that cold, sunshine."

I'm too busy tucking my now freezing toes under my legs to say anything. For a few minutes, we sit quietly, absorbing the peace of the water and the nature around us. The sun is sitting low on the horizon, making the sky bleed orange, yellow, and purple.

I break our peaceful quiet when I ask, "You're not going to try to pry into my feelings about the whole ghost debacle?"

He huffs out a laugh. "Nah. I figured you got enough of that from Luca and Bishop."

243

"And Cain," I mumble.

"Really? Cain?" When I look over at him, Archer's brows are sky-high in surprise.

"Yeah. I don't know why you're surprised. Cain's the sweet one who always wants to talk about my feelings." My lips tip up slightly, thinking about the thoughtful wolf. While he's gruff and quiet on the outside, he has a gooey marshmallow center.

Archer looks at me for a moment before bursting out laughing. He doubles over, he's laughing so hard. I just stare at him, wondering if he's lost his mind. Eventually, Archer gets his laughter under control. He turns to me with a wide smile. "Cain, sweet? That's fucking hilarious. I don't think he's ever been called sweet in his life. Unhinged? Definitely. Terrifying? That's more like it. Sweet? Absolutely not."

"What're you talking about? He's definitely the sweetest out of all of you, no offense or anything."

"Oh, babycakes, you're adorable. I'm not sure how he convinced you he's sweet, but he's not. You can ask anyone in the pack who the most unhinged member is, and they'll all say Cain." I look at Archer skeptically. While I don't have a problem with Cain being unhinged, I don't really see it. Archer sighs. "You heard of the Reaper?"

"Yeah." I only know of the Reaper because I do stuff for Elemental.

The Reaper is some psycho who goes around dolling out vigilante justice in extremely violent and gruesome ways. Rhys and Bishop are so jealous of him. While the Reaper gets to annihilate any supernatural scumbags they want, my brother and Bishop are stuck taking clients that pay. Elemental is a business, after all.

"That's Cain."

I whip my head around to stare at Archer in surprise. "No

way. Cain's not old enough to have been doing that for, like, fifteen years."

"Cain's the same age as Luca, but he started taking out shitty people when he was fifteen."

"Why?"

Archer blows out a breath and turns to stare at the rippling surface of the lake. After deliberating what to say for a moment, Archer tells me, "Cain was going through some stuff. It's not really my place to tell you about it, sunshine."

"That's fair." Even though I want to know everything about Cain, I respect Archer not telling me things that aren't his to share. My heart hurts for Cain, though. He must've been full of so much anger and pain to start taking out bad guys as a teen.

"Summer or winter?" Archer asks me out of nowhere.

"Fall." I can't help the grin at picking neither of the answers. It's fun to be difficult.

But fall is my favorite season. I love the chilly mornings and warm afternoons, the colorful leaves, any excuse to wear one of Bishop's flannels, and all the pumpkin things I can bake.

"Movies or TV shows?"

"Books." I'll happily watch good TV or movies, but I love reading. Books transport you to another world in a way nothing else really can.

"Batman or Superman?"

"Iron Man." I'd choose Tony Stark over Bruce Wayne or Clark Kent any day. Archer grins at my answers.

I shiver a little now that the sun's set. Even though I'm wearing Luca's sweatshirt, I only have shorts and a bra under it. Despite being a bit cold, I don't want to go in yet. "Tell me something no one else knows about you."

Instead of the silly response I expect, Archer thinks for a second before answering quietly. "I resented Luca for the

245

longest time. He's the perfect one. Luca's effortlessly good at everything he does, and everybody loves him. Our parents, teachers, the pack, and women. I was always the second choice, just Luca's shadow."

"What changed?" I whisper, unused to seeing the playful wolf so serious.

"Well, the first thing that changed it was that I got into Muay Thai at fourteen. I've never been very good at school. Teachers would always get frustrated with me struggling with the material. But Muay Thai and other martial arts were so easy to pick up. After a few months of practicing, I was winning against fully grown shifters. While Luca's good at MMA now, he had a much harder time learning it than I did. It was the first time I ever felt good at anything. It also taught me discipline."

Archer pauses for a moment, lost in his thoughts.

"I'd love to watch you fight sometime," I tell him earnestly.

A ghost of a smile crosses his lips before he shakes himself out of his thoughts. "Losing our parents was also a wake-up call. While we both lost our dads and mom, Luca was the only one who was expected to have it all together. The pack expected him to have all the answers. At twenty-five, Luca had to lead nine hundred people, while having no time to grieve for losing most of our family.

"I realized then why Luca was always perfect. He had to be. As the future alpha, everyone held him to higher standards than the rest of us. All this time, I'd been resenting my perfect older brother when he likely resented me, the goofy fuckup. Unlike him, I at least had some freedom to do what I wanted. Since then, I've been trying to pick up the slack. I want him to have more time to just be Luca, not Alpha Nightshade."

When Archer finishes speaking, I can't resist the urge to

hug him. In a clumsy move that makes an exorcism look smooth, I straddle the wolf and wrap my arms around him. "I'm sorry, sunny boy, about all of it. Coming in second your whole life and losing your parents are both awful in different ways."

My lips are pressed against the smooth skin of his throat, making my voice come out muffled.

He laughs softly while hugging me back. One of his hands spears through my blonde hair to hold my face to him. "It's not your fault, sunshine."

"I know. I'm still sorry, though. You should know, sunny boy, that anyone who couldn't see how awesome you are is stupid. Your joy and exuberance and zest for life is contagious. You know how to cheer me up, even when I'm at my lowest. You make any situation so much better and all the bad parts of life easier. While you may not see it, you add so much to your pack and to my life. Everything would be miserable and dull and gray without you."

"Fuck, Izzy," Archer rasps as he buries his face in my neck. I put one of my hands on the back of his neck and run my fingers through the silky strands at the nape of his neck. "Who knew you were so sweet under your thorns?"

"Tell anyone about it, and I'll kill you." I can't have anyone knowing I have a sappy side.

He snorts. "There's my girl." My heart beats a little harder in my chest at being called Archer's anything.

I stay on his lap for a while, soaking up his warmth and his vanilla citrus scent. We don't talk, content to sit in silence with each other. Eventually, I start shivering too hard to hide from Archer. "Sorry," I manage to get out through my chattering teeth.

"You cold, sunshine?"

"Just a little." It would be more convincing if I weren't shivering so hard my voice comes out wobbly.

"Let's get you inside, then." He waits for me to nod before standing. I squeak, expecting to fall. Archer's strong arms hold me effortlessly as he straightens. He lets me down, so we can both put on our shoes. Archer then picks me up again, and he wraps my legs around his waist before turning to the forest. With one arm under my ass and the other around my back, I feel secure in his arms.

As he starts walking to the forest, I remind him, "I have legs that work. I can walk."

"I'm aware, sunshine. Lemme hold you. Please?" His voice wavers on the last word, and my resolve to do it myself crumbles. I nod into his neck, and we walk the rest of the way back to the house like that.

I expect Archer to put me down when we reach their mansion. Instead, he supports me with one arm and opens the back door with the other. I'm impressed that he's able to carry me to the stairs, up them, and to Luca's room without even a huff or a puff.

He shuts the door behind us and lets me slide down him. When I turn around, I suck in a surprised breath at seeing my other four mates shirtless. Luca is in a pair of gray sweatpants at his desk. Levi is sitting on the edge of the bed in only basketball shorts. Cain and Bishop are whispering about something on the sofa but stop as soon as they see me. They're both in just sweats as well.

All of them are looking at me. "Um, hi?"

I glance behind me at Archer for some idea of what I'm supposed to do. But I find him stripping down to his boxers. He is one fine specimen of a man, all tanned skin, defined pecs, and rock-hard abs. My eyes momentarily snag on the wolf tattoo on his chest that both Luca and Cain have. It must have something to do with their pack if they all have it.

When I turn around, I'm startled by Luca standing right in front of me. I jump and press my hand to my racing heart.

"Jesus, fuck! Make some fucking noise, dude!" I need to put bells on the wolves. That way, they won't be able to sneak up on me.

Luca just chuckles at me, the asshole. "I made plenty of noise, wildcat. You just weren't paying attention." While he's talking, Luca puts his hands on my waist and pulls me tight against his front. I fight the urge to lean into the big wolf. "Are you ready for bed?"

As soon as he mentions sleeping, I realize just how tired I am. I woke up a few hours ago, but I'm already drained. I'm usually low on energy for a few days after using up all my magic, so it makes sense. "Yeah," I manage to answer around a big yawn. "Where am I sleeping?"

"In here. We all are."

I raise my eyebrows at him and turn to look at his king-size bed that definitely won't fit six people. Only, I don't see a king bed. Instead, there's a massive one taking up a sizable portion of Luca's huge room. A very smug-looking Levi is staring back at me.

"Is making beds massive a perk of being older than time itself?"

After snorting, Levi shakes his head at me. "I'm not that old, little raven. And it's a perk of my magic. It has nothing to do with age."

I guess that means I'll never get cool powers like him. Lame. I want a refund on my super uncool powers. Maybe there's a magic manager I can speak with to fix it.

While I'm lost in my tired thoughts, Luca lets go of me. He walks into his closet and comes out a moment later holding a deep blue T-shirt. It's slightly faded and looks super soft. Luca hands it to me. "You can sleep in this tonight. Go change in my bathroom, then we'll get you to bed."

Too tired to argue with him, I do as he says, much to his

surprise. When I walk back into the room, I see all of them already in the bed. There's a space in the middle between Luca and Cain that I'm guessing is for me.

Padding over to it, I knee walk toward the head of the bed. Luca holds the covers open for me. Once I'm under them, Luca turns me to face Cain and starts spooning me. Cain snags one of my hands, and someone else turns out the light.

"'Night, boys," I mumble, my eyes already feeling heavy.

I get a chorus of *good nights* from all my mates. My eyes then slip shut, and I fall into a deep, dreamless sleep, safe in between all of them.

CHAPTER 34

IZZY

"*I* hate this place," I grumble as I gaze up at asshole central. Oh, I'm sorry, I mean council HQ. Same thing, really.

For the past week, I've been oscillating between being completely and utterly terrified that all of my mates know what I am and being hopeful.

I know it's naïve to hope that there's some way we all make it out of this, so I try to crush the tiny flame of hope in my chest. Yet it's still there, taunting me with everything I want that's just out of reach.

Shaking myself out of my thoughts, I gaze up at the ostentatious council compound.

While the sandstone walls and slate roof are fairly tame, the fountains that bubble out front are made of pure gold. Inside, the floors are gold marble, encrusted with diamonds in some places. The gold theme continues with gold-leaf-accented ceilings, crystal and gold chandeliers that light every room, and gilt frame portraits of all the current and former council dudes that line almost every wall.

Along with all the gold, the council headquarters is also

massive. It's about a ten-minute walk to go from one end to the other of a single wing. The council compound has three separate wings. One wing is where they conduct council business, like the monthly council meeting, and councilor offices. Another wing is the mage prison, and the last is for experimental magic. I'm betting we'll find what we're looking for in the experimental magic wing.

Dad turns around and gives me a look to shut it while looking pointedly at the few stragglers rushing inside. I mime zipping my lips, and he just shakes his head at me. We're showing up late, so fewer people see us here. My dad is going to have to book it to get to the council chamber on time.

We walk up the stairs to the wrought-iron front door. The intricate scrollwork is dusted with gold leaf. Just in case you forgot that the council is rich for a moment. Dad pulls open the door and ushers us through.

Just inside the door are two mage security guards. They nod politely to Dad, Bishop, and Levi and sneer at me. I sneer right back because fuck them. The amount of power a person has shouldn't determine how they're treated.

Bishop subtly nudges me forward, probably worried I'll get in a confrontation with the guards. I may make bad decisions on the regular, but I'm not that stupid. The council headquarters is the absolute last place I'd choose to show magic. While I'm powerful, I don't think I'd win against the hundreds of mages crawling all over the place.

Rolling my eyes at Bishop, I glance down at my black Converse to avoid meeting anyone else's gaze. None of the mages will be happy that I'm here, so it's best if I just try to be invisible. There's only so much of their shit I can take quietly. But I can totally go an entire day without getting into a fight. Hopefully.

My dad insisted I dress up so I don't stand out. While I'm

wearing a black skater dress, I refused to wear heels. We compromised with my black Chucks instead of my white ones. See? I can be reasonable.

Bishop and Levi are both in black suits. While Bishop wears a white dress shirt with a black tie, Levi is wearing a blood-red button-up and black tie. Levi looks kind of like what I think Hades would if he were hot. Or real, I guess. I dig it, though.

We pause when we come to a crossroads. My dad wraps me up in a quick hug, his dark blue velvet robes swirling around him as he moves. "Be safe, Izzy. Don't take risks. Get out of here the second you sense any danger, okay?" he whispers into my hair.

Luca had me make similar promises before he let me head out today. The big wolf is not happy about me being in danger without him. He didn't try to stop me, though, which is a pretty big win in my book.

While I have no intention of bailing at the first sign of danger, I nod at my dad to ease his mind. Dad then takes off down the hallway directly in front of us.

The three of us turn right. That's where they house the magic labs. While the council says it's for developing new ways to keep mages safe, I highly doubt that's the only type of magic they're experimenting with. Most of the crotchety old men on the council would happily sacrifice the entire mage race for a drop more of power. These labs are probably more for power enhancement than safety advances.

None of us put up shields or cloaks because we don't know what magic detection measures they might have. The council is super paranoid, so we're operating on the assumption there will be lots of booby traps. There's also no way to portal in or out of the council headquarters to protect against a magical invasion. So, we have to enter and exit through the front entrance.

It's only a few minutes of walking before we see an industrial door that's out of place in the nineteenth-century extravagance of the rest of the council estate.

"You seeing this, Aiden?" I whisper, knowing the tiny earpiece I'm wearing will pick up my quiet words. A small camera on Bishop's dress shirt gives our support team a visual.

While we could talk with our team on the outside with magic, mages expect that. Security measures at council HQ are designed to stop magical attacks or espionage. They don't think about attacks with tech, even though they use magic-enhanced tech to secure everything.

Technology is one of the mage world's biggest blind spots. While magic can do everything tech can do and more, technology can now do a lot of what magic can do. Tech now replaces a ton of tasks that were huge magic sucks, like viewing places from a distance and keeping doors locked. Even as more and more mages use technology, they still don't think to guard against tech attacks or things like tiny microphones or cameras.

It's baffling but super convenient. Elemental makes use of the tech blind spot to get a lot done.

"Yes, sir. I'm looping the cameras now. Gimme a moment to unlock the door," Aiden's disembodied voice replies in my ear.

"I'm not a sir," I correct him.

"Oh, trust me, the wolves anxiously watching my every move are well aware of your titties."

"For fuck's sake, Aiden," I grouse at my embarrassing brother.

I turn to commiserate with Bishop about how annoying Aiden is when I find his gaze locked on my boobs. They do look quite nice in this dress, if I do say so myself. Bishop slowly drags his stare up my chest to my face. When we lock eyes, his baby blues are full of heat he doesn't try to hide. My cheeks grow pink under his intense stare.

"Doors unlocked. You're good to go." Aiden's voice shakes me free of Bishop's bewitching gaze.

I hurry toward the door to avoid any awkward conversation. I don't get more than a few steps before someone grabs the back of my dress to stop me. My arms windmill as I try to keep from falling over.

Bishop's rainy forest scent surrounds me as he presses his front to my back. He puts his hands on my waist to steady me. "Where do you think you're going? You agreed not to rush in first, sweetheart. I expect you to keep your word," Bishop rasps in my ear, his warm breath caressing the side of my face.

His deep voice feels like it arrows straight to my core. My thighs clench as I fight a shiver at his words. I bite my cheek to keep from asking *or what* because that's not a game I want to play with him. Not now and probably not ever. My horny self doesn't need to know whether Bishop would enjoy punishing me as much as I think I'd like it.

Fuck. Right now is really not the time to be getting turned on.

"Sorry," I manage to force out through my suddenly dry mouth. It comes out breathy, but it's the best I can do right now.

Bishop lets out a deep chuckle, knowing exactly what he's doing to me. With a warning squeeze on my waist, he strides calmly ahead of me to the door. It's entirely unfair that Bishop gets to be so unaffected while I'm trying not to combust.

"Are you okay, little raven?" Levi's voice is tinged with amusement. When I turn to glare at him behind me, one side of his mouth kicks up in a small grin.

"Just fantastic, screech owl. Thanks so much for asking." I

give him an overly sweet smile to go with my sarcasm. Levi huffs a quiet laugh before nudging me forward with his hand on my lower back. I go willingly because we really don't have time to waste. Who knows when someone could come wandering down this hall.

When we reach the door, Bishop is there, waiting for us. He heaves open the large metal door and peeks inside before waving us through. The sterile white room is empty. It's the end of the workday, plus a council meeting is going on. We were banking on the place being pretty deserted.

Things are going according to plan. At least, for now. Here's hoping our luck continues.

I glance around the room, taking in the white tiles, white walls, and white ceiling. The long tables in the center of the room are also white. Bright fluorescent lights harshly illuminate the windowless room.

Shelves line three of the walls. They're filled with an assortment of beakers, jars, and other scientific-looking lab equipment. Most of the glass containers are empty, but some have dried plants or murky liquids in them. We poke around the shelves for several minutes without finding anything.

"Think we should move on?" I don't turn around to look at the boys, because I'm having a staring contest with an eyeball floating in green liquid. Yep, an actual fucking human eyeball just chilling out on the shelf. I probably don't want to know why they have an eye in a jar.

I've worked on tons of potions with Anya. None of them ever called for any type of eye, much less a human one. The eye isn't for any normal potion, but maybe there's a reasonable explanation for it being here.

"Yeah, it doesn't look like there's anything here." Bishop's voice sounds to my left. I finally rip my gaze from the creepiest jar I've seen and glance at him. "You good, Izzy?"

I give him a sharp nod. "Yep." As weird as the eyeball is,

that's far from the worst thing I've seen while doing work for Elemental.

Bishop's sky-blue eyes bounce between mine a few times before he turns around. He heads down the hallway on the far side of the room. That's the only wall without shelving. The bland white wall is broken up by a large, cased opening.

Levi and I trail behind Bishop. We wander down the seemingly never-ending hallway until we reach a door on the right. Bishop jiggles the silver handle, but the door doesn't budge. "Can you open this, Aiden?"

"Yepperoni, bro." I sigh at Aiden. Why is he like this? I'm pretty sure he's deathly allergic to responding to anything like a normal person. After a beat, he tells us, "It's unlocked. Have fun, my guys."

"Thanks, man." Bishop pushes open the door and freezes. "What the fuck?"

CHAPTER 35

IZZY

*B*ishop is frozen in the doorway, so I can't see what he's looking at. I push lightly on his back to get him to move. My touch seems to break through whatever's going on in his mind. He turns back to me. "You don't need to see this, Izzy."

I raise my brows at him. "You don't get to decide that, St. James. I'm not yours right now. I'm just another mage on a mission with you." No one outside of my family and my mates should be listening in right now, but I'm careful not to say *mate* just in case anyone is.

While I get that he wants to protect me, I'm sick of everyone thinking I'm fragile. I don't need or want to be protected. All I want is to be respected as an equal.

He chuckles humorlessly. "You never stop being mine, sweetheart." Bishop scrubs a hand over his face before blowing out a breath. "Fine. Have a look. I don't think this is what we came for, though."

After Bishop steps farther inside the room, I'm able to get a good look at what he didn't want me to see. I gasp.

The room is more like a small warehouse than a room,

complete with a concrete floor, bare rafters, and no windows. It's probably around a hundred feet long and fifty feet wide. The part that stops me in my tracks are the cages lining the walls of the huge space. There have to be hundreds of cages filled with unconscious people.

All of the people are dressed in only hospital gowns. Their minimal clothing highlights the bruising, cuts, and dried blood covering them from head to toe. I'm not even sure some of them are still alive, with the amount of blood in their cages.

"What the fuck is this?" I whisper to no one in particular. Though the eyeball earlier wasn't close to the worst thing I've seen on missions, this definitely is.

I wander closer to the cage directly to my left. I'm not sure whether it's a good or bad thing that I can see the faint rise and fall of the woman's chest. It would probably be a kinder fate to be dead, honestly. Along with the cuts and bruises, she also has a broken arm, that's twisted the wrong way, and shattered fingers.

I clench my hands into fists, so I don't reach in there and heal her. Whoever is doing this to them would probably notice if her arm and fingers miraculously healed. That'd just mean more pain for her in the long run.

"I don't know, Izzy. Jesus fucking Christ. I knew the council was bad, but this is a whole other level of fucked up."

Bishop can fucking say that again.

"We have to leave them behind, don't we?" My voice is barely audible, but both Levi and Bishop hear it.

"Yeah, we do." Bishop stares at me like he's worried I'm going to lose control.

He's not wrong to be concerned. Pure fury at the council burns like acid through my veins as I take in yet another reminder of their corruption and depravity.

Losing control won't help anything, though. It'd be satisfying to storm into the council chambers and take out as many of them as I can. But that won't help these people or affect real change on the council.

Squeezing my eyes tightly for a moment, I try to gather myself. But the anger burning brightly in my chest isn't soothed. I open my eyes in defeat and slowly walk down the length of the left side.

As I walk, I memorize the faces of everyone I pass. I burn them into my memory, so they aren't forgotten. We may have to leave them, but I won't forget them. I vow to get them out as soon as I can.

On my walk through, I also realize why Bishop doesn't think this is what we're looking for. Most of the people in the cages aren't young mages. There are some kids in the cages, but I'm not sure they're even mages. Some of the people in the cages are too bulky, too pale, or have too pointed of ears to be mages.

How in the hell did they collect other races to experiment on?

When I reach the end of this side, I walk along the back wall and down the opposite side, doing the exact same thing. After I complete my walk through, I spend who knows how long staring sightlessly at the boy in the last cage.

"Say the word, and I'll get all of them out. Fuck the conse- quences. Just tell me what you need me to do." I turn around to see Levi standing right behind me. He's staring down at me with concern shining in his crimson eyes. I've only seen his eyes completely red a few times before, so this horror show must be fucking with his head too.

"We can't." My voice breaks. "Saving all of them means we won't ever figure out what's going on here or with the mage development program. We can't afford to tip them off right now."

Levi clenches his jaw before pulling me into a hard hug.

He squeezes me tight, and I inhale his smoky scent. "What can I do to help?"

"I don't know," I mumble into his dress-shirt-covered chest. "I just want whoever's doing this to pay." What I'm not saying is that I want to kill whoever it is. Painfully. I want them to feel every ounce of agony they've caused others.

"They will, little raven. Trust me, even death won't offer an escape. I swear it." He sounds absolutely convinced of that, even though there's no way to know what happens to people after they die.

I pull back to look at him. "You can't promise that."

"I can, and I will."

"How?"

Levi blows out a breath and shakes his head.

After staring at him for a moment, I realize he's not going to answer right now. With a nod, I step out of Levi's embrace. I need to get out of this room before I do something we'll regret. Stalking past a concerned Bishop, I make my way back to the unassuming white hallway. "You got all of that, Aiden?"

"Yeah." When even Aiden doesn't crack a joke, you know things are really messed up.

Without waiting for the boys, I angrily stride toward the next door. Testing the handle, I find that it's unlocked. When I go to push it open, Bishop is there to block me. "Fucking stop, Isabel. I get that you're angry. I am too. But being reckless and getting yourself hurt or worse won't fucking help them. You need to get it together, or you're done here."

If I were calmer, I'd recognize that all Bishop is trying to do is help. But right now, he's a convenient target for my anger. All the heartbreak and rage and helplessness come out at him.

My rage burns so hot that it turns into icy cold fury. Instead of yelling, I stare at him with the freezing anger in my eyes. My voice comes out detached. "We both know I'd win in a power fight, St. James. Try to bench me and see what fucking happens."

Bishop's eyes blaze with barely controlled anger at my defiance. He opens his mouth to lay into me when Levi beats him to it. "Little raven, I'm always on your side. But I have to agree with the mage on this. Rushing into situations when you're blinded by anger isn't smart. While you'd win on pure power alone against the mage, we both know you're not a match for the two of us together."

Levi's words pierce through my rage-induced fog and arrow straight to my heart. I can't keep the hurt out of my voice when I ask, "You'd choose him over me?"

"No. I'll always choose you, little raven. Even if it means going against what you want. Don't make me stop you. Please." Levi's eyes are back to pitch black, but the red rings around his pupils are bigger than usual. His eyes silently plead with me to calm down.

While Bishop's anger just eggs me on, Levi's quiet resignation starts to break through my rioting emotions. Sighing, I close my eyes and try to ground myself. Breathing through the anger helps it recede enough that I can think somewhat clearly.

We don't have limitless time. Every time Bishop stops me at doors, we waste what little time we do have. I need to calm the fuck down and go with the plan we agreed on. My anger isn't more important than finding out what's happening to the young mages.

Blowing out a breath, I gesture for Bishop to open the door. "Any time now, St. James. We have shit to do," I snark. I'm still unreasonably pissed at him and unable to say something that isn't snappy.

"We're fucking talking about this when we get home, Isabel. This isn't fucking over." With his warning delivered,

Bishop strides into the room without a single backward glance.

While I'm pissed off on the outside, I'm hurting on the inside. Bishop is never angry with me and never raises his voice at me. In the past month and a half, he's yelled at me more than the other fifteen years I've known him combined. I feel like I'm losing my best friend, and I don't know what to do about it.

A few tears trail down my cheeks, and I wipe them away before anyone can see them. This is not the time to break down. Pulling on all of the internal strength I have, I shove my heartache into the furthest corner of my mind.

I look up and see Levi waiting in the hallway, concern lining his handsome face.

"I'm fine." I try to blank my face, so he won't see that I'm lying.

Levi's lips twitch up in a small, sad smile. "You're not a very good liar, little raven."

"So I've been told. We don't have time for me to be anything other than fine, demon boy," I tell him quietly. "Can we just do what we need to do now and talk later?"

He searches my face for a moment. Eventually, he nods. "We can. After you, little raven."

I walk ahead of him into the room Bishop disappeared into. Unlike the house of horrors we were just in, this room is pretty standard fare for a lab. Tables, beakers, microscopes, and other lab equipment are all we find in the smallish space.

The other rooms we check in this white-tiled hallway are much the same. I'm beginning to think we aren't going to find anything about the mage development council when the hallway dead-ends at a steel door. It has locks upon locks upon more locks. Someone really doesn't want people stumbling on whatever is behind this door.

"Can you unlock it, Aiden?" I ask. "There's like eleven billion fucking locks on this thing."

"Can I? You wound me, Izzy, always doubting my skills. Of course, I fucking can. Just gimme a minute or two." I studiously avoid looking at Bishop as we wait silently for a few minutes. "Alrighty, the door's unlocked."

"Thanks, bro," I respond.

I let Bishop go first. He opens the door to a dark set of stairs. There's a bit of light coming from the bottom of the creepy staircase, but it's only just enough to see by. The three of us carefully pick our way down the winding stone steps.

When we reach the bottom, we're in another hallway. The walls, ceiling, and floors are rough gray stone, very unlike the sterility of the wing above us.

We can't go anywhere else other than directly forward, so we head toward the faint light. It's farther away than it looks. After walking for five or so minutes, we reach a large cavern. It looks like some sort of natural cave formation, with its rough gray walls and domed ceiling. It's empty, save for what looks like a hospital setup. There's a gurney, lines going from the person lying on the bed, and monitoring equipment that's beeping.

The guy on the gurney is in rough shape. He's bleeding from cuts all over his body, and his clothes are torn and bloody. His curly blond hair lays limply across his forehead, and his breathing is shallow.

I hesitantly walk closer to the guy. My heart stops when I see a face I never thought I'd see again. "Daniel?"

CHAPTER 36

IZZY

*M*y legs buckle underneath me as I'm bombarded by memories. Before I can hit the floor, strong arms band around me, with one arm wrapped around my shoulders and the other around my midsection. As I kneel on the floor, I'm held to a strong chest.

But I can't pay attention to any of that.

All I can see are flashes of him. His gap-toothed smile, bright enough to light up the whole town. His infectious laughter that helped me find joy when it felt like I hadn't smiled in years. His warm hand in mine, dragging me from adventure to adventure. His green dinosaur shirt he donned as often as he could, even after he wore holes in it. His perpetually grass-stained jeans because he loved being outside more than anything.

The happy memories play like a death march in my mind, moving closer and closer to that day. I want to scream at them to stop.

I want to stay in the good times, like when we played in the creek so long one fall day, our toes turned blue. Or when we tried to bake a cake for my mom and only succeeded in turning the kitchen into a disaster. Or when he'd sing like the angel he was while I clumsily played guitar to back him up.

No matter how hard I try to stay in the good times, I still end up at that day on the playground. I can smell the earthy scent of decaying leaves in the fall. I can feel the warm sunshine on my chilled cheeks. I can see his small body lifeless on the ground. I can hear my scream ringing out when I can't get him to wake up. I can taste the salt of my tears that didn't stop flowing for ages.

After I've spent what feels like an eternity reliving the proof of just how evil I am, I slam back into reality. Through the tears clinging to my lashes, my eyes sluggishly focus on Daniel's battered form on the gurney. I try to get to my feet when I realize I can help him this time, but strong arms keep me in place. I thrash around, desperately trying to break free.

"Let me go!" I scream, the sound full of pain and anguish. "I can fix it! I can save him this time! Please," I beg, my voice breaking.

"Hey. Hey, Izzy. It's not him, sweetheart. It's not Daniel. Look at his eyes. They're brown. They aren't blue." Bishop's rough voice tries to reason with me as he holds me tightly to him. It takes a moment to see that the boy's sightless eyes are open, and they're not sky blue. Bishop's strong arms are all that's keeping me from shattering on the cave floor when I realize he's right. It's not Daniel. My sobs echo through the cavern. With his lips pressed into my hair, Bishop whispers, "You're breaking my heart, baby."

It feels like I was given the most precious gift, only to have it ripped away seconds later. My heart shreds as I grieve again for the boy I didn't mean to hurt and wasn't strong enough to save. "No!" I wail in Bishop's arms, not wanting it to be true.

"Fuck, sweetheart," Bishop mutters as he holds me tighter.

He doesn't say anything else, because there's not a word in any language that can make any of this better.

I cry until I can't breathe. I cry until it feels like tiny daggers are stabbing into my eyes. I cry until my throat is hoarse and scratchy. I cry until it feels like I can't anymore. And then, I keep crying, silent tears tracking down my face. The pain won't let me stop.

At some point, Levi walks up to the kid. He gently closes the boy's eyes with one hand. I have to try a few times before I croak, "Is he dead?"

"Not yet, no." Levi shakes his head as he looks from the boy to the tubes of glowing orange liquid running from him to multiple IV bags. He seems just as perplexed about the setup as I am.

If he's not dead yet, then I can at least do something good today by healing him. I try to get up again, but Bishop keeps me anchored to his chest. Once again, I flail around, trying to get out of his hold.

"Stop, Iz. You can't go to him. We have to leave him here." At my pained noise, Bishop murmurs, "I know, baby. I know it goes against everything you are to leave him, but we have to. I'm so fucking sorry you have to do this, sweetheart. Fuck, you'll never know how sorry I am for putting you through this, but we have to go. Now."

I can kill bad guys without a second thought. But the part of going on missions that really gets to me is when we have to leave the good guys behind. My brain knows we need to leave the kid. Whoever is doing this will know someone is onto them if we save him. It also knows that there's little chance the kid would pull through, even if we did get him out. If we saved him, we'd be sacrificing who knows how many other kids.

But my heart? It's screaming to save him. The thought of

leaving anyone here, much less a kid, rends the already fractured remnants of my heart.

As I process Bishop's words, I realize there's a frantic voice screaming in my ear. "You need to fucking go, now! I don't care if you have to carry her, Bishop, but you need to get the fuck out of there!"

Bishop stands up while still holding me. My shaky legs struggle to support me when I'm fully standing up. By sheer willpower alone, I manage not to fall back to the ground. "Can you walk, or do you need me to carry you, sweetheart?"

"I can walk. Let's go. According to Aiden, we don't have much time." Bishop hesitates briefly as he takes in what an absolute mess I am. He gives me a sharp nod and snags my hand before turning back the way we came. Levi's warm palm grasps my other one as we hustle out of the cavern and back up the stairs. I'm grateful for the strength they're trying to lend me, but I'm not sure it's enough to ever put me back together.

We're just slipping out the steel door when Aiden shouts, "Fuck! Fuck, fuck, fuck. They're heading right to you. You guys need to hide, like yesterday! Goddamn it, why can't anything go right today?"

We quickly scan the hallway for somewhere to hide. Levi starts tugging me to the second room on the right. "This one's a storage closet. It's our best bet for right now. I don't see anywhere else to go."

"Good thinking." Bishop goes into the dark space ahead of us. He pulls me in after him. Levi steps in behind me and presses tight against my back. The closet is cramped, with two giant dudes and one slightly taller-than-average girl smooshed into it. My back is practically glued to Levi's front, and my front is plastered to Bishop's.

When Levi closes the door with a soft snick, I'm startled and jump. I let out a little squeak, and Levi covers my mouth with his hand to keep me quiet. My cheeks, cooled from the air brushing over the tear tracks, warm under his touch.

"We're in a closet," Bishop whispers to Aiden. "I'm turning off the coms and camera, in case they have anything to check for them."

"You better fucking get my sister out of there safely, Bishop," Aiden hisses.

"I will. No matter what." Bishop holds my gaze as he vows to sacrifice himself to keep me safe.

CHAPTER 37

IZZY

I shake my head at Bishop, since Levi is still covering my mouth. Rather than respond to me wordlessly telling him I'm not worth it, Bishop just reaches up to my ear to gently turn off my earpiece. He then turns off his own and the camera in his shirt button. Levi is moving behind me, and I assume he's doing the same.

The three of us strain to hear the people who were heading toward us. We needn't have worried, because they sound like a herd of elephants stomping down the hallway past our hiding place. Now, we just have to wait for them to walk back the other way before getting the hell out of here.

Our panting breaths and my heart frantically pounding in my ears are the only sounds in the tiny closet. While I try to calm my heart, I wiggle around slightly. We're going to be stuck in this closet for who knows how long, so I'd prefer to be comfortable while we are.

As I'm shifting around, I realize that both of my mates are hard. My eyes widen at that and snap up to Bishop's. He's not looking at me, though. Instead, Bishop's head is thrown back, and his eyes are closed. The tendons in his neck stand out starkly from how hard he's clenching his jaw. His hands are also balled into fists at his side.

Sensing my gaze on him, Bishop opens his eyes and stares down at me with heat burning in his baby blues. I'm still moving around, trying to find a good spot between them. Bishop's hands snake out and grab my hips, forcing me to still. "Stop fucking moving, sweetheart. My control's hanging on by a thread. Keep moving, and I'm going to fuck you in this closet, getting caught be damned."

I'm sure I look like a deer in the headlights with how wide my eyes are, but I can't help it. Bishop has kept everything strictly platonic for eight years. In the past week, he's threatened to fuck me twice. It's really not the threat he thinks it is, though.

Part of me wants to say *hell, yeah* and dive headfirst into the distraction of doing him, even though now is really not the time for that. I'd give almost anything not to feel the heartbreak that's trying to drown me. When I close my eyes, all I can see are Daniel, the kid in the basement, and the people in the cages. It's playing on a macabre loop in my mind, and it's slowly destroying what's left of my battered soul.

But I don't want to use Bishop like that. He deserves to fuck someone who's fully in the moment with him. Not someone desperately running from everything they're not strong enough to deal with.

Sighing, I nod and lean my head back against Levi's chest. Tears run down my face as I avoid Bishop's gaze. Even after all the crying I've done today, I somehow still have tears left. I wish it would all just stop.

"Don't cry, baby," Bishop murmurs as he presses his soft lips to my forehead.

I tap Levi to move his hand. He drops it to rest on the hollow of my throat, with his thumb tracing little circles there. "I just don't want it to hurt so much anymore," I rasp, the barely audible sound loud in the silent closet.

"Fuck, sweetheart." Bishop presses closer to me and palms the back of my head. He crushes me to his chest and holds me while my body shakes with silent sobs. Levi wraps his free arm around my waist and curves protectively against my back as I battle my tears.

After several long minutes, I'm able to stuff my feelings back into the dark corner of my mind where they belong. My heart isn't any less broken, nor my soul any less shredded. But the pain isn't as all-consuming as it was. I'm able to function well enough to get us out of here, which is all that really matters.

Bishop feels my frame stop shuddering. He takes a step back. His gaze bounces over my face, and he reaches up to wipe my tears away with gentle brushes of his thumbs. I try to lift my lips up a fraction to reassure him that I'm fine. When his forehead only wrinkles more in concern, I whisper, "I'm good."

"You're still not a very good liar, little raven." Levi's warm breath feathers over my ear, causing me to shiver. My lips do tip up ever so slightly at his comment. Bishop grins at my barely there smile, but it doesn't reach his eyes. I don't think any of us are okay after today. I'm not sure what I thought we'd find, but this shit show was certainly not it.

Loud footsteps thundering down the hallway cause me to jump in surprise. I don't squeak this time, so Levi doesn't move to cover my mouth. He leaves one arm slung low on my waist and the other collaring my throat.

As the footsteps fade, Bishop reaches up to turn his coms back on. "Are we clear?" he quietly asks. After listening for a moment, Bishop nods. "Okay. We'll head out."

Since we're likely in the clear, Levi and I both reach up to turn our coms back on. Bishop slowly eases the supply closet door open and looks around for any lingering council minions. When he doesn't see any, he quietly walks out into the hallway. Levi and I trail him.

It's an uneventful walk out of the experimental magic wing. Well, it is, other than the internal struggle as we pass the door that leads to the cages. I want so badly to go in there to free everyone, but I can't. Hurrying past the room, I'm the first to burst through the doors out of the entire wing. Bishop can chew me out about it if he wants, but I need to get out of there before I do something I'd probably regret.

Bishop doesn't say anything about it. Instead, he strides ahead, so he's in front and Levi is behind me. The only sound in the lavish hallway is the clack of our shoes on the gold-veined marble.

We've almost made it out of the hallway without being spotted when councilman Thomas Doyle appears out of nowhere. I'd know his thinning gray hair, cold bottle-green eyes, and hawkish face anywhere. He turns down the corridor, unaware of the three of us heading right toward him.

At the sight of the man who is probably behind all the fucked-up shit we found, my anger roars to life inside of me. It scalds my insides and coaxes my magic forth. My magic batters its cage in my chest, violently thrashing to get out. I'm so focused on trying to keep it from murdering the councilman that I don't even see him noticing us.

"Bishop St. James, my boy! It's a pleasure to see you!" Doyle shakes hands with Bishop, who isn't, in fact, his anything. They're not related, and Bishop hates his guts almost as much as I do. Doyle's eyes collide with mine over Bishop's shoulder, and his face twists into a sneer. The disgusting man seems to realize where we are for the first time. "What are you doing in this wing, son?"

"I caught those two sneaking down here. I know it's off-limits, so I went after them before they could cause trouble." Bishop aims a fake glare our way.

"How did you even get in the council building, *vilis*? I thought your kind weren't allowed in. None of the *vilis* or lower mages should be here. All you do is taint our sacred space." Doyle walks over to me and gets in my personal space. He's probably trying to intimidate me. It's hard to be intimidated when he's only an inch taller than me and has a massive beer belly.

I can't kill him. I can't kill him. I can't kill him, I chant in my mind. I hate the elitist rhetoric of the mages. Their inflated self-worth is what allows mages like Doyle to hurt people they deem beneath them without remorse. It's what allows them to torture children, like the kid we had to leave behind.

At the reminder, my magic once again goes ballistic. I grit my teeth and focus on stuffing it back down. "Through the front door," I respond as unhelpfully as possible, a sarcastic smile on my face.

Doyle's face turns thunderous. Bishop's eyes widen over Doyle's shoulder. His narrowed eyes silently tell me to play nice. *Sorry, my dude.* Being nice to shit people isn't a setting I've ever had.

When Doyle opens his mouth to say something that'd probably provoke my magic further, Bishop hurries to speak first. "I'll escort these two out before they can do anything to taint the council building. It was great to see you, as always." Bishop brushes past Doyle to put one hand on the back of my neck and the other on Levi's shoulder. He then rushes us past Doyle before the councilman can respond.

We walk in silence out of the council headquarters. Bishop drops his hands from both of us once we're out of the building, but we continue to walk quietly until we're past the gate at the end of the long driveway.

Once we're off council property, Bishop tugs me to a

stop. He spins me around to face him. His eyes are narrowed on me, and his mouth is set in a disapproving frown. "What the fuck was that, Isabel? Why the fuck did you think sassing Doyle was a smart idea?"

Instead of matching Bishop's anger with mine, I just feel tired. "Can we not do this, St. James? I can't take getting yelled at right now." My voice comes out small and defeated. I tilt my face up to the sun, hoping the bright light will keep the tears at bay. It doesn't work. Burning tears cascade down my cheeks, and I lower my head in defeat.

"I'm sorry," Bishop croaks. My gaze jumps up to his. I see the same anger and pain and devastation in his eyes that's probably in mine.

I reach out and grab one of his hands with mine to comfort him. "It's fine. Can we just get out of here?"

"Yeah, we can, sweetheart." Bishop tugs on my hand to bring me to his chest. He wraps me in a quick hug before stepping back. "*Aperire.*" A portal ringed with blue sparks sizzles into existence. Bishop is the one actually opening the portal. We don't want to risk me using my magic this close to the council.

I'm the first to go through the portal into the Nightshade Pack dining room. It's set up as a makeshift command center for this mission. As soon as I step through the portal, I'm smothered in Luca's embrace.

"I'm so fucking sorry, wildcat. And I'm so glad you got out of there safely." Luca rests his chin on my head as he squeezes me like he's worried I'm going to disappear at any second.

When I process his words, I realize that Aiden, Rhys, and the wolves all heard my breakdown. Fucking fantastic. I just love having an audience for absolutely losing it.

My cheeks heat in embarrassment, but Luca's massive chest hides my blush from anyone. Luca is only hugging me for a few moments before another hard body crashes into me. Archer wraps his arms around both his brother and me. "I'm sorry, too, sunshine."

I don't really know what to say to them, so I just quietly enjoy their warm bodies pressed against mine. When both of them reluctantly pull away, I see Cain standing behind Luca. He has one of his hands shoved in his black slacks. His dark green eyes stare at me uncertainly, like he's not confident I'd welcome a hug from him. It hurts my heart to see how unsure of himself Cain seems when it comes to me.

Approaching him with a soft smile, I wait for Cain to open his arms for me. When he does, I step into them and lay my head on his warm chest. He doesn't say anything. Instead, Cain holds me tight, like he can keep me from fracturing so completely that there will be nothing left of me.

Unfortunately, I'm not sure there's anything anyone can do, not even my mates, to keep me from splintering into a million pieces that'll never fit together again. I'm not sure anyone can save me from the roiling mess of emotions. I'm not sure anyone can stop pain and heartbreak from crashing over me like a tsunami wave, battering me until there's nothing left.

And the scariest part is, I'm not sure I even want to be saved. A larger part of me than I'd like to admit wants to lie down and just let the devastation consume me. But I refuse to give up until we break out all the people the council is hurting. I'll keep fighting until every last one of them is free.

CHAPTER 38

IZZY

"*I*t's way too early to be awake," Archer grumbles as he sleepily stares at his plate of eggs, sausage, and bacon.

"It's seven-thirty, sunny boy. It's really not that early." I hold in my laugh at the glare he gives me. I've got class in half an hour. Even though I told my mates they don't have to get up when I do, they all insisted. So, we're eating breakfast together in the Nightshade's dining room.

It's been three days since we broke into the council. I've been staying at the Nightshade pack house with all of my mates this weekend. I didn't want to be alone after the emotional roller coaster Friday was. Being alone with my thoughts is dangerous right now.

I thought my anger would've cooled over the weekend, but it hasn't. If anything, I've just gotten angrier at the council and mages as a whole. Somehow, I have to spend all day around the snobby mages at school and not murder any of them.

Speaking of the time, I should probably get going. I shove one last bite of yogurt into my mouth before I grab my backpack under my chair and stand up. When I turn around, I bump into Luca. "Be safe today, wildcat." Luca wraps me up in a hug, holding me tight, like he's worried something bad will happen.

"I'm just going to school, wolf boy. I'll be fine." I'm not sure if my soft words reassure him, but Luca reluctantly lets me go after a moment.

Archer, Cain, and Bishop all give me hugs as well. Their casual affection and concern for my well-being make my insides feel like goo. My secret sappy side laps it up, while I try to play it cool on the outside. I know I'm fighting a losing battle to resist my mates, but I also know it's safer for them not to mate me. My heart and mind are at war, and I don't know which one I want to prevail.

Shaking my head at my thoughts, I walk over to Levi. He's portaling us to school. We're heading to his office, so no one sees us arrive together. Dean Murphy would probably love to know I've spent the weekend with one of my instructors. I'm pretty sure that sleeping in the same bed as a teacher violates HGU's code of conduct, so Dean Murphy would take great joy in expelling me.

"Ready to go?" Levi asks as I reach him. I give him a nod, and he holds out his hand for me to take. Once my hand is in his, Levi walks through the portal and tugs me along behind him. I'm not sure I'll ever get used to his weird portals. They don't feel like anything. No stickiness, no thick air, no gooey feeling. It's just like walking in a normal room. Only, one second, we're in the dining room, and the next, we're in Levi's impersonal office.

"Thanks for the lift, screech owl."

"Anytime. Where's your ghost?" Levi perches on the edge of his desk and watches me with his otherworldly black-and-red eyes.

I shrug. "Hell if I know. Aggie does whatever the fuck she wants."

"Can you call her to you? I'd feel better if you had her just in case today." Levi is staring at me with worry in his eyes, so I can't help but want to reassure him.

"Yeah, I can do that. Everything's going to be fine, though. No one saw us on Friday." I pull on my magic that connects me to Aggie.

Aggie poofs into the room with a confused expression on her face. She looks around and lets out a small squeak when she sees Levi. "Kid, why'd you pull me to tall, dark, and scary's office?"

I snort. "He's not that scary, Aggie. I'm at least fifty-four-percent positive he won't hurt you."

"That's not reassuring, kid!"

"Simmer down, ghost. Little raven likes you. I'm not a danger to you, as long as you stay on her good side. If you hurt her? Well, now, that's a different story." Levi lets the red rings consume his irises as he threatens Aggie. It's unnecessary but also kind of sweet.

Aggie just stares at Levi in horror, making me chuckle. "You'll be fine, Aggie. Moving on, are you okay with following me to class? The boys are worried something's going to happen today, so demon boy wants you to follow me around." I don't know what has them so worried. I've done a ton of illegal things and haven't gotten caught.

After tearing her gaze from Levi, Aggie processes what I said. "It'll be boring, but I can do that."

"Cool. I've really got to get to class. Moore will flip his shit if I'm late." I give Levi a hug before walking out of his office because I'm apparently the type that gives out hugs now.

The walk to the Gallagher building and the first part of Moore's advanced magic class are uneventful. I'm struggling not to fall asleep out of sheer boredom when the classroom door bangs open. Six council guards in full tactical armor storm into the room. All the guards have military buzz cuts, stern expressions, and are bulky by mage standards. They're still not as muscular as my mates, though. They scan the room until every guard's gaze lands on me, one by one.

Oh, boy. This is so not good.

I subtly look at Aggie out of the corner of my eye. She's wearing the same *oh, shit* expression I probably am.

"Isabel Gallagher," the tallest of the guards booms. "You're under arrest." My classmates gasp in delight at the new juicy gossip they're about to have. I roll my eyes at them and try to tune out the quiet chatter that's already starting up.

"For what?" I ask, genuinely confused. I've done a lot of illegal things since I was a teen. They really need to be specific about what they're pissed at me for this time. Although, I'm pretty sure it's about our activities on Friday. I wonder if they had cameras we didn't catch or something because I'm one-hundred-percent sure no one saw us.

The tallest council dude looks me dead in the eye and says the phrase I've been dreading for fourteen years. "You're under arrest for being a spirit mage."

ABOUT THE AUTHOR

E. L. Finley is a Midwestern author of paranormal and why choose romance. As an avid reader, E. L. Finley writes about the sassy heroines, devoted heroes, and magical shenanigans she'd like to read about. She focuses on creating characters that pull you in and crafting worlds that you never want to leave. When she isn't writing or reading, you can find E. L. Finley baking anything with chocolate, bungling home improvement projects, or binging spy shows.

ALSO BY E. L. FINLEY

HAUNTED MAGIC SERIES

Veiled Spirits

Shadowed Spirits

WOLVES HOLLOW UNIVERSITY SERIES

Ruined Wolfsbane

Cursed Wolfsbane

Made in the USA
Columbia, SC
09 February 2025

53373952R00176